FOR THE THRILL OF IT ALL

Emily Mims

CHASING THE HIGH

From the first time she lays eyes on him, forensic chemist Amanda Blakeman is drawn to fellow cop Jack Vance, a fearless SWAT team officer who thrills her with his cocky good looks and peerless bravery, and himself by seeking out danger. Stock car racing, sky diving, rodeo riding—there's nothing the 1980s have that Jack won't do. And he's just as impressive behind closed doors. But as the pair joins forces against a serial killer hunting in the bars of San Antonio, Amanda realizes Jack's sweet and crazy nature isn't enough. She needs him to realize that life's best thrills can be found not just in defying death alone, but in living and loving together.

For the Thrill of It All

Emily Mims

www.BOROUGHSPUBLISHINGGROUP.com

FOR THE THRILL OF IT ALL
Copyright © 2015 Emily Wright Mims

ISBN 978-1-942886-48-8

Dedicated with love to my friend and co-worker Aleta Rhodes, who thirty years ago was my model for the character Amanda Blakeman. Aleta, you left us too soon. I miss you.

CONTENTS

Chapter 1
Chapter 2
Chapter 3
Chapter 4
Chapter 5
Chapter 6
Chapter 7
Chapter 8
Chapter 9
Chapter 10
Chapter 11
Chapter 12
Chapter 13
Chapter 14
Chapter 15

Epilogue
About the Author

For the Thrill of It All

Chapter One

1985

Amanda Blakeman looked down at the nonreactive blood on the microscope slide. "No, Dick, it definitely isn't the blood of a deer," she announced to the Texas Ranger who stood beside her.

"Cattle?" Dick Vaughan asked.

"Let me check for that," Amanda said as she transferred another spot of dried blood from the hunting knife onto a fresh slide. "Do you suspect cattle rustling?"

"Yes, and this knife is the first concrete evidence we have that will link the suspects to the crime," Dick declared. "This particular bunch has been very slippery so far."

Amanda added cattle blood antibodies to the slide. "What have they been doing?" she asked.

"Butchering them on the spot and driving away with the meat already cut up," Dick answered as Amanda put the slide under the scope. "That way, they leave behind the brand and any other identifying marks."

"Yes, it's definitely cattle blood." She examined the slide carefully before she removed it from the scope and put it in a holder. "I'll save the slide as evidence along with the rest of my documentation," she said, writing her observations in the notebook she kept. If the case ever did come to trial, she would be able to consult her records and have all the evidence there to review.

"Super! This is our first decent lead," Dick enthused. "Amanda, you're wonderful."

"If I'm so wonderful, why am I flat broke and without a date on Saturday night?" Amanda quizzed dryly as she returned the knife to the evidence bag Dick brought it in. "Do you want us to keep this, or do you want to take it back to Devine?"

"You have enough neat things in your evidence room without my piddling little knife here," Dick teased. "Why, some of the things the San Antonio criminals come up with absolutely put us country folks to shame. Seriously, thanks for the favor, Amanda. We keep hoping someday we'll get a lab that can compare with this one, but it may be awhile." He glanced around the spacious forensic chemistry laboratory of the San Antonio Police Department. "You've got a great setup here."

"Don't I know it," Amanda agreed. "Of course, we have enough crime to keep everyone in here busy." "Everyone" included Amanda, whose specialty was toxicology, her two assistants, three other chemists who were concerned primarily with identifying drug samples, and two ballistics experts.

"It's a shame there's so much crime, isn't it?" Dick asked, as much to himself as to her. "Say, did you mean it when you said you didn't have a date for the weekend? Are you free on Saturday night?"

"Have you left Eileen?" Amanda inquired pointedly. "I don't poach."

Dick's ears turned a little red. "Well, not really, but we haven't been getting along all that well. Aw, come on, Amanda. We could have a great time."

Amanda raised her eyebrow as she looked up and down the handsome officer. "Oh, I don't doubt that one bit, Dick. But I don't go out with married men. Sorry."

"So am I," Dick admitted, glancing down at Amanda's petite, shapely body and her attractive face, framed by short, dark hair. "I better get on back to Devine. Thanks again for the favor."

"Sure, any time," Amanda said as she watched Dick leave the laboratory. He always managed to ask her out, and he always took her refusal with good grace. She often became annoyed with him for asking, but today she had left herself wide open with that crack about not having a date on Saturday night. She knew she shouldn't have said anything, but she wasn't looking forward to spending the evening alone. Most of the time she didn't mind not having plans, but tomorrow was the anniversary of her divorce, and it always made her feel a little lonely.

Not lonely enough to go back to Brian, she thought ruefully. She would never do that.

Smiling grimly, Amanda pushed her feelings to the back of her mind and turned to the project she had been working on when Dick interrupted her. She had been painstakingly trying to match the chip of paint found on the clothing of last night's hit-and-run victim with the paint on an abandoned vehicle found near the scene of the crime. Amanda turned the first sample edgewise on the slide, so she could see each layer of paint in the chip. Within a moment she was totally absorbed in her work, her divorce and her dateless Saturday night completely forgotten.

Amanda Blakeman was one of those rare, fortunate individuals who thoroughly loved her work. A definite pioneer in the heavily male-dominated San Antonio Police Department, she had been a policewoman for the last five years. But she left the street patrol as soon as she could and put her degrees in chemistry to good use in the forensic laboratory, proving herself over and over to her somewhat skeptical male superiors and working her way up to supervisor in record time. She was something of a chemical detective, tracking down substances that would serve as clues or evidence in solving crimes. She spent her days identifying drugs, alcohol, and poisons in the bloodstreams of victims and analyzing anything left behind at the scene of a crime, including hairs, fibers, or perhaps paint, as she was right now. With her two degrees in chemistry she probably could have made more money working for a corporation somewhere, but Amanda didn't care all that much. She loved the sense of satisfaction she felt from solving a particularly baffling case, and she loved not knowing from one day to the next what to expect when she walked in the door.

Amanda had just made what she felt was a positive identification on the paint chip when she got a call to report to the courthouse to give testimony in another case. Irritated by the interruption, she nevertheless quickly shed the lab coat that protected her skirt and blouse of her newest power suit and put on the trendy blazer complete with the requisite shoulder pads. She reviewed this case yesterday after she received the subpoena, and the details were fresh in her mind.

Amanda hurried out of the building, the April breeze warm on her face. She made an attractive picture as she strode purposefully across the street, unaware of the many admiring masculine stares she received. Her figure was too short and softly rounded to be truly fashionable, but its appeal was not lost on the male of the species. Since her divorce Amanda had not lacked for dates or admirers. Contrary to what her ex-husband told her, men were attracted—not put off—by the combination of extreme intelligence and the somewhat sharp tongue that he found so intimidating. So Amanda dated and enjoyed her freedom, but she kept her relationships on a casual level. She felt she was not yet ready to become seriously involved with another man.

Amanda spent an hour and a half on the witness stand in a rape case, her testimony concerning the results of a semen test proving beyond a doubt that the accused was indeed guilty. As soon as the defense lawyer released her, she hurried back across the street. The increased number of cars on the road told her that rush hour was beginning, and Amanda checked her watch. She would be free to go home in a half hour herself, since she wasn't working on anything that couldn't wait until tomorrow. She ran back up the stairs to her lab and was hanging up her blazer when the door opened. Eddie Gutierrez, one of her favorite homicide detectives, leaned over the counter that separated the inner sanctum of the laboratory from the rest of the department. "Hello, gorgeous! Want to run away with me?" Eddie invited, his voice a soft, sexy put-on. "You and I could take off and not come back for a month."

"Sorry, I heard you invite Molly down in dispatch earlier," Amanda teased as she logged Eddie in and opened the counter for him. "I refuse to be second choice. Now, if you had asked me first…"

"Loused it up again, huh?" Eddie asked, grinning. "Well, I tried. I guess I'll have to take Sylvia and the kids." Eddie was a shameless flirt but totally harmless, and Amanda and most of the women in the department put up with his teasing rather than hurt his feelings. "Here, I've got a whole bag of stuff for you," he said as he handed Amanda a sack. "This is off that stabbing we found early this morning. See if you can find more than one kind of blood on his clothing."

Amanda glanced down in the bag, making a face at the blood-spattered garments. "Nearly five years in the lab, and it still bothers me to see something like this," she confessed. She sat down and carefully logged in each article of clothing.

"You better hope it doesn't stop bothering you," Eddie remarked with conviction. "There would be something wrong with you if it didn't."

Amanda glanced up at Eddie. "You mean they still get to you, too?"

"Not all of them," Eddie admitted. "A couple of thugs cut themselves up outside a bar, and I could care less. But some of them do upset me. I went home last week after that child abuse murder and was sick."

"I think everyone who had to deal with that one felt the same way," Amanda said. She cataloged in the last piece of clothing, a pair of tattered jeans. "Have any plans for the weekend?"

"Not really, now that you've said no," Eddie replied as his beeper went off. He picked up Amanda's telephone and dialed his sergeant's extension. "Amanda, I've got to go," he told her as he hung up the phone a moment later. "I've got another murder to check out."

"Lucky you," Amanda said, taking off her lab coat and tossing it across her chair. "I think I'll go ahead and knock off. Bring me all the goodies in the morning."

"Want to help me collect them?" Eddie asked as they left her office. "Do you have to be home early?"

"No, not particularly. Would you mind if I tagged along?"

"Why not?" Eddie answered. He and his fellow homicide detectives knew that Amanda enjoyed going along to help them collect evidence when she could get away from the lab, and they appreciated the fact that sometimes she picked up on something they overlooked.

"Super," Amanda responded. She checked the .38 that was constantly with her, buried in the depths of her shoulder bag, and followed Eddie out to his car. "Where are we headed?"

"Fancy part of town. One of those swanky subdivisions out on the north side. Family violence—it looks like some dude's shot his wife."

"I'm always surprised when a family in that situation resorts to violence," Amanda said, shaking her head sadly.

Eddie fought to get on the expressway and jockeyed the bumper-to-bumper traffic that glutted the lanes during rush hour. The traffic slowed them considerably, and it was nearly a half hour later when Eddie finally entered the subdivision where the shooting had taken place. He turned onto the proper street and was rewarded by the zing and whistle of two bullets as they hit the pavement near the car and ricocheted off. "What the *hell?*" Amanda shouted as she ducked her head.

Eddie slammed on his brakes, and they peered cautiously out the windows. At that moment four more police cars drove up and were similarly greeted from the two-story house, the second house on the block. Up ahead a patrolman trapped behind his car motioned for them to get back. All five cars backed to the end of the street and parked lengthwise across the intersection and down the side street, forming a barricade that stretched from one corner house to the other. Eddie and Amanda crawled out of the car and crouched behind it. "What's going on?" Eddie called to the uniformed officer who was behind the next car.

"The officer up there, the one who's trapped, radioed that the man returned with a young girl, supposedly his daughter. He dragged her inside and is using her as a hostage. Over the telephone he told the negotiators that he would shoot her if anyone tried to storm the house."

"SWAT team?" Amanda asked.

"They're assembling now," the officer said. "Over there."

Amanda glanced in the direction the officer had indicated. Behind the wide garage of the house next door to the two-story, completely hidden from the man in the upstairs window but clearly in Amanda's view, a group of officers were assembling. They were dressed in combat fatigues, and the weapons they carried were more like those of a soldier than those of a law enforcement officer. "Are they going in after him?" Amanda questioned.

Eddie shrugged. "You know as much as I do."

Amanda flinched as another round of bullets peppered the patrol cars blocking the intersection. "Come on, we're getting behind that house," Eddie announced quickly. He and Amanda half walked, half crawled down the row of cars, staying as flat to the side of the cars as they could, until they were behind the large brick house that sheltered the SWAT team. "I thought you said the murder had already happened," Amanda remarked dryly. "I didn't realize you wanted an eyewitness."

"Cute," Eddie shot back. "That's all right. You need something to wake up your tired blood."

The captain of the SWAT team stepped over to Eddie and Amanda. "What are you two doing here?" he interrogated, obviously not happy to see them.

"I got a call to report to a homicide," Eddie returned. "And Amanda came along to help me collect evidence."

"Oh, you're police officers," the captain said. "I'm Mike McCormick. As long as you're here and stuck for the duration of this mess, could I draft you into keeping the press from getting too close? One of those hotshot cameramen is liable to get his head blown off."

"Sure, but they're going to scream bloody murder," Amanda said, thinking of San Antonio's love of gore on the six o'clock news and the willingness of young, careless camera crews to supply the gore with almost no thought to their own safety. "There comes the first live-eye now."

The live-eye van was halted by a couple of whizzing bullets and quickly backed up behind the red ranch house across the street. Amanda and Eddie bent over and made their way back across the row of cars blocking the intersection to the same relative shelter that the broadcasting van had sought. Eddie showed his badge to the shaken driver of the van. "Young man, you'd be safer if you stay back here, out of the killer's line of fire."

"You bet, sir," the young man affirmed. "But my boss will be fit to be tied if I don't get some good shots of this."

At that moment the back door of the ranch house opened and a frightened-looking elderly woman peered out. "Are you folks all right?" she asked.

"Yes, ma'am. Are you?" Amanda queried in return.

The old woman nodded and introduced herself as Martha Southerland. "I've been watching from the living room since it started. I have a plain view of everything."

The cameraman's face brightened. "Ma'am, would I be imposing if I came inside and shot a little footage from your window?"

Amanda opened her mouth to protest that his camera shooting might draw attention—and hence gunfire—to the house, endangering Mrs. Southerland, but before she could do so, the little woman had ushered him inside. "I wonder if she'll offer him tea and cookies?" Eddie asked dryly.

"Look, he's safer in there than he would be wandering around out here," Amanda asserted as the second television van drove up. This team was also quick to accept Mrs. Southerland's hospitality. And before long, reporters from the third television station were also cautiously peering out Mrs. Southerland's large picture window, ready to watch the drama unfold from relative safety.

Amanda and Eddie waited until all the reporters were settled in before they cautiously made their way back across the row of cars that blocked the intersection. The various police officers who had responded to the call had blocked traffic further down the side street to avoid endangering innocent drivers and pedestrians, but the house didn't appear to be surrounded yet. "What's happening?" Eddie inquired of Joe Turner, one of the plain-clothesmen who had appeared since they had left the SWAT team.

"He demanded a face-to-face confrontation with a policeman and hung up," Joe answered. "We haven't gotten word from the psychologist yet on whether or not we should try to reason with this guy. Say, how did you get that homeowner to let the reporters in?"

"Get her to? She volunteered!" Amanda exclaimed. "I don't really like it, since that idiot might shoot up her house if he sees them in there."

"At least it gets them out of our hair," Joe returned.

At that moment Mike McCormick motioned them over. "We just got a call from downtown," he said. "The psychologist thinks this guy's beyond reasoning. We have the green light."

Amanda shuddered at Mike McCormick's declaration. The "green light" gave the SWAT team the authority to go after the killer. They had to keep the safety of the hostage uppermost in their minds, but otherwise they had free rein.

Considering the state of mind that this killer appears to be in, there is probably no way he can get out of it alive, Amanda thought. The only question now was whether or not the hostage and all the SWAT team would.

Amanda and Eddie drifted as close to the clustered SWAT team officers as they could without being obvious about it. Amanda listened to Mike's discussion of their options. "The way I see it, there are several things we can try. We can storm the house, of course, and we may have to eventually. But if we do that at this point, the little girl's dead."

"Is she still alive?" one of the officers asked. "Or has he shot her already?"

"As far as we know, she's alive, and we want to keep her that way," Mike responded.

"What about slipping around the other side of the house and breaking in?" another man quizzed.

"He's got windows all the way around. Besides, that's too noisy," Mike countered.

"How about giving him what he asked for?" a third man broke in. "He wanted to talk to a policeman. So…how about sending somebody to talk to him?"

"Vance, you're crazy!" the first officer piped up. "That man would shoot a cop so fast it would make your head swim. Which one of us are you trying to get rid of?"

"No, listen to me," the man named Vance replied, his voice intent. "He's asked to speak to a cop. So we send him one, out in the front yard, and lure him to the window. When he's in view and distracted, somebody else shoots him."

The group of officers stood quiet for a moment. "That's a suicide mission," Mike answered slowly. "I'd never ask one of my officers to do that."

"I'm volunteering," Vance replied coolly.

Amanda glanced up then, wanting to see which officer would be willing to put himself in danger like that. She was half expecting a large, brawny man to match the cool strength of the deep voice and was surprised that the man was only a few inches taller than her, barely meeting the department's minimum height requirement for men. He wasn't heavy either. Although he seemed fit and healthy enough, he appeared to be rather thin and wiry. Amanda cringed inwardly at the thought of bullets ripping through the man's small body.

Mike glanced down at him. "I should have known you would," he said thoughtfully. "But you're taking a hell of a chance, Jack— you know that. He's killed once today, and he's shot at everything moving for the last hour."

"But what other option do you have?" Vance asked quietly. "If you storm the house, you may lose several officers, and you lose the hostage for sure. The shrink says he's beyond reasoning with. If we don't try it, what are we going to do? Starve him out?"

"He has a point," one of the plainclothes officers spoke up. "The people in the houses around here are in danger, too. You have to think of them."

"All right, we'll try it," Mike acquiesced. "Sam, radio downtown and have them call him on the phone and tell him Jack's coming. Otherwise, he'll just start shooting."

The officer named Sam reached into a patrol car and flipped on the radio. The rest of the SWAT team scattered, taking sheltered positions from behind which they could shoot. Calmly, apparently no more concerned than if he were alone in his bedroom, Jack Vance put down his rifle and started unbuttoning his shirt. Eddie motioned for Amanda to move a little farther away from the edge of the garage, and the two of them ducked into a patrol car that was well behind the house. Amanda leaned over and whispered in Eddie's ear. "That little guy really intends to go out there and let that maniac shoot at him?"

Eddie grinned and nodded. "Sure, he does," he whispered back. "Don't you know who that is?"

Amanda shook her head. "Who is he?"

"That's Jack Vance. He's almost a living legend in the department."

"I hope he holds on to the living part of that legend for a while longer," Amanda chimed in dryly. "Is he the one in the news every year or so? The one who does all those daring things?"

"Yeah, that's him. I'm surprised you've never met him."

"I'm holed up in the lab," Amanda reminded him. "I don't meet anybody but homicide, remember?" For someone who had been on the force as long as she had, Amanda really didn't know too many of her fellow officers. "So how has this guy earned his reputation? Doing what he's doing right now?"

"Stripping to his underwear in front of God and everybody?" Eddie asked.

"Eddie!"

"All right, all right. He has a reputation as a first-rate officer, second to none. But he's also known for his willingness to risk his own life. You notice that he didn't propose this scheme and then expect someone else to do it. He thought it up and then immediately volunteered to be the decoy himself."

"I remember him now," Amanda said. "He's the one who dove in a flooding river last year to save that little kid and nearly drowned himself." She watched as Jack calmly removed his uniform pants and tossed them on the ground. "This is a lot more dangerous than diving in the river."

She bit her lip as she stared at Jack's body. Now that he was stripped almost naked—so that the killer could see that he carried no weapon—she could see that although he was far from being a big man, he was more muscular than she had originally thought. His chest was broad and firm and covered with blond hair that was a couple of shades darker than the honey-colored hair on his head. His firm, flat stomach rippled with layers of fit, trim muscle, and his narrow hips and calves were well shaped.

He isn't heavy, but he's hard…and tough, Amanda thought, realizing that no amount of fitness or strength would make this brave man invulnerable to the killer's bullets. She shivered at the thought that if things did not go well for Jack Vance in the next few minutes, she might have to watch the medical examiner dig bullets out of his hard, fit body before the night was over.

Sam put the radio back and spoke to Mike and Jack. They nodded and Jack calmly stepped out from behind the garage and started slowly toward the house next door.

Amanda tried to wait but couldn't stand it. "I'm moving to where I can see something." She and Eddie both eased out of the car and carefully approached the edge of the garage, where a group of police officers were already gathered, trying to see what was going on while still staying out of the line of fire themselves. Amanda could see the various SWAT team members crouched behind cars and trees and completely surrounding the house. Surely one of them could shoot the killer before he shot Jack Vance.

Slowly, calmly, Jack Vance crossed the yard of the house they were behind and stepped onto the killer's property. Amanda and her fellow officers behind the garage could not see the upstairs window, but they could see every step Vance took as he slowly moved into the middle of the front yard. He cocked his head and stared into an upstairs window.

"Hey, you," he called, cupping his hands to his lips. "You asked to talk to a police officer," he said. "Well, I'm a police officer. So get over to the window and talk to me!"

They waited tensely for a moment. Jack Vance stood calmly, almost arrogantly, clad only in his blue boxers. "What's the matter? Cat got your tongue?"

"Damn! Is he trying to get his head blown off?" Mike muttered.

"I told him the negotiators said the man was worse than ever," Sam snapped.

"Yeah, well, maybe Jack thinks that's the only way he's going to get him out of there," Eddie mused.

Jack waited for another couple of minutes—minutes that seemed to last forever. "Hey, if you're going to talk to me, come on, man. I'm standing here in my skivvies giving the ladies a show, and I'm getting a little chilly!"

"If Vance ever gets as big as his mouth, he's going to be the biggest man I have on SWAT," Mike quipped.

At that moment a shot rang out from the house and Jack dove to the sidewalk. Rifle fire erupted from five or six different SWAT officers positioned around the front of the house. They fired almost simultaneously into the window, the sound of shattering glass mingling with the echo of rifle fire. Amanda stared in horror at Jack's prostrate body. Was the daring officer all right, or had the killer's bullet hit him?

"We got him!" one of the SWAT snipers called as one by one they stepped from behind houses, trees, and cars. Much to Amanda's relief, Jack Vance sat up and pushed himself to his feet. "Are you all right, Vance?" one of the snipers inquired anxiously.

"That idiot couldn't have hit the broad side of a barn at three feet!" Jack called out as he brushed the dust from his chest.

One at a time the police officers stepped from behind the garage, looking as if they were not quite able to believe it was all over. Amanda discovered that her hands were shaking. And if the pale, tense faces around her were anything to go by, the others found the experience as harrowing as she had. Maybe there was something to be said for working in the lab all day.

In fact the only person who didn't seem shaken at all was Jack. He spoke briefly to Mike, telling him that he had seen the killer hovering in the background and felt that the only way he could draw him to the window was to taunt him. Just as he was telling Mike that he was pretty sure he had seen movement in the room behind the killer, Mrs. Southerland's front door opened and the three teams of television reporters and camera crews descended on the police officers, surrounding Jack. "Officer, could you—why, you're Jack Vance!" one of the young women gushed. "We should have known!"

Jack nodded and grinned rakishly, and Amanda noticed that dimples flashed in his cheeks. "Yes, ma'am, I'm Jack Vance."

"Mr. Vance, what was it like to look up and see the killer in the window?" one of the other reporters asked as she shoved a microphone into Jack's face, her cameraman catching them both in the shot.

"Something else. And speaking of looking, would you mind shutting that thing off until I have my uniform back on? My mother lives in Pearsall, and the folks back there are a little more modest than we are here in the city."

"Oh," she said abruptly.

The cameraman obligingly quit taping, and Jack made his way over to where Eddie and Amanda were standing by the garage. "Good work, Jack," Eddie offered warmly, extending his hand.

"Thanks," Jack responded as he shook Eddie's hand and held his out to Amanda. "Are you a fellow officer, or has Eddie here finally succeeded in getting somebody to go out with him?"

"No, Eddie hasn't been so lucky," Amanda returned as she gripped Jack's hand, the rough calluses on his palms curiously pleasant. "I'm Amanda Blakeman, forensic chemistry."

"I'm Jack Vance," Jack said, his blue eyes dancing. "So you're our forensic chemist. I knew there was a reason I wanted on homicide."

"Jack is in the process of transferring to our department," Eddie interjected. "He should be coming by with evidence for you soon—that is, if he can come up with a murder to investigate."

"I don't think I'll be waiting that long to see her," Jack volunteered. "Look, let me get my clothes back on. I wouldn't want to give Amanda high blood pressure, standing here like this." He grinned as he picked up his pants. "Sorry for the informal attire," he teased. "I hope I didn't shock you." His manner told Amanda he wasn't sorry at all but was enjoying the attention.

"Oh, I didn't mind a bit," Amanda assured him. "And you're going to have to go a lot further than standing around in your skivvies to shock me. Tell me, though, does all your underwear match your eyes?" She gazed innocently at him and was rewarded with a tinge of red on Jack's cheeks.

"I should have warned you, Jack," Eddie laughed. "Amanda sharpens her tongue every day at lunch with a straight-edged razor. You aren't going to make a thing off her."

"She's going to keep me on my toes, huh?" Jack asked as he put his shirt back on. "Are you on duty, or were you in the neighborhood?"

"I was in Amanda's office when I received a call to report to a homicide," Eddie said. "Amanda came along to help me collect evidence. I think she got more than she bargained for."

"I thought for a minute we were going to be among the bodies," Amanda admitted. "I guess we better get on with it, hadn't we? We've got to collect on two, now, at least. Do you really think the little girl's all right?"

At that moment Sam left the house, leading a girl who looked to be about ten by the hand. "She made it," Amanda breathed. "Thank goodness!"

"And Sam will be as gentle as he knows how when he questions her," Eddie said. "She's been through quite an ordeal. She may be all right physically, but I wonder what it's done to her emotionally."

"A lot," Jack uttered grimly. He sat down on the driveway and pulled on his socks and shoes.

Mike McCormick approached the three of them.

"Helluva job, Vance. I want a report on my desk by eleven in the morning."

"I'll write it tonight if you need it," Jack offered.

'Tomorrow's soon enough," Mike assured him. "Maybe you don't need to go home, rest, and drink a few beers, but I sure do." He left them and got into one of the patrol cars.

Jack watched as Mike drove away. "Say, why don't I go inside and help you gather evidence?" Jack volunteered as the paramedics, the coroner, and an investigator from the medical examiner's office parked in front of the house. It would be the medical investigator's job to preserve all of the physical evidence on the bodies in preparation for the thorough examination and autopsy that would be performed later by the coroner. "For some strange reason," Jack added, glancing at Amanda, "this case interests me a great deal."

"Not ready to go home?" Eddie asked. Jack shook his head. "Sure, come and help us, then. The more people we have, the faster this will go."

"Your help will be welcome, Jack," Amanda interjected warmly. "That is, as long as you promise to keep your pants on."

"Scouts' honor," Jack assured her.

"Oh, darn it," Amanda teased, winking at Jack. She, for one, wouldn't mind a bit if the handsome officer helped her and Eddie.

Jack followed Eddie and Amanda across the yard to the house where the murder had taken place. He could feel the adrenaline still pumping through his veins, the adrenaline high he'd learned to love a long time ago. The adrenaline high that came with proving himself once again by putting himself on the line and living to tell the tale. He admitted to himself—as he admired Amanda's sexy stride—that his dedication to the department, as considerable as it was, had nothing to do with his sudden interest in staying to investigate the brutal murders that had just taken place. What he was really interested in was a chance to flirt with Amanda Blakeman a little more.

Chapter Two

Amanda followed Eddie into the large, expensively decorated home, holding the screen door so that it wouldn't slam in Jack's face. The patrol officers were already cordoning off the house, and no one else—not even the other officers—would be allowed inside until the three of them had painstakingly gathered each and every bit of evidence surrounding both the killer's victim and the killer himself. Amanda glanced into the elegant living room, noting that nothing was out of order. She could hear the paramedics in the family room, so she followed Eddie in, gasping a little when she saw the gory mess awaiting them. "Somebody's going to have a lovely time cleaning this place up when we're finished here," she muttered as she stepped aside so Jack could enter the room.

Jack let out a long, slow whistle. "They must have had one wingding of a fight before he shot her," he said as he glanced around at the scattered furniture and broken dishes.

"We'll eventually reconstruct the events," Eddie ventured confidently. "I'm going out to the car for the camera and the bags. Amanda, you take that end of the room. Jack, over there, since that's where most of the evidence is. I'll try to get the rest of the room."

"I think we ought to check upstairs first," Amanda suggested. She and Jack went upstairs and into the front bedroom where the killer lay. He had been a tall, slim man and was dressed in a three-piece business suit. Amanda burned with curiosity as she stared down at the dead man. "What on earth do you suppose is the story behind this?" she asked, more to herself than to Jack.

"Like Eddie said, we'll find out sooner or later," Jack responded. They left the room and passed the medical investigator and the coroner on the stairs, each taking a small stack of the special airtight evidence bags—similar to zip sandwich bags—with them into the family room. Jack stared for a moment at the dead woman's face, beautiful and cultured even in death. "Yes, Amanda, there's bound to be a story behind this one," he said as he knelt to make his part of the meticulous search for evidence.

The three of them fell to the task of collecting everything that might in any way relate to the crime. Eddie photographed the entire room, section by section, so that the department would have detailed pictures of the room and the dead woman. When Eddie finished, they resumed their search, going over each section inch by inch. Amanda found the shell casings in her section and carefully sealed them away, knowing that they would be matched with the weapon upstairs that had fallen from the killer's hand. Jack dug two bullets out of the wall in his section and put them in a separate bag. They very carefully took a sample of each bloodstain in the room, on the off chance that there was more than one blood type present. They fingerprinted all of the broken dishes as well as all of the wood surfaces in the room. Amanda found some hair on the woman's clothing and carefully bagged it.

The paramedics returned a few minutes later. "Are you ready for us to take the bodies?" one of them asked.

"This one, but we haven't even started upstairs," Eddie said.

"We can go ahead and put her in the ambulance, but we may as well wait for you to finish," the older of the two suggested. "No sense in making two trips downtown."

The paramedics packed up the body—careful not to disturb the medical investigator's handiwork—and disappeared with it. Amanda and her companions spent the next hour in the family room, making sure that they hadn't missed anything that might prove relevant to the shooting. She learned from the address label on a magazine that the man's name was Steve Morely, and that the woman's name was Caroline. She also thought that if the room prior to the struggle was anything to go by, cruelty and violence was not a way of life for these people. Of course, domestic violence occurred in every level of society and in every kind of dwelling imaginable, but somehow it just didn't fit in this home. The furnishings, the books and magazines, the fine china that now lay broken on the floor, all indicated a civilized, gracious existence.

Amanda stood up with her last evidence bag and glanced at Jack, who was still taking hair samples from the carpet. He was frowning with concentration. Amanda thought he was doing an excellent job collecting evidence, especially for a homicide detective who had just been promoted. He glanced up and his frown turned into a warm smile. "Come here and tell me if you think this should go in," he said, gesturing to a small piece of cloth on the floor.

Amanda bent over and peered at the small square of fabric. "It looks like a sewing scrap, but you never can tell," she responded as she handed him a fresh evidence bag. He put the fabric in the bag and added it to his growing collection. "You've done a very thorough job," she complimented Jack as he got up off the floor. "Most new men on homicide aren't half that careful."

"Thank you, my lady," Jack gallantly returned, bending low at the waist. "I would kiss your hand, but I'm not sure where that hand's been in the last hour."

Amanda laughed and resisted the urge to rub her hand on her skirt. "True, dashing knight. Can't be too careful with the noble tonsils."

Jack took Amanda's hand and kissed the air above it. "Will that hold you?" he asked. "Seriously, I wish I had your expertise." He had admired the ease with which Amanda had made her collection, while he had agonized over what to include in the bags.

Eddie rose from the floor and sealed his last bag. "That does this one," he said. "Let's put these in the car and tackle upstairs." They trooped out to the car, leaving the bags in the trunk, and were on their way back into the house when Sam drove up. "Have you already finished with the little girl?" Eddie asked.

"Yes. Apparently the man and woman had been arguing over money for days. He desperately wanted to buy a new Corvette, and she was opposed to the idea."

"All this over a *car?*" Jack questioned incredulously, thinking of the dead woman's beautiful face.

"Not entirely. From what I read between the lines, the man had been having severe emotional problems for the last several months and refused to seek help. Five will get you ten that the medical examiner finds evidence of brain disease."

"What a waste!" Amanda lamented. She followed Jack and Eddie back into the house and they repeated the process upstairs, combing every square inch of the spacious bedroom for evidence. When they had finished with the area immediately around the dead man, the paramedics moved the body to the waiting ambulance. Amanda ignored the rumbling in her stomach, mentally scolding herself for being hungry at a time like this, and blushed when a particularly loud rumble caught Jack's attention. "That orange for lunch didn't go very far," she admitted.

"Maybe we can do something about that later," Jack suggested. They finished with the upstairs room and put the bags in the trunk of the car with the others. Eddie gave the word that the cordon could come down, and the three of them got into Eddie's car. The news media were long gone, but groups of neighbors stood around in the warm night and talked about what they had seen and heard.

Eddie pulled into the parking lot of the police station. "You're going to have a busy day tomorrow," he teased as they checked the bags into the evidence room. Amanda would type all the blood samples and analyze the hairs that had been found on the woman's clothes and near her body, although it looked to her like the case was pretty well solved. She would have bet a month's salary that ballistics would confirm that the bullets in the wall and Caroline Morely's body were from the gun that Steve Morely was clutching as he died.

"That's all right. I haven't got anything better to do," Amanda quipped as she squirted a liquid disinfectant into her hands. She held out the bottle and squirted some for Eddie and Jack.

"We could fix that, *juera,* if you would go out with me tomorrow," Eddie said suggestively as he sidled up to Amanda. "You're my *juera,* you know that?" *Juera* was an affectionate term meaning "Anglo" or "fair one."

"Eddie, you wouldn't know what to do with *a juera* if you caught one," Amanda countered, laughing good-naturedly.

"I could try," Eddie returned hopefully.

Amanda blushed as her stomach rumbled again. "All right, stomach, I'm going to feed you," she murmured.

"I think you better make it soon before you swoon," Jack suggested as he rinsed his hands. "Eddie, where would you like to go?"

"Home. Sylvia will have something waiting for me. But thanks and good night."

"Night, Eddie," Amanda said as she rinsed her hands.

"Where would you like to go, then?" Jack asked as Amanda handed him a paper towel from the stubborn dispenser.

"Why don't we walk down to Market Square? There's bound to be something open down there."

Jack checked his watch. "It's only ten. There'll be several places open."

They left the police department and walked toward Market Square, the old market that had been converted into an elegant collection of shops and sidewalk restaurants. Jack gave the hostess his name at one of the most popular restaurants in the area, and they sat down on a low brick wall to wait. Fatigue swamped Amanda as she sank down gratefully beside Jack. "Tired?" Jack inquired quietly.

"Exhausted," Amanda admitted. "Aren't you?"

"A little. I guess it's been a long day for me, too."

"And I must say that it was more stressful than most," Amanda declared. "I don't usually get shot at in the lab."

The hostess called Jack's name, and they followed her to one of the outside tables, illuminated by the soft glow of candlelight. The table was quiet, the noise of clanking dishes and singing mariachis much less intense than it would have been in the restaurant. Jack barely glanced at the menu before he shut it. *"Fajitas?"*

"What else?" Amanda asked. *Fajitas,* or marinated skirt steaks, were the restaurant's specialty. The dish had only recently appeared in Tex-Mex restaurants in south and central Texas and had been an instant hit.

Their waitress came almost immediately to take their order. "So you don't like getting shot at?" Jack teased as the waitress disappeared into the restaurant.

"No, not that this is the first time it's happened. I got shot at once before on a family disturbance call the first year I was on the force. It scared me, but not like tonight."

"It's happened to me so often I don't think anything of it anymore," Jack said.

"How often is 'so often'?" Amanda asked.

"Maybe once a year. Make that times ten years on the force—so I guess nine or ten times. I've lost count," he finished with a casualness that amazed Amanda.

"I knew there was a reason I liked being in the lab," Amanda said. "I didn't mind a normal patrol, but I transferred as soon as I could. Brian was very relieved."

"Brian?" Jack asked.

"My ex-husband. He worried about me constantly when I was out in a patrol car."

"Has he been an ex long?" Jack persisted, hoping that he sounded properly casual and not as desperately interested as he was.

"Two years this week. Brian decided he preferred a wife who didn't talk back and who was willing to stay at home and cater to his whims. And I decided that if he could find a woman that stupid, he was welcome to her." Amanda grinned wickedly. "He hasn't, yet. And according to my former sister-in-law, it's driving him crazy. How about you? Ever been married?"

"No, I've never taken the plunge," Jack answered. Their waitress brought the beer they had ordered and Jack took a big swallow of his. "I have nothing against the idea, though."

"That's nice to hear," Amanda said. "So many bachelors are convinced that they want to stay that way forever." She sipped her beer. "What made you transfer to homicide?"

"I was ready for a change," Jack admitted. "Ten years of working a rotating shift got old."

"Did you get tired of never knowing what you had to face next?" Amanda asked. "Did you get tired of the constant danger?"

"No, that didn't bother me at all. In fact, I kind of liked that part of it. But I think I'm going to like solving murders just as much. And I can still stay on SWAT—they don't get called out all that often."

"You liked the danger?" Amanda quizzed him. "Weren't you frightened?" She thought of the calm way Jack had faced possible death tonight.

"No, not really," Jack said thoughtfully. "I'm always surprised when people make a fuss over something I do," he added. "Like tonight. That was no big deal."

No big deal? Amanda thought as their waitress placed a large platter of in front of them. He had come to within inches, literally, of having a bullet hole in his head. Inwardly she shook her head. It just didn't seem to bother him.

They stuffed *fajitas* and hot sauce into fluffy flour tortillas, and they spent dinner on shoptalk. Jack had Amanda cringing in her chair with tales of some of his exploits over the last ten years. Besides several daring escapades with the SWAT team and the river rescue last year, he had once braved live wire from a fallen electrical pole to rescue a tiny toddler, knowing that one brush against the hot wire would mean death for both him and the child. Another time he disarmed a two hundred and fifty pound drunk in a parking lot by throwing the man over his shoulder in a judo maneuver and sitting on him until he had pried the knife out of his hand. And yet another time he pursued a drug smuggler down an expressway during rush hour. Jack didn't seem particularly proud of his brushes with danger—the way a show-off would—but rather matter of fact about them. He admitted that they always seemed to bother others much more than they ever did him.

About halfway through the meal Jack cleverly steered the conversation around to Amanda. He learned about her two degrees in chemistry, and that she had been on the force for five years—ever since earning the second degree. She had joined the force with the understanding that she would be assigned to the laboratory as soon as she had put in her requisite months in a patrol car. Not particularly shy about her personal accomplishments or those of the department, Amanda admitted that a number of convictions had been obtained purely as a result of her testimony, and that her department had developed a test that would identify blood or semen to within a one percent possibility of failure. Consequently, a number of rapes had been solved, as well as several robberies where the thief had cut himself entering or leaving the house. Amanda told Jack that she was particularly proud of solving the difficult hit-and-run of a small child last year, where she identified a chip of paint on the child's clothing as being from the 1982 Mercedes of a prominent local businessman.

They waded through an entire platter of *fajitas,* and Jack ordered a few more strips of meat for himself. When Amanda teased him about it, he confessed he had a hollow leg and could eat tremendous quantities of food without gaining weight. Jack paid for the meal, refusing Amanda's offer to split the bill, and the two of them walked down the quiet sidewalks toward the parking lot of the police department. The soft April breeze stirred the hair at Amanda's temples, and she was achingly aware of the handsome, virile man by her side. Jack Vance was warm, and personable, and funny, and he stirred her more than any man had in a long time. Amanda wondered more than once on the walk to the police station what his lips would feel like on hers. She did not object when he took her hand and cradled it lightly in his as they crossed the street and made no attempt to remove it when they were safely on the other side.

"It looks like the graveyard shift is already on duty," Jack commented as he and Amanda walked across the parking lot. Most of the patrol cars were gone, and they were the only two people in the lot. "Where's your car?"

"Over there." Amanda pointed out a lovingly restored 1965 Mustang convertible.

Jack whistled. "Good Lord, I've admired that car every day for the last five years! It's beautiful, Amanda."

"Why don't you get one if you like it so much?" Amanda asked.

"I've already got one old vehicle I've spent a fortune on," Jack rebutted.

Amanda whirled around. "The '52 Ford pickup!" she said. "I bet that's yours." The old Ford had been restored much the same way her Mustang had been.

"Yes, that's mine," Jack admitted. "If I offer to let you ride in it, will you accept a date from me for two nights from now? I'd take you out tomorrow, but I'm directing traffic at the convention center."

"Making some of that nice part-time money, huh?" Amanda asked. Most of the officers in town, herself included, earned extra income directing traffic for private businesses or working off duty as a security guard a few hours a week.

"That's right. So how about it? Are you free on Saturday night?"

"You bet," Amanda responded quickly, not caring if she sounded eager. "What time?"

"Sixish," Jack said as he leaned over her. And before Amanda could move away he had planted a hard, quick kiss on her lips. "That's in case you don't kiss on the first date," he added, grinning. "See you Saturday." He waved as he walked away.

Amanda got in her car and put the top down. She sat for a minute, the tip of her finger lightly touching her lips where Jack had kissed them just a moment earlier. There was no doubt about it: she was very attracted to Jack Vance, and if he hadn't left so suddenly, she very probably would have reached up and kissed him back.

Amanda got on the expressway and drove toward her northside apartment, the wind whipping her hair around her head. She could hardly wait until Saturday night so that she could see Jack again. And if his eagerness to make a date with her was anything to go by, he was just as excited to see her. That was just fine with her. Amanda admitted to herself that Jack was the most attractive man she had met in a long time. And she found his attitude toward danger interesting and a little intriguing, even if she didn't understand it.

***

Amanda slammed the door of her apartment behind her and hurried toward the bathroom, unbuttoning her shirt as she went. Jack had said sixish, and it was already a quarter of. What a time to get stuck behind a freight train. She thought she was going to be only a few minutes at the store. Cursing under her breath, Amanda shed her clothes, leaving them in a neat little heap on the counter. She hopped into the shower, quickly washing and shampooing away the grime that covered her after a day of cleaning house. She knew she wasn't going to be ready when Jack rang her bell, but she wanted to at least be dressed.

Amanda was just wrapping a towel around herself when the telephone rang. She muttered a swear word, hoping it wasn't her long-winded best friend, and picked up the receiver. "Hello!" she answered rather sharply.

"Used a good razor on that tongue today, huh?" Jack returned, laughing over the wire.

"Oh, thank goodness it's you," Amanda said. "You won't be knocking on the door while I'm standing here dripping wet trying to get rid of whoever. Did you get held up, too? Are you going to be a little late, I hope?"

"Something like that. We just got a call that there's been a very suspicious death at Penny's restaurant, and they want somebody from homicide to investigate it. Everybody is either tied up or has gone home already, so I'm going to have to answer the call."

Wonderful, Amanda thought. There went tonight. It would take Jack at least two hours at the restaurant, and he was probably going to ask for a rain check.

"So I thought I would give you a choice," he continued. "We can either postpone until another time, or I can pick you up on the way to the restaurant and we can go out after I get through. Since you're in the business, I thought you might not mind coming along."

"You just want help collecting evidence if it is a homicide," Amanda teased, glad that Jack didn't want to cancel. "Sure, Jack, come on and get me. But if I have to help you collect evidence, I get a steak."

"If you have to collect evidence, I'll even throw in a lobster," Jack promised. "See you in a little bit."

We'll be through in a couple of hours, and the rest of the evening will be ours, Amanda thought as she returned to the bathroom. What should she wear to a murder? She selected a tan pleated skirt and a shiny peach blouse with small shoulder pads. But before she put them on, she dropped her towel and stared at her naked body in the mirror. Not bad, but she would look better without those extra five pounds she could never quite shed. She made a face as she thought of Jack's small, hard-muscled body and the way he could put away food without gaining an ounce. She would have to try to get rid of those pounds before it got warm enough to go swimming.

Amanda dressed quickly and was putting the finishing touches to her makeup when Jack rang the bell. She checked for her .38 and her keys and met him at the door. "I'm ready," she announced as she stepped out on the porch. "I'll keep you waiting a fashionable fifteen minutes another time."

"You look great," Jack said as he smiled appreciatively at her.

Amanda returned Jack's look of admiration. "So do you," she returned, taking in Jack's crisp khaki safari jacket and brushed jeans. "Perfectly attired for collecting evidence." She laughed a little. "How many of your dates have you taken to a murder?"

"I must admit you're the first," Jack confessed as he opened the door of the pickup for Amanda. "I don't think too many of them would have appreciated it. I just hope it doesn't really turn out to be a murder. Maybe they choked on a bone or something like that."

"Do you have any idea what happened?" Amanda asked.

"No, my boss didn't say," Jack replied. He drove to Penny's, a small, family-style restaurant that Amanda had patronized many times before, and they made their way through the crowd that was milling around the door and trying to peer through the police cordon to see what was going on inside. They showed their badges and the patrolman let them through and held the door for them as they entered the restaurant. Amanda was surprised that Sergeant Tony Pehachek, Jack's boss, had arrived with another homicide investigator. "Bigger than you thought at first?" Jack queried.

"A tableful dead or dying," Tony responded grimly, raising his voice over the roar inside the restaurant. Unlike most murder scenes, the establishment was crawling with paramedics and policemen, trying desperately to keep anyone from entering or leaving the premises. "There are already two dead, and the paramedics just rushed four out of here barely hanging on to life."

"What happened?" Jack demanded as they made their way toward the center of the restaurant.

"We won't know until Amanda makes tests, but we suspect it's some kind of poison," Tony said. "I'm glad the bosses called you in tonight, Amanda. I'd like a confirmation and identification as soon as possible."

Amanda groaned inwardly—they weren't going to be out of here in any couple of hours. "I'm here unofficially, Tony, although I'd be glad to run some samples tonight," she offered. "This is Jack's idea of an evening out."

"Sorry about that, both of you," Tony said. "But look at it this way—it'll be a cheap date for Jack, and neither one of you will have a hangover in the morning. I guess we better get cracking on this."

Tony led the way to the table where dinner had been interrupted so tragically. Two bodies lay covered with sheets, and a middle-aged couple sat at the table, deep in shock, staring at the shrouded forms on the floor. The woman, obviously the boy's mother, was wringing a napkin as tears rolled down her face. The remains of eight dinners cluttered the table, and a birthday cake sat untouched, the candle melted to the base. A part of Amanda sized up the situation professionally, whereas another part of her hurt for these people. "Who were the victims?" she asked.

"Bert Carroway, age twenty, and Winnie Carroway, forty-five," Tony said crisply. "He was her nephew. Apparently the family was celebrating the boy's birthday. They all became sick, almost simultaneously, within a few minutes of finishing their dinner."

Amanda glanced around at the diners, some of whom were nibbling at their food. "Stop these idiots from eating anything else," she snapped. "Somebody else may end up dead if there was something in the food."

Tony nodded to one of the patrolmen, who stood up on a chair and spoke into a bullhorn. "Ladies and gentlemen, do not—I repeat, *do not*—eat anything else. These people may have been poisoned, and if they were, the poison may be in something that's on your plate."

A horrified gasp went up from the crowd, and some of the patrons started to get up from their chairs. The uniformed policemen managed to persuade them to sit back down, but they could not persuade one hardheaded old man to stop eating. "It tastes all right to me," he said belligerently when one of the policemen took his plate away. "You give that back to me, young man! That food was perfectly all right."

"Sorry, sir," the policeman murmured impassively. Amanda and Jack turned their faces away so that the man would not see their grins.

"The first thing we need to do is test for poison," Amanda said as she knelt beside the bodies. "Tony, I didn't come prepared. Could one of the paramedics draw blood from each victim?"

Tony motioned over one of the paramedics. "We need a vial of blood from each of them."

The paramedic nodded and knelt beside the bodies. He reached under the sheet and withdrew the lifeless arm of the young man. *"No!"* the woman sitting at the table cried suddenly. "Don't hurt Bert. He hates needles."

"Don't worry, ma'am, he won't feel a thing," the paramedic declared callously as he jabbed a needle in the man's arm.

The woman gasped and flinched, and Jack and Tony shot a disgusted look at the unfeeling paramedic. Amanda put her arm around the woman. "It's all right, ma'am," she said soothingly. "We have to take a sample, so I can find out what happened to them. You do want to know what happened, don't you?" The woman nodded.

"I'll know by the end of the evening what happened to your boy," Amanda assured her. "He was your son, wasn't he?"

The woman nodded again, too deeply in shock to even speak. The paramedic finished with Bert and pushed up the sleeve on the arm of the dead woman. Amanda positioned herself between the mother and her dead son and picked up the sheet that covered his face. She cringed inwardly as she stared down into his handsome features, hating the waste of this young life as she searched for a clue as to why he had died. Thoughts raced through her mind as she noted the blue tinge of his face and the almost purple hue of his lips. She covered his face and withdrew one of his lifeless hands, finding the same blue under his nail beds. Amanda wasn't sure, but she thought she detected a faint smell of almonds. She checked the aunt and found the same telltale coloring and odor. "Tony, I think I know what happened here, but I need to get downtown and check it out. I'll have you the results within the hour."

"What do you think it was?" Jack asked as he knelt beside Amanda.

"One of the cyanides. Can I borrow your truck?"

Jack handed her his keys. "Tony, Amanda's pretty sure it was poisoning," he said. "Should we start taking statements and collecting evidence? We're going to have to interview everybody as well as take a sample of everything in the kitchen. We'll be here half the night as it is."

"I see your point, but my boss will get my tail if we don't stick to procedure," Tony objected. "Amanda, call us the minute you know anything for sure."

What a horrible ending to my first date with Jack, Amanda thought as she took her precious blood samples to Jack's truck. She was pleasantly surprised to find a rather powerful engine under the hood and suspected that the old vehicle had been rebuilt as well as restored. She hurried downtown, and as quickly as she could prepared blood samples to go into the mass spectrometer, which was in turn hooked up to a computer link. She ran the aunt's first. In just a moment the computer generated a list of the ten most probable substances the poison might be, followed by the percent odds that it was that chemical. Amanda looked down the list and was not surprised by the results. The substance on the top of the list was sodium cyanide, with a 98.4 percent rating. Potassium cyanide was second, with a 2.1 percent probability, and the other eight were all less than 1 percent. Amanda then tested the young man's blood. Again sodium cyanide was the overwhelming computer choice.

Amanda called the restaurant three times and each time heard a busy signal. Abandoning that tactic, she called downstairs to homicide and had Tony paged. A moment later her telephone rang. "Is it cyanide?" he demanded.

"Sure is," Amanda confirmed.

"Any possibility of it being accidental?" Tony asked.

"Highly unlikely." Amanda explained, "Cyanide isn't found under sinks and in supply cabinets like a lot of things that lead to accidental poisoning. You have a homicide for sure."

"Just what we needed tonight," Tony said. "Thanks for the rush job. Will I see you in a few minutes?"

"I guess so," Amanda answered. She drove back to Penny's, nearly colliding with Jack as she opened the door of the restaurant.

"Here, let me," Amanda offered as she took several of the evidence bags, all filled with the remains of the ill-fated dinners. "Does Tony still need me?"

"No, but he wants you to go in early tomorrow and get started. The media's onto this one." Jack opened the door of the cab and pushed the bags in. "Some date, huh?" he asked as Amanda climbed up in the truck.

"I've got to admit that it's been unique," she put in dryly.

Jack backed out of the parking lot. "Amanda, I'm sorry," he apologized. "I'm going to be half the night at the restaurant. I may as well take you home."

"That's all right," Amanda responded, even though she was quite disappointed. "But only if you let me fix you a quick sandwich at my place. Ten minutes won't matter."

"I'll take you up on that," Jack said. He parked in front of Amanda's apartment and poured them each a glass of iced tea while Amanda hastily threw together ham and cheese sandwiches. "This hits the spot," he said as he wolfed down his sandwich. He took another.

"Real gourmet fare," Amanda teased. "So the search for a killer is on."

"Yes, and the public's going to be real interested in this one," Jack said. "You do know who the boy was, don't you?"

"The name seemed vaguely familiar, but no, I don't," Amanda admitted.

"He was a Baylor football star. Was supposed to have a good chance for the Heisman Trophy his senior year."

"He would have had such a wonderful life," Amanda whispered.

Jack finished the last of his second sandwich. He stood and pulled Amanda to her feet. "You're a mighty good sport, you know that?" he said as he ran his hand down the side of her face. "I'm sorry about tonight. I really am."

"I'm as disappointed as you are," Amanda admitted.

"I'll make it up to you next weekend, if you'll let me," Jack proposed as his fingers feathered lightly across her chin. "I'm off Saturday. If you'll save the afternoon, I'll treat you to a real relaxing good time."

"Sounds great," Amanda murmured, her breath suddenly uneven. Jack's fingers on her face were rough but gentle, teasing the sensitive nerve endings on her face. "I'll look forward to it."

"Thanks," Jack said as he bent slightly and pressed his lips to hers. He kissed her tenderly, gently at first. Then his kiss began to grow in intensity astonishing Amanda. Swamped with desire, she started to raise her arms when Jack suddenly pulled away. "If I keep kissing you, I won't be able to stop, and I have to get the evidence bags downtown," he said, his cheeks flushed. "I can hardly wait until next weekend."

"Neither can I," Amanda murmured as Jack left her. She sat down on the couch and kicked off her shoes. Some first date. It wasn't his fault or hers that the murders had turned out to be something that would keep Jack all night. Still, she was disappointed he was gone. At least she would see him during the week, especially if he was assigned to the poisonings, and they would be going out next weekend. He had promised her a relaxing afternoon. Amanda wasn't sure what he meant by that, but she was sure it was going to be long and lazy and perfectly lovely.

Chapter Three

Amanda hunched her shoulders as she stared at the computer console. "Well, that's it," she said as she scanned the list of substances the computer read as being present in the bottled mayonnaise. "There are enough food additives in it to kill you, but no cyanide."

"Is that everything out of the restaurant?" her assistant, Samantha Johnson, inquired as she peered over Amanda's shoulder.

"Yes, this is the last of it," Amanda responded. "But we knew by Tuesday that the cyanide didn't come from anything on their plates. All their scraps came up clean."

"So why did we test everything in the kitchen?" Samantha complained good-naturedly. "I had no idea a restaurant had so many bottles and jars!"

"Because Tony and Jack wanted us to. They had to be sure, absolutely sure, that those people didn't get that cyanide in the restaurant. And I'm sure the owners of the restaurant don't mind having the name of their establishment cleared, although I'm afraid the bad publicity's already wrecked their business."

"That's too bad. Lionel and I have eaten there several times and liked it a lot," Samantha volunteered. "So what are Jack and Tony going to do now? If the poison wasn't in the food, where could it have come from?"

Amanda shrugged. "It's days like today I'm glad I'm a chemist and not on homicide. I honestly don't know what they'll do next."

The telephone rang and Samantha answered it while Amanda took her sample from the mass spectrometer. "Amanda, it's that weirdo again," she said, her hand firmly across the receiver. "He's asking to speak to you."

"Wonderful," Amanda remarked dryly. Sometimes the laboratory got the strangest calls. Lately they had received several from a man who insisted that he was hearing voices from outer space and wanted her to tell him what to do about it. Amanda realized that he had a problem and had tried to tell him that her department could hardly help him. But he insisted that only she could make the voices go away. "Couldn't you tell him I've already left?"

"That doesn't work, remember?" Samantha reminded her. "He'll just start calling on Monday morning. I wish there were something we *could* tell him—just to get rid of him."

Amanda stared at Samantha as an idea took hold in her head. "Maybe there is."

"Are you thinkin' what I think you're thinkin'?" Samantha drawled.

"What do you think?" she asked, her eyes sparkling with mischief as she took the telephone from Samantha. "Hello? Yes, Mr. Smith, I remember you. You're the gentleman who keeps hearing the strange voices, right?" Amanda had to be sure it was her kook before she proceeded. "Yes, sir, I've done some thinking since you called me last week. It hasn't gotten any better, is that correct? It's gotten worse? That's a shame, but I think we may be able to help you. I checked with the UFO department of the Air Force, and they said that there might be a temporary solution we could pass along to you if you'll give us your word that you'll see a Dr. Ruben Sanchez just as soon as you possibly can." Dr. Sanchez was one of San Antonio's leading psychiatrists. "Now, sir, do I have your word?"

Amanda winked at Samantha, who was trying not to laugh out loud, and turned back to her caller. "The UFO department said that you weren't grounded. That's right, sir. What can you do to ground yourself? It's easy to take care of temporarily, but you must remember that this will not take the place of going to Dr. Sanchez. You just need to go to the store and buy a box of paper clips. When you get home with the clips, make a chain of them and run them from your belt to your shoe. That should ground you well enough to stop those voices for now." Amanda paused a minute. "No, sir, you don't have to get the fancy paper clips that they sell in the office supply stores—just the ordinary ones from the grocery store will do. Now remember, you need to see Dr. Sanchez as soon as possible. Glad I could be of help." She grinned as she hung up the telephone. "I hope he doesn't tell Dr. Sanchez who referred him."

Amanda heard several hands clapping behind her. She whirled around to find Jack, Tony, and Samantha applauding enthusiastically. "Grounded? That's priceless!" Samantha giggled.

"Tell me, in which of your chemistry courses did you learn about grounding?" Jack teased.

"Try Comedy 103," Amanda retorted, laughing.

"And I thought we got some kooky calls in homicide," Tony sputtered. "What were you grounding him for, by the way?"

"He thought he was hearing voices from outer space. 'Extraterrestrial transmissions,' I think he called them," Amanda said. "I do hope he sees the doctor, though. He sounded very nice—very strange but very nice."

"ET probably loves him," Tony quipped. "What have you turned up in the kitchen supplies from Penny's?"

"Absolutely nothing," Amanda answered. "I've tested everything you brought in, even the detergent. And I found nothing. Penny's is clean."

"The owners will be glad to hear that, but it sure makes our job that much harder," Jack admitted.

"Where do you go from here?" Amanda asked.

"We keep thinking, and questioning, and digging, although I must admit my mind's a blank right now."

"Say, what about the table linens?" Tony asked. "Has anybody checked them?"

"No, I hadn't thought of that," Amanda said slowly. "Do you want it right now? It will take me an hour or so to set up."

Tony glanced at his watch. "Monday morning's good enough," he said. "The press has that city council fight to keep them busy and out of our hair for the next few days. See you Monday, Jack. I'm taking off."

"I'm leaving, too," Samantha chimed in as she took off her lab coat. "Lionel and I are trying that new nightclub that opened last week. We're gonna boogey the night away!"

"I heard that place was just a pickup joint," Jack teased. "What's a nice old married couple like you two doing in a place like that?"

"So? We'll pick each other up," Samantha retorted. "See you later." She was already dancing as she shut the door behind her.

"Where does she get the energy?" Amanda groaned. "She's put in just as hard a week as I have, and I can barely put one foot in front of the other."

Jack sat down on one of the laboratory stools and pulled out a cigarette. "The fact that she's considerably younger than we are might have a little to do with it. Got any more coffee?"

Amanda poured them each a cup from the coffeemaker. "The bane of the policeman," she said, handing him his cup and sitting down across from him. "Coffee and cigarettes."

"Want one?" Jack asked as he held out the pack.

Amanda shook her head. "No, I gave it up two years ago and promptly gained ten pounds, most of which I still have. Sometimes I'm tempted to start up again and see if I can lose them."

Jack looked up and down her body appraisingly. "I like you better with the weight," he announced matter-of-factly. "Don't go back to these things—they're a nasty habit."

"Ever thought of quitting?" Amanda wondered. "Not that I'm pushing you to."

"Yes, I've thought about it, but then I put in a week like this one, and I'm ready to admit I need the crutch," Jack confessed. "Either Tony or I have talked at length to everybody that was in that restaurant, and we're firmly convinced that nobody there was involved in the poisoning. Yet, *somebody* had to have done it. It's enough to drive a cop to drinking—never mind smoking." He ran his hand across his face. "Thank goodness I have tomorrow off. Are you ready to spend a relaxing afternoon with me?"

"More than ready," Amanda said as she sipped her coffee. "My week's been as bad as yours. We not only got hit with the poisonings, but we had that double shooting and two hit-and-runs on Sunday. I admit that I'm looking forward to relaxing as much as I am to spending some time with you."

"You need some of both," Jack teased. "Come on, I'll walk you to your car."

Amanda locked up the lab and together they walked to the parking lot. "Dress casually," Jack suggested as she got in the car and lowered the top. "See you about noon."

A relaxing afternoon, Amanda thought happily as she drove toward her apartment, not even bothering to get angry when a BMW cut in front of her. She was ready for a quiet day. There were a million things they could do to relax. San Antonio was full of museums and had a fantastic zoo and several lovely parks where they could go on a picnic. Or maybe they would just put on their swimming suits and lounge around the pool at her apartment complex. It really didn't matter to her what they did—as long as she could relax and they could be together.

So Amanda needs some time away from her work as badly as I do, Jack thought as he put his old truck in gear and drove toward the small tract house he bought last year as a tax break. His week had been slow and, he had to admit, a little boring, as he had questioned suspect after suspect and found them all innocent. In some ways homicide was interesting, but he missed the action he was used to seeing on the street. But that was all right. He would see some action tomorrow at the track. He would get the adrenaline flowing again. He would get the rush, the high that he couldn't seem to live without. His hands tightened on the wheel of his truck as he thought of his other vehicle, parked in his garage. He hadn't driven her in a month or more, and he could hardly wait to get behind her wheel again.

***

Amanda was ready when Jack rang her bell. "Hello," she said as Jack reached down and planted a soft kiss on her lips.

"Hello, yourself," Jack returned as he gripped Amanda's hand. "Are you ready to go?" He looked approvingly at her tight stirrup pants and soft slouchy cotton sweater.

"Yes, I'm ready." She locked her door, and they held hands as they walked to Jack's car. "I meant to ask, did you want to stay here and use the pool? If you're tired and just want to goof off, I can't think of a better way to do it."

"We'll do that another time," Jack answered. "I have something else in mind for today." He held the door of the truck for Amanda.

"What?" Amanda asked.

Jack got in on his side. "We're going to the stock car races."

"The what?" Amanda asked, not sure she had heard him correctly.

"The stock car races," Jack repeated. "Ever been?"

"Uh, no," Amanda admitted. Watching a bunch of souped-up old cars race around a narrow track had never been her idea of fun, but why not give it a try? She might be wrong about the fun part, especially if she was watching the race with Jack.

"You'll love it," Jack predicted confidently.

They chatted as they drove across town and down the road that led to one of the local racetracks. Amanda tried to remember everything she could about racing. Finally she gave up. Jack would have to explain to her what was going on. She doubted he would mind—men usually liked to show off their knowledge. Besides, that would make it just that much more fun for the both of them. They turned into the dirt parking lot, and she and Jack walked toward the track. But instead of buying a ticket at the gate, Jack turned off and started walking around to the back. "Where are we going?" Amanda asked, slightly bewildered.

"Around to the pit," Jack replied cheerfully. "My car's back there."

"Your what?" Amanda asked.

"My car," Jack repeated. "I brought it out this morning. I'm in the third race."

It took a moment for reality to register. When it did, Amanda's eyes widened. "You're *racing?*"

"Yes, isn't it great?" Jack said enthusiastically, his eyes flashing with excitement. "I've been looking forward to this all week. You're going to love it, Amanda."

I am? Amanda wondered as she followed him. Did Jack really intend to drive a car in one of the races? Wasn't that kind of dangerous? Amanda looked at Jack's face and shivered at the excitement she saw there. He was really looking forward to the race.

Amanda said nothing to Jack as they approached the pit. *He knows more about this than I do,* she told herself. *Maybe it's not really as dangerous as I've been led to believe.* Jack greeted several men who looked like drivers or mechanics before he led her to an old orange Dodge Charger that had been altered for racing. "Amanda, this is 'Debbie,'" he said solemnly as Amanda peered doubtfully into the car. "Debbie, Amanda's going to watch us this afternoon, so we're going to have to do our best for her." He gazed at the car proudly. "What do you think of her?"

"Very nice," Amanda said admiringly. The car really was something to look at. "Is she safe?"

"As safe as any other stock car," Jack replied. "She has all the standard safety equipment along with her other modifications. She's where all my overtime money goes."

At that moment a voice came over the loudspeaker and announced that the first race would begin in five minutes. Jack gave her a quick kiss on the lips and directed her to a seat on the edge of the stands. Here she could see but would be able to slip to the pit when his race was over. Amanda sat down on the wooden bench and watched as the cars entered in the first race took their places at the starting line.

Amanda kept one eye on the track and another on the pit as the first race proceeded. It looked like fun and it didn't seem all that dangerous. All the drivers, even though they were amateurs like Jack, seemed to know what they were doing. Jack left the pit for a few minutes and returned wearing an orange jumpsuit that Amanda sincerely hoped was fireproof. The first race was over in a matter of minutes, and was won by a green Malibu. As soon as the track was clear, the cars that were scheduled for the second race took their places at the starting line. That race began, but Amanda ignored it completely as she watched Jack pull on gloves and an orange helmet that matched his jumpsuit. He spoke with a man that Amanda guessed was his mechanic and got into the Charger.

A collective gasp from the crowd drew Amanda's attention from Jack to the race. She looked but she couldn't see what had startled the crowd. "What happened?" she asked the man next to her. "I was looking down in the pit and I missed it."

"Number 25 cut in front of 17 and nearly creamed him," the man informed her. "Great move! I love a thrill like that."

I'm not sure I do, Amanda thought as she politely thanked the man. The second race was longer than the first, but it, too, finished without incident. Then the loudspeaker was calling for the contestants in the third race to take their places.

Amanda stared at Jack as he got out of the car and blew her a kiss. She blew one back to him, and Jack disappeared into the Charger and joined the starting lineup.

The signal came for the cars to start their engines. Amanda's eyes were glued to the orange Charger, and she cheered with the crowd when the flag went down and the cars pulled out onto the track, each maneuvering to take the lead. Jack's Charger quickly slipped into fourth or fifth place. His position kept changing as he and an old GTO passed one another over and over again. Jack finally cut in front of the GTO and stayed there, but he missed hitting the GTO by inches. His daring move had the crowd gasping. Without meaning to Amanda cringed.

The race was over quickly. A red Fairlane won, but Amanda barely glanced at the victor. She watched closely as Jack slowed his car and drove back into the pit. She wasn't sure, since she hadn't really paid much attention to the other cars and drivers, but she didn't think Jack was all that good. A better driver might have had a close call on the track, but he probably wouldn't have had the kind of near disaster that Jack had.

Amanda left the stands and tried to make her way through the pit, but it had filled up with cars and drivers and Jack was at the other end. Rather than push her way through, she waited patiently while the cars scheduled for the fourth race one by one left the pit. Seeing a path starting to open in Jack's direction, she was about to cross over to him when she heard Jack's name on the lips of the man who was standing directly in front of her. "What did you think of Vance's near miss?" he asked the man next to him as he drank from a bottle of beer.

"I think he's a lousy driver," his companion returned.

"I wouldn't call him 'lousy,' exactly," the first man said. "'Mediocre,' maybe, but not 'lousy.'"

The second man shrugged. "He could be pretty good if he got out here more often," he commented. "He doesn't get in enough practice."

"He doesn't have the time, from what I gather," the first man said. "He only has about one Saturday in three or four free."

"Oh, yeah? What's he do for a living?"

The first man launched into a description of Jack's job, but Amanda walked on. She had heard all she cared to hear. So she had been right. He wasn't a very good driver. She shivered a little, even though it was quite warm in the pit. Could his lack of skill really cause an accident?

"What did you think?" Jack asked eagerly as Amanda approached him. "Wasn't it the greatest?" He took her by the hand and led her over to his mechanic. "Tom, I want you to meet Amanda Blakeman. This is Tom Martinez, the best mechanic in the pit."

"Glad to meet you," Tom said as he wiped his greasy hand on his pants before he offered it to Amanda.

Amanda exchanged a little polite conversation with Tom while Jack changed back into his jeans and shirt. They climbed up into the stands, and Jack took Amanda's hand. "Did you enjoy the race?" he pressed eagerly.

"Sure," Amanda said, forcing more enthusiasm into the word than she felt. She would be damned if she voiced her misgivings to Jack "It looks like a lot of fun."

"It is," Jack enthused. "And it's exciting down there, just me and my machine."

Amanda glanced over at Jack. "Don't you ever think about getting hurt?"

"Lord, no," Jack responded, laughing. "Racing's not really very dangerous."

"If you say so," Amanda murmured. And maybe it wasn't. She started to say something else to Jack, but at that moment another race started and it captured Jack's attention completely.

The sun was low in the sky when the last group of cars roared across the finish line. Amanda's head ached a little from the smell of exhaust fumes and the whine of engines, but she had actually enjoyed the races—once she didn't have to worry about Jack.

"How'd you like it?" Jack asked as they climbed down from the stands.

"It was interesting," Amanda hedged.

"You're a good sport," Jack said as he looped his arm around her shoulders. "And for that you've earned a night on the town, no expense spared," he proclaimed. He steered Amanda into the pit. "Tom, would you mind parking Debbie in your garage for the week? It seems silly to take her all the way back across town when I'm going to race her next weekend." Jack turned to Amanda. "Tom lives just a couple of miles from here."

"Sure, if you don't mind if my cat sleeps on the seat," Tom said.

Jack gave Tom the keys to his trailer, and he and Amanda joined the slow, lazy exodus to the parking lot. Amanda breathed in the fresh country air and stopped to pick a bluebonnet. "Shame on you— that's illegal," Jack teased as she fingered the delicate flower.

"It's only illegal along the public roadside," Amanda corrected him. "This is private property. Here." She tucked the flower in Jack's lapel, her fingers lightly brushing the warm skin of his chest. She withdrew her hand reluctantly, wanting to maintain the intimate contact just a little longer.

They watched the sun go down in red and orange splendor as they drove across town. The sky gradually darkened, and the lights of the city winked on. Jack parked in front of Amanda's apartment and walked her to the door. "How long do you need to get gorgeous?" he asked.

"Passable or gorgeous?" Amanda teased.

"How long does gorgeous take?"

"Six weeks—my plastic surgeon said it would take at least that long for the swelling to go down."

"Smart ass," Jack retorted, laughing.

"Seriously, give me an hour, and I'll be ready to outdo Samantha," Amanda said.

Actually, it was only fifty-three minutes later when Amanda stepped in front of her mirror and put on her opal necklace and ring. The milky greens and whites of the stones glowed against the golden tan of Amanda's skin, and they picked up the soft mint-green of her dress. It had demure cap sleeves but plunged in the front, showing a hint of provocative cleavage. Her eyes, subtly shadowed, sparkled. She looked pretty tonight, prettier than she had in a long time, and she knew that it was because she was excited about her evening with Jack.

Jack rang her doorbell promptly on the hour. Amanda's eyes widened as she stared at him, dressed to the nines in a silky European-cut shirt and pleated slacks. He looked more like a jet-setter than a policeman tonight. "You look absolutely wonderful, Amanda. Were you thinking the same thing I was thinking?"

"You did say something about dancing," Amanda said.

"I did and we will, but first, where would you like to eat?"

Amanda tossed out several suggestions, but in the end they settled on one of the many small, interesting restaurants on North St. Mary's, an area that had recently become the trendiest gathering place and watering hole in San Antonio. The restaurant specialized in homemade pasta and had a belly dancer every Friday and Saturday night. Amanda ordered a bowl of linguine, and Jack ordered fettuccine. Their waiter brought them a carafe of wine and Jack poured Amanda a glass. "Is this better than the races?" he teased as Amanda sipped the rich red wine.

"Yes, I must admit that it is. But I had a better time than you think I did."

"You didn't look all that enamored when you came down to the pit." Jack said as the waiter put huge salads and a loaf of garlic bread in front of them. "I thought I had really blown it with you until we got up to the stands."

"Is that why you came on so enthusiastically about the races?" Amanda asked dryly. She was rewarded when a bright red blush crept up Jack's neck.

"I guess so," Jack confessed, breaking off a piece of bread and handing it to her. "I wanted you to give the racing a chance. You didn't find it a real bore, did you?"

"It was fun," Amanda insisted. She was not about to admit to Jack that she had misgivings.

"I'm glad," Jack said. "I love to race. It's an unbelievable adrenaline rush, and it's not even dangerous."

Amanda raised an eyebrow. "It's not?"

Jack shrugged. "Well, maybe there's a little danger involved. That's what makes it fun. But it's not all that dangerous—not like my skydiving."

It took a moment for that to register. "Your *what?*"

"I always wanted to be a paratrooper, but the war in Nam was over before I got a chance to enlist," Jack admitted cheerfully. "So I took some lessons a few years ago, and I go out every other month or so. I belong to a club that charters a plane and jumps nearly every weekend. I jump with them when I'm not racing."

"I can't believe it," Amanda breathed, more to herself than to Jack.

"Now, I have to admit that gets a little dangerous," Jack said. "Or maybe it's not. Maybe it just feels like it is."

The waiter brought their dinners, and Amanda wound some linguine around her spoon and popped it in her mouth. "Why do you keep doing it if it makes you feel frightened?"

"For the rush. I love the rush. And I don't feel frightened." Jack sampled his fettuccine. "Delicious. This place was a good idea."

"I've never gone wrong in here," Amanda agreed. "I'm almost afraid to ask, but what else do you do for fun?"

"I love Travis McGee novels, I watch every cop show on television—*Cagney and Lacey, Hill Street Blues, Magnum, P.I.*— and tape them if I miss, and I chase pretty women in my pickup." Jack sipped his wine and helped himself to another chunk of bread. "Oh, yes," he said almost as an afterthought, "I ride wild bulls."

"Cute, Jack," Amanda shot back, grinning.

"No, I really do. I don't know why I didn't mention it first. It's my favorite sport. I've competed in amateur rodeos all over the state."

Amanda's jaw dropped. "Good grief, doesn't *anything* scare you?"

Jack nodded and looked shamefaced. "I fainted at my first autopsy. It wasn't the sight of a dead body, or of blood. It was the knives they use on them to cut them up. I still can't stand to watch."

Despite herself Amanda laughed. "You're kidding. You mean you can jump out of a plane for fun, but you can't watch an autopsy? I'm sorry for laughing, but that's hilarious."

Jack laughed along with her. When Amanda asked him how on earth he had become interested in bull riding, he told her that he grew up in Pearsall and became involved in amateur rodeo in high school. Amanda learned that he was the only son of a schoolteacher and that his father, whom he idolized as a child, died from cancer when he was in college. She was touched by Jack's deep love and respect for his widowed mother, who had never remarried. Amanda in turn told Jack all about her older sister's lovely family and bragged a little about her recently widowed mother's successful reentry into the job market. She said that her relationship with her father had been a little stormy but admitted that she missed him now that he was gone. They exchanged a few stories about high school, and Amanda related some of the funny things that had happened in her college chemistry courses. Jack said that he had never gone to college, and that he regretted it now.

The waiter had just cleared their plates when a bearded man stepped to the small platform and began to pound a set of drums in rhythm to a strange-sounding music coming from the stereo system. Amanda giggled at the way Jack ogled the blonde belly dancer who slithered out from the back. Bouncing and jiggling, the girl gyrated her hips as she weaved her way through the tables, stopping long enough for the men to put money in the top and skirt of her costume. Amanda couldn't keep from laughing when it took Jack three tries to get a dollar bill in her skirt.

They were still laughing twenty minutes later when they walked back to Jack's truck. "I can't believe the way that girl can move," Jack marveled.

"Yeah, she wiggles places I don't even have," Amanda complained.

Jack put his arm around Amanda's shoulders. "There's nothing wrong with your moves, believe me."

Amanda blushed in the darkness. "Are we still going dancing?" she asked. "Do you have to work tomorrow?"

"Sure, we're going," Jack answered as they got in the truck. "A few cups of hot coffee and I'll be fine."

Jack took Amanda to a brand-new nightspot that wasn't too far from her apartment. The smiling hostess showed them to a table on the edge of the dance floor, and as soon as they had ordered drinks Jack leaned over to Amanda. "Are you a duffer or a pro out there?" he asked, pointing toward the gyrating dancers.

"A pro—definitely a pro," Amanda assured him. They waited for the music to end, and as a rock song faded into a lively reggae Jack led Amanda to the dance floor. Moving as gracefully as if they had danced together for years, they twirled and whirled. Amanda was glad she had worn high heels—they made her almost the same height as Jack, and he could slip under her arm almost as easily as she could slip under his.

The reggae faded into a dreamy ballad, and Jack pulled Amanda into his arms as a twinkling mirrored ball rotated from the ceiling. Amanda put both her arms around Jack's neck and held him close to her, as the lonely wail of a saxophone filled the air. She could feel her breasts crushed against his hard chest, and the warmth of his legs cut through both his clothing and hers. Jack's hand pressed against the small of her waist, holding her close to his hips as his lips lightly brushed her temple. *He feels so good next to me,* Amanda thought as she gave herself to the dreamy sensuality of the moment.

All too soon, the music began to change, this time to a lively Michael Jackson number, and Jack led Amanda back to the table. "You're not dressed for break-dancing," he teased as his eyes ran down her sheerly-stockinged legs. The waitress had left their drinks, and Amanda sipped her scotch and soda, savoring the lingering response she felt to Jack's nearness.

In spite of the fact that Jack had to work the next day, he and Amanda danced until the wee hours of the morning. They discovered they were naturals together. Both had rhythm and flair, and neither of them was shy about displaying their dancing talent. They actually received applause for their wildly sensuous rendition of Tina Turner's latest hit. When the music turned slow and dreamy, they clung together, aware only of each other and the haunting throb of the music. It was with real reluctance that Amanda finally reminded Jack that he had to be at work by seven. Still, he insisted on one more dance before he would take her home.

Jack parked in front of Amanda's apartment. "Thank you for a wonderful evening," he murmured gently as he took Amanda's hand and stroked it lightly with the tip of his fingers.

"Thank *you,* Jack," Amanda said. "I loved every minute—well, almost every minute."

"Was tonight special?" Jack asked softly.

"You know it was," Amanda answered as she held Jack's face between her palms. "I haven't had such a wonderful time in quite a while."

"Good," Jack said as he grasped Amanda's shoulders, "because I haven't spent an evening this special in a long time, either. And I haven't wanted to kiss a woman this badly in I don't know how long."

"So what are you waiting for?" Amanda asked as Jack lowered his lips to hers.

"Absolutely nothing," Jack breathed as his lips brushed hers once, twice, before kissing her in earnest. Amanda groaned a little as she pressed her body against Jack's, her fingers curling around his head to nestle in the soft hair at his nape. Greedily, hungrily, they clung to one another, the taut thread of awareness that had stretched between them since the first moment they had laid eyes on each other, ensnaring them as they gave expression to their emotions. Jack caressed the soft skin of her shoulders, the tender flesh that he had wanted to touch since the first time he had seen Amanda. Amanda stroked the firm chest that she had wanted to touch since the day she had first seen Jack. She felt his waist through the fine fabric of his shirt and remembered the way he had looked that day without it, tanned and bare and gleaming with fitness and health. Jack ran his finger down the provocative dip of her dress, lightly brushing the edge of her breasts as he tried to imagine what she looked like without her bra. He tantalized her with the tip of his finger, not going beyond the edge of her dress, yet every tender stroke was pleasurable torture.

Amanda made a quiet sound of protest when Jack lifted his lips from hers. But rather than pulling away from her, he placed gentle, feathery kisses all along her temple. His uneven breath stirred her short hair, and Amanda caressed his face with her lips. "Are you real, or are you the sum total of all my sensuous daydreams?" Jack whispered.

Amanda took his hand and placed it lightly over her heart, which he could feel pounding in her chest. "I'm real," she said. "Only I don't feel real right now. I feel like it's magic or something. You're magic—we're magic."

"Oh, Mandy," Jack breathed as he kissed her again, once again drawing a deep response from Amanda. This time when he removed his lips from hers, he gently slid away from her. "I have to go," he insisted gently. "I wish I could stay for a drink, but I can't."

"I know." Neither of them had any illusions about what would happen if Jack stayed "for a drink," and neither of them was ready for that to happen yet. Jack walked Amanda to her door and waited patiently for her to find the key. "Thank you again for a wonderful evening," Amanda said. She reached up and gave Jack a gentle kiss on his cheek. "Good night."

"Good night," Jack said. He walked to his truck, a bemused expression on his face. He had never been so bewitched by a woman in all his life.

She was so much fun to be with, he thought as he sped down the expressway. And she was a trouper. She'd tried to hide her misgivings about the racing this afternoon, but Jack wasn't fooled. She wasn't all that fond of the racing, but she hadn't made a fuss the way his mother used to when his father took his old Chevy out on the track. She'd gone along and managed to have a good time anyway. Amanda would come around, Jack promised himself. She would learn to love the racing. She would learn to love all of his sports.

Amanda waltzed around the apartment for a minute before she ended up in the bathroom. Wishing the beautiful evening didn't have to come to an end, she slowly took off her clothes and showered. Smiling to herself, she got into bed, pulled up the covers, and turned off the light. As she lay in the darkness Amanda realized it would be a long time before she would be able to fall asleep. Her mind was too full of thoughts of Jack.

He was nice—he was *so* nice. And unlike many nice men, he was also a lot of fun to be with, and he could be something of a charmer. He actually managed to make watching the stock car races fun, and dinner and dancing with him had been absolutely divine. The sensual attraction they felt for one another was almost overwhelming. Amanda couldn't ever remember feeling that kind of longing for another man, not even the man she had been married to for five years. Jack Vance was pretty close to perfect.

Pretty close…but not quite. Although she tried to push the memory away, Amanda envisioned him as he had looked this afternoon, climbing into his race car and speeding around the track. She pictured him skydiving and riding a wild bull and shuddered at the thoughts. But the scene that was most vivid in her mind was Jack stripped to his underwear, taunting a killer. Amazingly none of it frightened him. He didn't really seem to comprehend the danger he put himself in.

Amanda sighed as she turned over. She liked Jack, and she was attracted to him, but she didn't understand him. But she'd be damned if she would share her misgivings with Jack. No, she would play along. She was not going to let her fear for his safety ruin what could be a wonderful relationship with the man.

***

Amanda reached down into the swimming pool and splashed a handful of cool water over her bare stomach. She tested her skin with a forefinger, decided she had sunned her front enough, and flipped over so that her back was exposed to the bright sunshine. She slept until almost noon and let the warm sun and sparkling water of the pool lure her away from the housecleaning she planned. She had been out for nearly an hour, soaking up the sun and gossiping with the people in her apartment complex. They barely saw one another during the winter, but come spring they would congregate around the swimming pool and get caught up on what everyone was doing. Beer, wine, and soft drinks fueled the conversation, and a few brave souls tested the water and declared it chilly but invigorating.

Amanda lay on her back until it was hot with the warmth of the sun, and she, too, was persuaded to give the cool water of the pool a try. Once in the water, she joined in a lively game of chase and tag with the college boys in the apartment across from her until she could feel her nose turn red. Since she was getting chilled, and she didn't want to pay for too much sun with a week-long sunburn, she excused herself and was loping up her steps when she heard the telephone ring. She fumbled with her key and grabbed the jangling phone on the fifth ring. "Hello, mom! How've you been?"

"Amanda, sorry, I'm not your mother. Where have you been? I've been trying to reach you for the last hour."

"Jack! How are you today? I've been at the pool for most of the afternoon." Amanda was pleased and surprised to hear from Jack, since she hadn't expected to see him until tomorrow.

"I'm a little sleepy but otherwise all right. Look, I hate to do this to you. I know you were enjoying your day off, but we really need you down here this afternoon."

"Sure, Jack. What's happening?" Amanda asked, immediately businesslike, as she started to shrug out of her wet bathing suit.

"We've had another poisoning. We need you to identify it for us."

Chapter Four

Jack was waiting at the lab when Amanda arrived. "What happened?" she asked as she unlocked the door.

"A bunch of the residents at the Village Heights apartments were having an impromptu pool party when they started getting sick. There are seven or eight of them who are ill, and some of them are sicker than others." Amanda took the blood samples Jack thrust at her and left him to log in.

"Why did they call you in? Did one of them not make it?" Amanda asked.

"One of the women didn't," Jack said grimly. "And the paramedics said that a couple of the others were really iffy when they took them in."

Amanda wasted no more time on conversation. Jack watched patiently as she prepared a blood sample for the mass spectrometer and inserted it into the machine. The computer console flashed a list of possibilities a moment later, and 2, 4-dinitrophenol topped the list at 95 percent. "There's your poison," Amanda declared as she ran her finger across the screen. "A rather effective one, I might add."

"I've never heard of it," Jack admitted as he peered over Amanda's shoulder.

Amanda thought a minute. "You're right. It isn't a well-known poison. In fact, very few people have ever even heard of it, much less know that it can kill."

"Is it possible that the poisonings were an accident?" Jack inquired.

"No, this had to be deliberate," Amanda responded with conviction.

Eddie Gutierrez walked into the room fumbling with several large evidence bags filled with the party food and drink. *"Juera,* how did your nose get so red?" he asked as Amanda took the bags from him.

"I was just coming in from a pool party at my place when Jack called," Amanda explained as she put the bags on the cabinet.

"I'd love to come to a pool party with you," Eddie teased as Amanda started to sift through the first bag. It contained a sack of potato chips that had been dusted with fingerprint powder. "Do you wear one of those little string bikinis?"

"Yes, and I probably look better in it than you would," Amanda flipped as she poked her finger into the slight paunch Eddie had developed in the last year.

"It's all Sylvia's fault," he complained good-naturedly. "If she would stop fixing me all those tortillas, I wouldn't have this problem. Then all the girls would like me."

"The last time I talked to Sylvia, at the Christmas dance last year, she said she put you on a strict diet and that she hadn't made a tortilla in a month," Jack chimed in dryly.

Amanda giggled as she prepared the potato chip sample to go in the machine. "Why don't you give up and admit that you just love to eat?" she asked. She inserted the potato chip sample into the machine, and a minute later the results flashed onto the screen. "All you could get from those potato chips is fat," she announced as she removed the sample. "They're all right."

"Lord, I hope this doesn't turn out to be like the one last week," Jack murmured to Eddie. "We still haven't figured out where that poison came from."

"Patience, patience," Amanda cautioned as she opened the second evidence bag and removed a half-empty bottle of strawberry wine. She uncorked the bottle and shuddered at the smell. "You wouldn't need to poison this stuff—it would kill you on its own," she said as she prepared a sample of it.

Jack picked up the bottle and read the label. "Isn't this the stuff that's a famous ingredient of freshman drinking parties?"

"Sure. How do you think she knows it kills?" Eddie put in as he sniffed the bottle.

"I have vivid memories of being sick on it," Amanda admitted. "I can't even smell the stuff without gagging." She put the sample into the spectrometer. "Nothing," she said a moment later. "I'll keep going."

Amanda tested her way through a bag of corn chips, a couple of bottles of jug wine, and three half-empty cans of soft drinks. She could tell that Jack was getting anxious, and she knew that he was thinking of the lack of progress they'd made in the cyanide killings. *Come on, onion dip!* she thought as she prepared a sample for testing.

"Bingo!" she called quickly. "Fellows, come take a look. This stuff is loaded."

Jack and Eddie peered over her shoulder. "It sure is," Jack said as he stared at the console. "How could they not taste it?"

Eddie picked up the tub and sniffed it cautiously. "I can't smell anything."

"You wouldn't," Amanda explained. "The smell of onions in the dip would disguise almost any flavor or odor." She removed the sample from the machine. "Whoever did this poisoning knew what they were doing."

"Whoever did the last one did, too," Jack declared ruefully. "We couldn't even find the vector there," he said, referring to whatever the poison had been hidden in. "At least this time we have *something* to go on."

"Are you taking this case, too?" Amanda asked.

"For today, I guess," Jack said. "I don't know who Tony will want to take it tomorrow."

"He'll probably assign us both," Eddie said. "He usually does that, if we start a case together. Think you can stand it?"

"Only if you promise not to call me your *juera,*" Jack chided.

"All right, honey," Eddie said. Jack rolled his eyes and gave up.

"I wish I could wrangle my way into being assigned to this one," Amanda remarked longingly. "Maybe I shouldn't admit it, but I find both this poisoning and the one last week fascinating, even though people died. I don't know, I guess it's because they were done with chemicals rather than with knives or guns."

Jack and Eddie looked at each other over Amanda's head. "Think you can stand her sharp tongue?" Jack teased.

"I don't know why not. She's been sharpening it on me for the last two years," Eddie said. "You want to be in on it on an informal basis, Amanda?"

"I'd love to! But how would I manage that?"

"Well, today we're going to do as many of the interviews as we can," Jack began. "You come along, listen, and ask any questions you think of that we don't. Then, if Tony does put us on the case together, we can keep you up with what we find out during the week, and you can come along on any evening work. Would you like that?"

"Sure, that would be great," Amanda answered enthusiastically. "Where to this afternoon?"

"I'm going back to the apartment complex and start with the people at the party who didn't get sick," Eddie said. "It's possible that the poisoner was at the party and knew not to eat the dip."

"And I'm headed out to Medical Center Hospital," Jack announced as he grabbed Amanda's hand. "Sorry, Eddie, she's coming with me. You can have your *juera* back another time."

"Aw, shucks," Eddie lamented, winking broadly at Jack as he left the lab. Jack smiled inwardly as he watched Amanda make careful notes of the afternoon's test results for later use. He was delighted that she was interested enough in the poisonings to get involved in the investigation. He had every intention of taking her out again, of course, but this would give him an excuse to see her almost daily until the case was solved. He wanted to see her daily. As a matter of fact he wanted to see her as much as possible.

They took Amanda's car out to Medical Center Hospital, the large public hospital where all emergency cases were taken in San Antonio. The sun felt good on their faces, and the wind blew their hair—so much that they both had to use a brush before they were respectable enough to enter the hospital. All of the patients had been taken to intensive care, where they were being treated and monitored until the poison could be removed from their systems. "The first one on the list is a man named Perry Price," Jack said. They showed their badges to the nurse, and she pointed to the first room on the right.

"Mr. Price, we're from the police department," Jack explained as they showed him their badges. "We'd like to ask you a few questions."

"I'd like to ask somebody a few myself," Perry rasped, the oxygen tubes in his nose making it difficult for him to talk. He was a big man and was sunburned as well as sick. "What in hell did we get hold of?"

"2, 4-dinitrophenol," Amanda said. "That's a poison—a potent poison. It was in the onion dip."

"Mr. Price, we'd like to ask you a few questions about this afternoon. Do you know who brought the dip to the pool?"

Mr. Price was very cooperative, but he couldn't contribute much in the way of information. He had only come down to the pool a few minutes before the first of the swimmers started getting sick. He had been trying to cure himself of a hangover and thought maybe some food and some sun might help. He had no idea who brought the dip. In fact, he had only moved into the complex a couple of weeks earlier and didn't know many people at the party.

Jack and Amanda peered into the next room, but the young woman there was still suffering from the worst effects of the poison. The nurse was adamant that she not be disturbed. The next patient, a very pretty young woman, had more or less organized the spur of the moment party and knew who contributed most of the food, although she couldn't remember who brought the onion dip. She had been quite worried that something she contributed had done the damage and was much relieved when Amanda assured her that her food was blameless.

Jack shut the young woman's door behind him. "Surely somebody knows who brought the onion dip!" he exclaimed. "How could anybody just slip it in unnoticed?"

"Come on," Amanda told him reassuringly. "We still have three more to talk to. Somebody's bound to know where it came from."

They entered the next room and showed their badges to the young man who lay sweating in the bed. "Mr. Salazar, the poison was found in the onion dip. Do you know who brought the dip?"

Juan Salazar nodded. "Onion," he whispered.

"Yes, we know it was onion dip," Amanda said. "But do you know who brought it?"

"Onion did," Juan repeated.

Jack looked at Amanda. "I'll come back and talk to him tomorrow. He's in no shape to answer our questions now."

"Maybe the next one will be," Amanda ventured hopefully.

Jack read the name on his notepad, and they showed their badges to the handsome young man in the next room. "We're from the SAPD and would like to ask you a few questions, Mr. Burns. Oh, could I have a first name, please?"

"I'm Onion," the young man rasped.

"What was that, sir?" Jack questioned, startled.

"Oh, my real name's Clarence, but I go by Onion," he replied.

Jack and Amanda looked at one another. Juan Salazar hadn't been out of it, after all.

"Mr. Burns, did you bring the onion dip to the pool this afternoon?" Jack asked.

Onion nodded as he clutched his abdomen and grimaced with pain. "Oh, God, don't tell me it had gone bad," he groaned. "I just brought it home on Friday."

"It hadn't gone bad, Mr. Burns," Amanda spoke up. "It had been poisoned."

They watched as shock, astonishment, and finally fear transformed Onion's face. "Poison? But how could it have been poisoned? Oh, no, surely you don't think that I put it in there! If I wanted to commit suicide, I would have found a less painful way than this!"

Amanda looked at Jack, who shook his head slightly. "No, Mr. Burns, I think it highly unlikely that you would put yourself through this kind of misery to kill yourself or anyone else. Tell me, how did you get your nickname?"

"I love onion dip," Onion said. "I eat three or four tubs a week."

"And is this a well-known fact?" Amanda asked.

Onion nodded. "Almost the first thing somebody asks me is where I got the nickname—the same as you did. I guess just about everybody who knows me knows about it."

"Sir, ma'am, could you step out in the hall for a couple of minutes? I need a few specimens," a lab technician explained as he carried his tray into the room.

Jack and Amanda stepped out in the hall. "I'll bet he was the intended victim," Amanda said.

"Yeah, if he was known to love onion dip that much, the killer would leave it there, knowing it would be consumed fairly quickly. Smart. Deadly…and smart."

The technician left the room and a nurse entered. She stopped to speak to Jack and Amanda when she stepped out a moment later. "Don't stay more than a few minutes," she warned them. "He's still very sick."

"We won't, ma'am," Jack assured her. They returned to Onion's bedside. "We can't stay much longer," Jack said. "Mr. Burns, we think that you were probably the intended victim in all this. Can you think of anyone who would want to see you dead for any reason?"

"No, officer. I don't know of anybody who has a grudge against me. Even my ex-wife likes me. She doesn't want to live with me, but she likes me."

"You're sure?" Amanda pressed.

"Positive," Onion assured them.

"All right, let's talk about the dip. Did you buy it at your usual store under the usual circumstances?" Onion nodded. "And when did you bring it home?"

"Friday afternoon," Onion said. "I unsealed it, ate a little, and left it in the fridge. I didn't eat any more of it until today."

"Can you give me a list of all the people who were in your apartment between Friday afternoon when you brought the dip home and today when you took it to the pool?" Jack asked, his pencil poised. Hopefully, Onion Burns had not thrown a party Saturday night.

Onion thought a minute. "My mother came over for a few minutes yesterday morning. My best friend and his little girl came over just about sundown. She played in the water while he had a drink with me. And one of my former students came by for a little while."

Jack wrote down the names and addresses of all Onion's guests. "Anybody else?" he asked.

In spite of his illness, Onion's cheeks turned a little red. "Lori spent the night Friday night," he said reluctantly.

"Lori who?" Amanda pressed.

Onion shrugged. "I don't know—if you want to know the truth. I picked her up at a bar on Friday night, and we never got around to last names."

Jack bit back an audible curse. "Where does she live?"

"I don't know. She insisted on taking the bus," Onion continued. "And she didn't leave a phone number. It was like she didn't want me to call her back."

Jack and Amanda exchanged glances. It was possible, of course, that one of the friends or relatives might have done it, but it was unlikely. "Can you at least describe Lori for us?"

"She was sort of tall and very shapely. She has a gorgeous body and a little brown birthmark right on her bottom, and—"

"Mr. Burns, we're not going to be able to identify her in a crowd by the mark on her bottom," Amanda said dryly. "What did her *face* look like?"

"Kind of thin. Her hair is long and dark, and she had on a short skirt and long fingernails painted red."

"Facial features?" Amanda prodded.

"Not pretty, not plain. Just there. I hardly looked at her face. Her body was what I couldn't believe."

"We can put her between two Playboy centerfolds in the lineup," Jack whispered to Amanda.

The nurse stepped into the room and asked that Jack and Amanda finish questioning Onion tomorrow. They left the room and leaned against the wall outside his door. "You think it was the woman, don't you?" Amanda demanded.

Jack nodded. "We'll check out the others, of course, but it sounds like it was her. A faceless pickup—somebody who insisted that she take a bus home rather than let him drive her and see where she lived."

"But *why?*" Amanda asked. "Why would anyone want to kill Onion Burns?"

"God only knows. I've seen every reason for murder in the world, and half of them aren't rational," Jack said as he pushed himself away from the wall. "Come on. We've got one more interview before we knock off here and go home."

"Where did these clouds come from?" Amanda wailed as she and Jack stepped out onto the darkened parking lot. A thunderstorm was blowing in from the southeast. "It was sunny when we came in."

"You know how it is: if you don't like the weather, give it five minutes," Jack quipped as a gust of wind blew in their faces. "So much for driving with the top down."

"I hope it will be sunny again by morning," Amanda said as she unlocked the car. "I enjoyed today so much."

The first drops of rain were just beginning to fall when Amanda pulled into the parking lot of the station. "Thanks for coming down this afternoon," Jack said. "Going into the investigation knowing what we do will be a big help. I'll come by the lab every day and keep you informed."

"Do you have to do the report tonight?" Amanda asked.

"Yes, but it won't take that long," Jack replied. "How about you?"

Amanda turned up her nose. "A TV dinner and the housecleaning I skipped to go out to the pool."

"What an evening to look forward to," Jack commented, laughing. "I can't let that happen. I'll take you out for a bite when I get through down here."

"I wasn't hinting, Jack," Amanda said quickly. "I didn't mean—"

Jack stopped her protest midsentence with a hard, sweet kiss. "I know you weren't. Shut up and don't bother to change your clothes. We'll go someplace simple." He jumped out of the car and ran toward the building in the rain.

"Bossy man," Amanda murmured under her breath. But she was smiling as she drove home in the noisy thunderstorm. Apparently, Jack was as eager to spend time with her as she was with him. That was a thought that pleased her very much.

Amanda had picked up and vacuumed and was just dusting the last piece of furniture when she heard Jack running up the apartment steps. The porch light caught the sparkle of rain on his hair. "Ready again," he said as Amanda picked up her shoulder bag. "You're a paragon."

"It's pretty easy to be ready when I don't have to change." She locked the door and together they ran through the rain to Jack's truck.

"Where to?" Jack asked.

"I'm dying for a burger," Amanda admitted. "How about that place on the expressway?"

"Not worried about being poisoned?" Jack teased.

"With all the jalapeño they put in the cheese sauce, how could I tell whether I was poisoned or just had a bad case of indigestion?" Amanda said, laughing. "Seriously, though, this is the first time in my years on the force that we've had two poisonings this close together. It's a strange coincidence."

"Yes, it is," Jack agreed thoughtfully.

"Unless the second poisoner read about the first one in the paper," Amanda mused. "But enough shoptalk. Have you seen that new movie 'Prizzi's Honor' yet?"

Jack and Amanda quickly discovered that they had vastly different taste in movies, and they were still sparring good-naturedly when Jack pulled up in front of the Hamburger House, which proudly proclaimed on its neon sign that the patties weighed a quarter of a pound after cooking. Jack reached into the waistband of his jeans and removed his .38, which he tossed into the glove compartment of the truck. "Ready to go?"

Amanda looked at Jack a little strangely. "Jack, why did you put your .38 in the glove compartment? We're supposed to carry them in public at all times."

Jack grinned and shrugged. "I get tired of messing with it. Come on, the rain's slacked off some."

"Jack, not having your gun with you is punishable by a suspension," Amanda reminded him.

Jack's lips pressed into a thin line. "Don't be ridiculous. I don't need to carry it tonight. The chances of that place getting robbed tonight are virtually zero."

"But why take the risk? "

"I get tired of the thing, that's why," Jack said a bit shortly. "Besides, you have yours."

"Fine. Get yourself fired. I could care less," Amanda said dryly, a bit taken aback that Jack could be so cavalier. "Just don't come crying to me when it happens. I don't like to have a soggy shoulder."

Jack's irritation faded, and he grinned wickedly. "Come on, let's not fight over a ridiculous police regulation," he cajoled her. "Let's go eat burgers." Jack locked his pistol in the glove compartment, and they got out of the truck. The fresh-faced hostess took their order and motioned them to the end of the line of hungry families waiting to go through the cafeteria-style serving line.

The restaurant was noisy and conversation was impossible. Jack took Amanda's hand and stroked her palm softly. They finally reached the counter and the cook put their burgers on trays. "I love these do-it-yourself fixings," Amanda said as she speared a round, fat slice of tomato. "It gives me a chance to fill them up like my mother does." She stared a minute at the bottle in Jack's hand. "Jack, are you going to ruin a perfectly good burger with catsup?"

"Ruin it? This is the only way to eat it." Jack declared as he shook out several dollops onto his burger.

In spite of their earlier intentions, Jack and Amanda spent dinner on shoptalk and police department gossip and both loved every minute of it. The rain had begun again in earnest while they ate dinner, and they were pretty well soaked by the time they had run across the parking lot to the truck. "You don't melt, do you?" Jack asked as he opened the passenger door and pushed Amanda into the cab.

"No, but I'm sure glad I'm not dressed like I was last night." She opened Jack's door for him and he slammed it shut. Suddenly they were enclosed in the privacy of the small cab, the heavy rain on the windshield sheltering them from the outside world. Amanda's breath caught in her throat as she stared into Jack's damp face.

Jack grasped Amanda's shoulders and pulled her toward him. "I need to kiss you. I've needed to kiss you all day long."

Amanda wound her arms around Jack's neck. "You weren't thinking about kissing me this afternoon," she teased. "You were all business."

"I was all business on the outside," Jack corrected her. "Inside, I wanted to hold you and to touch you." He caressed her face lightly before he gathered her to him. "Oh, Amanda," he breathed as their lips met in a kiss of sweet passion. Amanda groaned as Jack unleashed a storm within her, a response so fiery and profound it left her gasping. His arms crept around her waist and pressed her closer, as close as she could get in the awkward confines of the cab. Amanda ran her fingers through his damp hair, brushing the blond tendrils from his forehead. She could feel the tautness of his thighs where they were clenched tight with passion and desire, and she could feel her own body tense in response to his passionate caresses. If a simple kiss could stir her this way, what would it do to her to make love to him?

Jack ended his kiss abruptly and pushed her a few inches away. "Let's go back to your place," he said as he started the engine. It took both his hands to drive the truck in the blowing storm, but his shoulders brushed hers as the truck swayed back and forth in the gusting wind. Jack parked under a tree in Amanda's parking lot and pulled her back into his arms. "I wanted to get you in out of the rain, but I can't wait," he murmured as he captured her in an embrace as passionate as the first.

The night was dark, and the tree and the rain effectively curtained them from the rest of the world. Amanda melted into Jack's arms and gave herself up to the intimacy of his embrace. His lips were tender and seeking as they touched and caressed hers, drawing the sweetness from her depths. Amanda gave of herself willingly, wanting to share her essence with Jack in this way.

Jack groaned when he felt her tremble in his arms, his own passionate response soaring just that much higher. Amanda was like dynamite—a simple kiss had never made him feel this way. He could tell that she shared the same wondrous, sensual feelings. His fingers trembled as they traveled down the side of her face, past the softness of her neck, and down to the smooth warmth of her shoulder, until he encountered the fabric of her shirt. Slowly, so as not to alarm her, he pushed her down on the seat and followed her, his fingers ever so nimbly unbuttoning her top buttons.

He's going to touch my breasts, Amanda thought as she felt Jack's fingers on her buttons. Deftly, more quickly than she could have, he had her shirt unbuttoned almost to the waist, and his fingers found the tip of her breast through the thin cotton bra that she wore. He tormented it with the pad of his thumb until it was a hard little knot under the fabric. With a murmur of impatience he unhooked the front closure of her bra and pushed aside the offending material, baring her to his touch and gaze. "Beautiful," he breathed as he caressed the tip of her breast almost reverently. He lowered his lips and explored the hardening bud. "Do you like that?"

"Oh, Jack, yes," Amanda gasped. Jack caressed it gently for a moment until it was hard and round. Then he turned his attention to her other breast until it, too, was a hard knot of desire. Amanda wiggled beneath him, the desire she felt for Jack expressing itself in sensual little motions over which she had no control. "Oh, Jack, I…" Amanda's voice trailed off as words failed her.

"I know, Mandy," Jack whispered as he laid his head between her breasts. "I've never felt like this either."

"Do…do you want to come up?" Amanda asked hesitantly. She had never been one for casual sex, but if Jack wanted her tonight, she wouldn't deny him.

Jack was quiet for a moment. "You don't usually invite men up on the second date, do you?"

"Never. But you're different."

"So are you," Jack replied. He sat up and hooked Amanda's bra. "So special, in fact, that I'm going to deny my baser instincts and decline your very lovely invitation." He pulled Amanda up to sit beside him.

"Why?" Amanda asked quietly.

"Because I don't want to jump the gun and screw up something that could be very good," Jack explained. "Oh, I'm attracted to you, all right. I want you like I've never wanted a woman before, and I could make love to you all night long. But it might not be the best thing for our relationship to do that tonight."

"It probably wouldn't be," Amanda agreed softly. A part of her was disappointed that Jack wasn't coming in, but a part of her was surprised and relieved that he had sensed and understood her reservations.

"Can I take you out next weekend?" Jack asked as he buttoned Amanda's shirt.

"I'm working a high school dance on Friday night, keeping the creeps out and the kids in, but I'm free on Saturday."

"Save it for me," Jack said. They got out of the cab, the rain quickly soaking them as they ran across the parking lot. Jack paused at the foot of her outdoor stairs. Amanda stared up into his dripping face as the rain pounded them both. Wordlessly, they came together for another passionate embrace, kissing for long moments as the rain poured down on them. They clung together, their wet clothing a thin, almost nonexistent barrier between them.

Finally Jack held her shoulders and pushed her away. "Go in before I forget my good intentions," he whispered.

Amanda nodded and ran up the stairs. She waved to Jack from the window and watched as he ran across the parking lot and drove away. Amanda could feel herself start to shiver in the air-conditioned room, but she stood at the window until Jack's taillights were out of sight.

Amanda stared out into the rain a moment longer before she went into the bathroom. She stripped the wet clothing from her body, but before she stepped into the hot shower she stared at herself in the mirror. Her face was flushed, and her nipples were still hard and firm from Jack's passionate caresses. Jack stirred her tonight, more than any man she had ever been with. He could have made love to her, and she wouldn't have protested.

But she was glad he hadn't. It was still too soon for her, and she was glad that Jack sensed it. He had chosen to take the cautious route—to let their relationship grow a little more before they became lovers. Amanda was pleased he had wanted to wait, and she was more than a little surprised. She hadn't thought Jack was capable of being cautious about *anything.*

Amanda showered and put on an old cotton nightgown that had seen better days. She poured herself a glass of wine and sat down on the couch, propping her feet on the hassock. She frowned a little as she sipped her drink—noticing the ever-so-slight tingling as it ran down her throat—and thought about the man who had invaded her life so suddenly. She liked Jack. She liked him a lot and had high hopes for the direction their relationship might take. But if she were honest with herself, she had to admit that his cavalier attitude toward taking chances bothered her. He seemed to be determined to do things that were foolish and/or dangerous, both on the job and on his own time. Amanda was not timid, but she knew what an unnecessary risk was. She also knew that Jack took them on a regular basis. What she didn't know was if she could learn to live with it for the sake of their relationship.

Chapter Five

"Amanda, are you still here?" Jack asked as he stuck his head around the door of the lab. "It's time to knock off. Woman, you work too hard."

"Haven't you heard I'm getting rich in here?" Amanda called out from the back room. "Log yourself in and come on back. I've got a couple more minutes on this test."

Jack wandered back and peered over Amanda's shoulder. "Whatcha testing there?"

"I'm trying to do a blood matching," Amanda replied. "Burglary's trying to pin down a sneaky little cat burglar. They've known who it is for some time but haven't been able to come up with any concrete evidence. Anyway, he apparently cut himself on his way out last week and they're hoping to nail him."

Jack watched while Amanda ran the serologic assays. "Oh, *no!* There's no match," she moaned as a totally different set of blood factors appeared in the blood taken from the broken windowsill. "It wasn't him last week, after all." She dialed burglary and asked to speak to the sergeant. "This is Amanda Blakeman in the lab. Sorry, but your man didn't do this one." She listened a minute and her face took on an angry expression. "Listen, Hanson, the blood types don't lie. It wasn't his blood on the window." She paused a minute. "Hanson, I'm sorry if your fair-haired darlings down there can't catch the man you want, but he *didn't break into that house.* Now, I suggest you quit insulting me and my department and get up off your fat rear and come up with something else on the weasel." She paused. "Same to you, sweetie pie," she flipped, smiling, and hung up the phone.

"You didn't really say that to iron-pants Hanson," Jack asked uncertainly as Amanda slammed down the telephone. "Nobody talks to him like that."

"I do—all the time," Amanda answered calmly as she carefully noted the results of the test.

"And he lets you?" Jack pressed incredulously.

"Are you kidding? He loves it," Amanda said, shedding her lab coat. "I'm the only one in the department with enough nerve to tell him where he can go. He'll be up here Monday morning trying to worm his way back into my good graces. He'll probably even bring me a sack of doughnuts as a bribe—which I need like I need a hole in my head. You've been feeding me too well lately." She and Jack had been seeing one another for the last month, and they had dined out a lot. "I'm gaining weight."

Jack patted her bottom lightly. "Still feels all right to me," he replied thoughtfully. "Come on. Eddie's waiting for us."

Eddie was already seated at one of the outdoor tables at their favorite bar along the Riverwalk. Jack and Amanda sat down in the vacant chairs, and Amanda slipped out of her shoes. "This was a good idea, whichever one of you came up with it. It's perfect out here tonight." The air on the street level was warm, even for May, but their table was shaded, and a gentle breeze blew along the river.

"It beats sitting in my office drinking coffee out of a Styrofoam cup," Eddie said. "I'm calling this official unofficial meeting of the onion dip poisoning investigation to order." Jack and Amanda laughed. "Seriously, Jack, Amanda, do either of you have any more ideas on the onion dip poisonings? I'm completely stymied."

"I'll second that," Amanda added dryly. "I'm fresh out of ideas." Jack and Eddie were officially assigned to the case, as they had predicted, and Amanda had continued as an unofficial participant in the investigation. But in the last month they had turned up nothing. Jack and Eddie had even returned with Onion Burns to the bar where he picked "Lori" up, but no one had seen her there since the night she had left with Onion.

The waitress came to take their order and placed a basket of bread sticks on the table. "Have either of you thought that this poisoning just might be connected to the cyanide killings?" Jack conjectured. Jack and Tony had thoroughly investigated those poisonings, too, but again turned up nothing.

Eddie shrugged and Amanda shook her head. "Not really," she said. "There's no pattern that I can see."

"And why would the killer use a different poison?" Eddie asked. "I don't think they're related. Any other ideas?"

Jack and Amanda both said no just as the waitress brought their drinks, and the three of them started discussing the affair one of the young women officers was supposedly having with her married sergeant. Eddie finished his drink and excused himself, saying that he was going to find the young officer and persuade her to have the affair with him instead.

Jack and Amanda laughed as they said good-bye to Eddie. "Do you suppose he means any of it?" Amanda asked once he was out of earshot.

"I doubt it. Under all that carrying on, he's a great person, and he's crazy about Sylvia and the kids. He was just showing off his son's football team picture to me the other day."

"I'm glad," Amanda answered, relieved. "Do you suppose that girl and her boss know everybody's talking about them?"

"Do you know that everybody's talking about you and me?" Jack replied. "I've had three different people say something to me about you."

"Yes, I do, and I don't mind," Amanda said. "Neither of us is married, and we're not even doing anything we shouldn't. Darn it," she added as an afterthought.

Jack chortled at Amanda's words. He reached across the table and put his hand over hers. "Would you like to remedy that?" he asked softly.

"Not in public," Amanda managed as she fought down an embarrassed blush.

"No, seriously, Mandy," Jack continued, "I'm sorry I laughed, but you were thinking exactly what I was thinking," His face sobered. "I'm spending the weekend in Burnet at the lake. Would you come with me?" He stared into her eyes, mesmerizing her.

"And finish what we started a month ago?" Amanda whispered.

Jack nodded. "I think we're to that point—I know I am."

"I am, too. I'd love to come with you, Jack."

"Great. I'll pick you up on Saturday morning about eight," he announced enthusiastically. "Do you want to go to the dance on Saturday night?"

"Maybe…" Amanda hedged, thinking that she might rather spend the evening quietly with Jack in their motel room.

"On second thought, maybe some other time," Jack said, grinning, correctly interpreting her hesitation.

"Can we go fishing?" Amanda asked eagerly. She was an avid fisherman and never passed up a chance to indulge in her favorite sport.

"Uh, Mandy, could we postpone the fishing until Sunday?" Jack asked. "Some buddies and I wanted to get together for a couple of hours on Saturday, if you don't mind. Just for a little while. Is that all right with you?"

"That's fine as long as I get to meet your friends," Amanda agreed. She started to ask what he and his friends would be doing on Saturday, but Jack changed the subject and she never thought to ask again. They had a second drink, these nonalcoholic, and Jack walked her back to the parking lot of the police station. Amanda lowered the top and drove home, the little particles of dust in the air stinging her face. She changed into a pair of shorts and a tank top, made a fat sandwich, and opened a bottle of beer for supper. She started to turn on the television, but the sun was just setting and the breeze was cooling down some, so Amanda carried her supper out to the pool and sat down in one of the lounge chairs.

So she and Jack were going to become lovers. It was inevitable—they had been moving in that direction since the day they met and would have become lovers long before now if her innate sense of caution and Jack's respect for her feelings hadn't held them back. She would not have denied Jack earlier if he had insisted, but until recently she had reservations about him— reservations that the last month had pretty well laid to rest. Although she hadn't been able to forget Jack's love of danger, she was beginning to think that perhaps he didn't take as many chances as she had been led to believe. He had not raced the weekend after she watched him. Instead, she and Jack spent the day floating down the Guadalupe River in a canoe. And as far as she knew, he hadn't indulged in anymore of his dangerous pastimes—he spent nearly every free moment with her. They had seen several movies, eaten out quite a few times, and burned up several more dance floors. But they had done nothing that would risk life and limb. Amanda was beginning to think that Jack exaggerated his love of danger to impress her with his daring, and that her earlier worries were groundless. And what chances he did take, she would be able to handle.

Amanda finished her sandwich and beer and spent a few minutes going through her wardrobe for clothes to take with her to Burnet. She had plenty of shorts and jeans and pretty underwear, but she groaned when she reached the bottom of her drawer and came up with nothing but old, faded cotton gowns. This would never do! Grinning wickedly, she took her charge card out of the drawer where she kept it and drove to the mall, emerging an hour later with a black lace nightgown that was guaranteed to give Jack a provocative view of one Amanda Blakeman.

"Amanda, are you ready?" Jack called softly as he knocked on her door.

Amanda opened the door and handed Jack a steaming cup of coffee. "I've broken my perfect track record," she yawned as she sipped the other cup of coffee she held. "That wedding reception I was providing security for lasted until nearly two, and I was so tired I forgot to set my alarm. Sorry."

"What? You're not ready?" Jack said in mock anger. "That's despicable."

"You want me to put the rest of this coffee in an interesting place?" Amanda inquired dryly.

"No, in the cup's just fine," Jack assured her as he sipped his. Amanda was dressed, but her bedroom door was ajar and he could see that her suitcase was open on the bed. "How was the wedding, other than long?" he asked as he followed Amanda into her bedroom.

"It couldn't have been lovelier. The families were mostly worried about gate-crashers." She stuffed in several pairs of panties and a new peach bikini.

"Gonna model that suit?" Jack teased as he sat down on the bed.

"Sure am," Amanda said, feeling a little embarrassed. By the end of the weekend, Jack would have seen her without a stitch.

Jack picked up the black nightgown and let out a long, slow whistle. "Good grief, this thing's heart attack material!" he exclaimed as a blushing Amanda grabbed the gown from his hands and folded it into the suitcase.

"Would you care to check out my makeup kit, also?" she asked pointedly.

Jack laughed, but he didn't get up. Amanda packed the rest of her clothes and snapped the suitcase shut. "The makeup kit's ready. I'm taking a little fishing gear—if that's all right?" she added questioningly.

They stowed her gear under the specially made camper that fit Jack's old truck. Amanda noticed a pair of disreputable western boots and a beat-up old straw hat at the back of the camper and wondered what Jack wanted with them this weekend. *Perhaps he wears the hat while fishing,* she thought. Amanda locked her apartment and before long they were out of the city, driving up Highway 281 to the cluster of man-made lakes that provided Central Texas with one of its best recreational areas. Jack told Amanda that he had rented a motel room right on the shore of Lake Buchanan but that they could see the rest of the lakes, too, if she wished. Amanda had always heard that Buchanan had the best fishing and was perfectly content to stay there.

The drive through the rolling Texas countryside went quickly, and before long they were checking into a picturesque little motel on the edge of the water. The woman at the desk, who Amanda suspected also owned the motel, looked at them disapprovingly when they wrote their last names on the registration card. Feeling slightly embarrassed, Amanda was happy when Jack signed over two traveler's checks and the woman slapped the key down on the desk and turned her back.

Amanda giggled as she carried her suitcase into the cheerful motel room. "I don't think she entirely approves of us," she sighed theatrically as she dumped her suitcase in the closet.

"That's all right. She didn't mind my money," Jack responded, laughing. He put his suitcase in the closet beside Amanda's. "Do you want to get into that skimpy little suit and shock her some more?"

"I don't usually wear a swimsuit to fish in," Amanda said.

"Are you sure you don't mind about this afternoon?" Jack asked.

"Of course not," Amanda replied. In fact, she was downright curious about Jack's friends. The only people she had ever really seen him associate with in San Antonio were either fellow policemen or the people at the racetrack.

"Thanks." He stared at Amanda and she moved to him, opening her arms as he opened his. They met by the window, their lips touching as they stood shoulder to shoulder, hip to hip, sharing a foretaste of the passion they knew awaited them tonight. Amanda moaned and buried her fingers in Jack's hair, her heart—or was it his—pounding loudly. Jack groaned as Amanda's knee found its way between his legs, pressing firmly against his inner thighs. "Stop it, woman," he begged as Amanda's hands drifted past his waist and rode low on his hips, "or you'll never make it out for a swim. We have all night for this."

Amanda nodded and pulled away from him reluctantly. She put on her new swimsuit in the bathroom, and she and Jack earned themselves several more disapproving looks from the motel owner as they played on the sandy beach for over an hour, laughing and squealing and dunking one another with great abandon.

Finally Jack declared that they needed to go in if they were going to be in time to meet his friends. Amanda showered and changed into a new pair of jeans and stared with dismay at the faded old pair that Jack donned. "Am I overdressed?" she asked, wondering why clothes-conscious Jack would wear those awful looking things.

"No, you're fine," he assured her. His eyes sparkled with suppressed excitement, and a prickle of unease slid down Amanda's spine. She tried to persuade herself that he was only excited about seeing his friends, and about being with her, but she was pretty sure there was more to his excitement than that.

They drove through the friendly little town of Burnet and down a dirt road that led to a rambling old farmhouse. "Buddy and I went to high school together," Jack volunteered as a huge man, running to fat, ambled out to greet them. "Buddy, you old son-of-a-gun, how are you?"

"Jack, you skinny rat, get out of that truck and introduce me to your friend." Buddy pumped Jack's hand enthusiastically and turned to Amanda. "Hello, there. I'm Buddy Ecbert," he said, working her hand up and down.

"Amanda Blakeman," Amanda said, wondering if her blood had turned to butter yet. "Glad to meet you."

Buddy finally let go of her hand and turned to Jack, who was getting his boots and his hat out of the back of the pickup. "I'm glad you could make it this time," he said. "I bought another real mean Brahma at the Gonzales auction last week. Somebody's ridden this one before —he's as mean as a cornered rattlesnake."

"Fantastic!" Jack exclaimed. "I've been practicing at the ring outside town. I'm going to show you country bumpkins who can ride a bull."

"Okay, city slicker, you're on."

Buddy and Jack continued to tease one another while Amanda stared at them in astonishment. Yes, he'd mentioned it once, but she'd only half-believed him. Apparently he really meant to get on the back of a bull this afternoon. She turned round eyes on Jack. "When have you been practicing?"

"Oh, I've been going out there a couple of evenings a week, mostly when you were moonlighting," Jack responded cheerfully, oblivious to Amanda's shock. "For three dollars a go, they'll set up a bull for you."

"Jack, are you sure you—" Amanda bit her lip. No way was she going to say something to embarrass him in front of his friends.

"Jack, come on! The guys are waiting," Buddy called.

Jack grabbed the hand Amanda had laid on his arm and started toward the back of the house. "Come on, Mandy, I want you to meet the rest of the guys."

A small cluster of roughly dressed men waited beside a large pen. Jack made introductions and Amanda murmured a greeting, but she kept sneaking looks at the chute at the other end of the pen. She couldn't have remembered any of the men's names if she tried. Was this group of sane-looking, sane-acting men really going to take turns getting up on a bull and let it try to pitch them off? Jack introduced a big, friendly looking woman as Melissa Ecbert. Melissa sat down on a tall stool and motioned for Amanda to sit on the one beside her. Melissa had a stopwatch in one hand and a clipboard in the other. "I'm the unofficial score-keeper."

Amanda perched on the stool beside Melissa. "Have any of the men ever been hurt?" she asked.

Melissa thought a minute. "Yes, Dan Voight broke his arm last year, and Buddy had to spend the night in the hospital a couple of years ago because of a concussion. But nothing serious—at least not yet."

"Doesn't it bother you to watch them do it?" Amanda pressed.

Melissa thought a minute. "Yeah, it does, a little. But Buddy's life out here's so tame otherwise, I hate to make a fuss about it. This is the only thing he does that could remotely be considered dangerous."

Amanda considered Melissa's attitude. Would she be less worried if this were the only dangerous thing Jack was into? But that was the problem—this wasn't the only risky activity Jack was involved in. Suddenly Amanda could no longer ignore the doubts that she'd tried so hard to deny. Jack did dangerous things—lots of dangerous things—things that could get him badly hurt or killed.

And he absolutely loved doing them all. So did she really have any business getting involved with a man who thrived on putting his life and safety on the line?

Amanda watched as Jack and Buddy shooed a big, mean-looking bull into the chute and wound a rope with a bell on it around the animal's flanks. Melissa called out a name, and the man mounted the bull. She fired a pistol with a blank in it and the chute was thrown open. Immediately the big white bull pitched out into the ring, bell clanging, and dumped the man flat on his back in the middle of the pen.

"That didn't take long," Melissa said, laughing. She recorded the time while the man hightailed it out of the pen.

The next two men did a little better, although neither of them made it the eight seconds the rodeo riders aimed for. In spite of her desire not to react Amanda's heart leaped into her throat when Buddy brought out a huge black Brahma and pointed to Jack. "Here's the new one. You get to break him in today."

Jack laughed and chatted while they secured the rope around the bull's flanks. Amanda's hands tightened into fists, and her fingernails cut deeply into her palms without her being aware of it. Melissa reached over and patted Amanda's arm. "Don't worry. He's going to be fine."

Amanda nodded as Melissa raised the gun. The chute flew open and the black bull emerged, twisting and pawing, his back heels flying high into the air as he tried to rid himself of his unwanted burden. Amanda watched, the quick movements of the bull registering as slow motion in her brain, as Jack hung on to the ride for dear life, gripping the rope with one hand and his other flying in the air. He seemed to stay on top of the bull forever. Then the bull gave a particularly vicious twist and Jack flew off.

But he didn't land in the dirt as the others had. His hand had become entangled in the rope, and Amanda watched with horror as he was dragged behind the kicking heels of the angry bull, dodging the dangerous hooves as best he could. Jack gave a shout, but before the others could reach him he managed to untangle his hand and slide to the ground. A hoof missed his head by inches as he rolled away from the huge animal.

Buddy and Melissa grabbed broom handles and got into the ring to distract the bull. Meanwhile, a couple of the cowboys jumped over the fence and ran to Jack, who was lying facedown in the dirt. "Don't touch him!" Amanda commanded as she climbed over the fence. "You could hurt him if he has broken bones."

"Ma'am, we've got to get him out of here," one of the men spoke up. "That bull ain't too pleased with him right now."

"At least let me check him first," Amanda said as she knelt beside Jack's still body. "Jack, can you hear me?" she asked as she ran her hands over his arms and legs, hoping that her inexpert fingers could tell if anything was wrong.

Jack heaved a ragged breath. "Knocked the wind out of me," he croaked.

"I guess it did," Amanda returned tartly as she finished his back. "Jack, I'm going to turn you over and check your ribs," she said as she eased him over, wincing when he groaned. She ran her fingers over his ribcage. "I don't think you've broken anything, but the doctor will be able to tell for sure."

"Don't be ridiculous," Jack wheezed. "I don't need a doctor."

"Naw, he's all right," Buddy chimed in. The bull was nowhere to be seen, and Amanda assumed that Buddy and Melissa had driven it from the pen. "He's just got a few scratches on him."

"When did you get your medical degree?" Amanda asked pointedly. She knew she was being rude, but at the moment she didn't care. "Let's get you in the truck, Jack, and I'll get you to the doctor."

Jack sat up and glowered at her. "Damn it, woman! I'm *all right,*" he insisted as he struggled to his feet.

"Sure you are," Amanda breathed, stepping away when he reached out to take her arm. Jack swayed and she relented, holding him around the waist and letting him lean against her. "I'm taking him back into town," she announced curtly as they started toward the truck.

Buddy helped her get Jack into the cab. "I'm sorry he got hurt, ma'am," he said uncertainly as Amanda got into the driver's seat.

Amanda softened at the hang-dog expression on Buddy's face. "It wasn't your fault—not really. It was nice meeting you."

"Pleasure to meet you, too, ma'am," Buddy said.

Amanda turned around in the driveway and started back down the bumpy dirt road that led to the highway. Jack groaned and winced with every thump and jostle of the truck. "Oww, do you have to hit the bumps so hard?" Jack complained when they bounced into a particularly deep hole. "At this rate I *am* going to need a doctor."

"Hold on and be quiet," Amanda directed as she pulled onto the highway. "And you *are* going to see the doctor."

"Amanda, I'm fine," Jack ground out. "I just fell off a bull—that's all."

"You just got dragged across a cow pen, nearly were stomped, and had the wind knocked out of you."

"None of which the doctor can do a thing about at this point," Jack said shortly. "So lay off and take me back to the motel. I'll wash up there."

Amanda glanced over at Jack. His color was returning, and he didn't seem nearly as stunned as he had a few minutes ago, so she shrugged her shoulders and drove them back to the motel. She eased Jack out of the cab and helped him to the door, glowering back when the owner gave them a dirty look. Jack unlocked the door and collapsed on the bed, wincing when he hit the mattress. "It hurts a little," he admitted.

"You don't say." Amanda pulled off Jack's boots one at a time. "You better let me tend to your cuts and scratches," she said as Jack sat up.

"If you're sure you don't mind," Jack answered dryly as he started unbuttoning his shirt. His hand and arm were badly burned from being tangled in the rough rope, and Amanda was sure that by morning his chest and back would be a mass of bruises. "I didn't bring anything with me—do you have a first aid kit?"

"No, I guess I'll have to ask Miss Pruneface in the office. Why don't you take a shower, and I'll fix you up when you get out?"

Jack nodded and got up, groaning a little as he did so. Amanda went to the office and borrowed a bottle of iodine and a box of Band-Aids from the owner, who was dying of curiosity and trying not to show it. She returned just as Jack was stepping from the bathroom, clad only in a pair of white boxers. "See—they don't all match my eyes," he quipped, hoping that a little joke would restore Amanda's good humor.

Amanda just stared at him. "Sit down," she directed, pointing to the edge of the bed. "All she had was iodine, and it's going to hurt. Is your tetanus vaccination up to date?"

"I don't know. Why?"

"You might have gotten something in one of these cuts," Amanda explained as she dabbed iodine on the first of the skinned places. She heard Jack suck in a quick breath, but he said nothing. "That's how people contract tetanus—through wound infection. Soil is loaded with bacteria—sometimes the really harmful kind. You really should go get a shot on Monday morning. Under the circumstances, you need it."

"All right, all right, I'll go get a booster," Jack groused. "I wish you weren't carrying on so about it."

"I wouldn't have had to carry on about it if you hadn't gotten thrown off in the first place. Riding that bull was a fool thing to do, Jack." She dabbed iodine on a second cut, ignoring Jack's involuntary flinch.

"No, it wasn't," Jack countered. "I enjoyed it."

"You *enjoyed* coming within an inch of getting your head stomped on?" Amanda asked incredulously. "Pardon me, but you have a strange idea of fun."

"I like the challenge," Jack continued defensively. "Is that so wrong—*oww!* What are you doing to my hand?"

"I'm trying to disinfect it," Amanda said as she dabbed the rope burn as gently as she could.

Jack jerked his hand away from hers. "Stop that."

Amanda grabbed his hand and held it out in front of her. "It will hurt a lot worse if it gets infected," she threatened as she squeezed on a liberal amount of iodine and ignored Jack's pained gasp. "Maybe you'll think next time before you crawl up on one of those crazy animals."

"Is that why you're acting like a bear with a sore paw?" Jack demanded. "Because I fell off the bull?"

"You didn't fall off—you were thrown off by a very large, very angry animal. And he missed your head by just about this much." She held her thumb and her forefinger up in front of his nose. "Why do you insist on riding them in the first place?"

"I like to," Jack said simply. "I love the challenge and the excitement."

Amanda looked at Jack searchingly. "Really? Is that the only reason you ride? Or is there more to it than that?"

"What else would be going on? It's plain and simple. I like the thrill. I like the rush."

"Holy Moses, don't you get enough excitement on the job? You take enough chances there to become San Antonio's living legend. Why do you have to look for more?"

"What business is it of yours if I do, anyway?" Jack countered. "What I do for fun is my business—and mine alone."

"Fine. If it's your business and yours alone, doctor the scratches on your back…alone." She slapped the bottle down in his good hand.

Jack slammed the iodine down on the nightstand. "Damn it, woman. What's wrong with you? Why are you coming so unglued, anyway? I thought you were having a good time with me."

"Most of the time I do have a good time with you. Just not when you do something stupid like this afternoon. And no, don't bother arguing with me about that," she said when Jack opened his mouth. "It is stupid, *damned* stupid, to risk your life for the sake of a thrill."

"So you weren't having fun that afternoon at the race track," Jack said slowly. "Isn't that a little dishonest? Pretending to have fun when you weren't?"

"I tried to tell myself I was," Amanda admitted. "And it was all right once you got off the track. But did I enjoy watching you race? I tried to but no, I did not. And I sure didn't have a good time this afternoon. I don't have fun watching you put yourself in danger for no good reason."

"Sure, I got a few bumps and bruises, but I could have gotten those playing touch football," Jack said pleadingly. "It's not all that dangerous, honest."

"Not if you don't mind hoofprints in your head," Amanda responded levelly. "Jack, bull riding is dangerous, and so is racing, and so is skydiving. They're *all* dangerous."

"I know," Jack agreed, "but they don't frighten me."

"Pardon me if I just don't understand," Amanda said. "You admit that they're dangerous. Yet you say that you aren't frightened. That doesn't make sense, Jack."

"It makes perfect sense to me, Amanda. Look, I'm willing to admit that they're dangerous if you don't know what you're doing, or if you're frightened yourself. But I do know what I'm doing and I'm not afraid, so I don't see what you're concerned about."

"I see what I'm concerned about," Amanda said softly. "Your argument makes about as much sense to me as Greek. You say that because you're not frightened, that you're not in danger? Did that bull who nearly ran over you know that you weren't frightened of him? Did he know that you were a good rider when he nearly walked all over you?"

"Amanda, come on," Jack reproved. "All right, so there is an element of danger involved. Does that make something off limits? Lots of hobbies have an element of danger in them. Motorcycling, horseback riding, surfing—people get killed at those all the time. And then what about all the swimmers and divers who drown every year? People get their necks broken on *trampolines,* for heaven's sake. Do you think everybody ought to swear off those, too?"

"You're rationalizing, Jack. Yes, people get killed doing all those things, and they also get killed getting out of the shower. But the odds are a whole lot worse racing or trying to stick on the back of a bull. Can't you see that?"

"No, I can't," Jack answered, his voice maddeningly calm. "And if you want the truth, I don't really care to continue this discussion. They're my hobbies and my business."

"Fine," Amanda said, equally calmly on the outside, although she was trembling inside. She got her swimsuit out of the bathroom and put it in a plastic sack. "Take me back to San Antonio, Jack. I've changed my mind about the weekend."

"Amanda, you can't do that. You can't let this change your mind."

"I can and I did. You obviously don't care about your own safety, and yes, that's your business. But how it makes me feel when you take damn foolish chances with your life is *my* business, and I'll be damned if I'm going to spend all my time worrying about what hair-brained stunt you're up to next. Get your clothes on, and I'll drive you home."

Jack calmly lay back on the bed. "No way. I'm not going to let this tiff get in the way of our weekend together. Come sit down and let's forget about the bull riding." He patted the bed beside him. "Come on, Mandy. We'll talk about something else."

"I suggest you take your patronizing attitude and shove it. I said it was off, and it is. So get some clothes on and let's get out of here."

"I said we weren't going anywhere," Jack repeated, equally calmly. "You'll get over your snit if you give yourself a chance."

"Suit yourself," Amanda said mildly. She picked up her overnight bag and her makeup case and walked out the door.

"Have a good walk," Jack called after her. She would think twice when she realized that there was no way she could rent a car out here.

Jack lay back on the bed but jumped up a second later when he heard the familiar roar of his truck engine. She still had the keys. He threw open the door and ran after the truck. "Amanda, you bring my truck back here! Woman, you can't walk out on me like that. Get back here and we'll talk about it."

Jack stood in the driveway and watched his truck pull onto the highway and slowly disappear. She had done it. She had walked out on him—and in his own damn truck. Angrily he kicked a rock, swearing a little when he stubbed his bare toe, and turned around to face the owner of the hotel and two other elderly women. They were staring at his boxers with horror on their faces. "She…she left and took my truck," Jack stammered.

The motel owner nodded her head approvingly. "Couldn't go through with it, could she? I thought she looked like a decent sort of girl. Mind you, young man, if you offered her a ring and a preacher, she wouldn't be running off like that."

"Uh, yes, ma'am," Jack mumbled, blushing to the roots of his hair. Swearing under his breath, he went inside and slammed the door of the motel room behind him.

**

Amanda sniffed and rummaged around with one hand in her purse for another tissue. She swore when she found there were none left and told herself she could have a good cry once she got home. She roared around an old couple in a Cadillac and fumbled around until she found the knob for the headlights. She would be back in town within the hour if the traffic stayed light, and she could leave the truck in Jack's driveway and the key in the mailbox. Eddie would meet her at Jack's house and take her home, and she could cry after he was gone. She needed to cry—she hadn't been this hurt and disappointed in a long time.

Amanda stared down the long, lonely highway. She'd tried, she really had, with the racing, but the bull riding was taking things too far. She was angry with Jack for taking so many chances and at the same time angry with herself for not being able to ignore the fear and be more accepting of Jack's dangerous hobbies. And she was disappointed, so disappointed that they hadn't taken their relationship to the next level. But she wasn't about to take the risk that becoming his lover would entail. She was beginning to care for Jack deeply, but she simply wouldn't risk loving a man who seemed bent on self-destruction. She would be worrying about him constantly, and that would eat her insides out. There would be angry words, and blowups like today, and Amanda knew better than to think that kind of situation would ever work. It was better to break things off now—before she became involved too deeply.

***

Jack finished his bourbon and poured himself another generous drink. Every bone and muscle in his body was sore, and the ache in his hand hadn't been dulled by the whiskey yet. Once Buddy got through laughing, he brought Jack a full bottle of Wild Turkey and lent him an old Fairlane he could drive back to San Antonio. Jack appreciated both the car and the liquor, and since he didn't have to go back to work until Monday, he intended to get thoroughly drunk tonight in the privacy of his motel room. The alcohol would numb his aching body as well as his hurt feelings.

Jack sipped his drink, letting the liquid burn down the back of his throat. He still couldn't believe Amanda really walked out on their weekend together. But she had. Jack tried, but he simply couldn't understand why she had been upset enough to take his truck and go home.

Maybe it was too much to expect Amanda, or any woman for that matter, to understand. How strong and powerful it felt for a man to put himself on the line like that, what kind of a rush it was to get behind the wheel and win, or best the bull, or stare down the gun barrel of a killer and walk away. A small smile touched his lips when he remembered the pride in his father's eyes the first time Jack had crawled on top of a bull. "There are no pipsqueaks on the back of a bull," he'd reminded Jack that afternoon. "I'm proud of you, son." Jack bolted down the rest of his drink and poured himself another. It was too bad Amanda couldn't accept the bull riding and the racing, but if that was the way she felt, she could just take her sexy nightie and her skimpy little bikini and go home. He would find somebody else. He didn't need a fretting, fearful woman in his life who got upset every time he raced his car or rode a bull. He had spent years fending off the needless carrying on and smothering concern of his mother, first for his father and then for him, and he didn't intend to go through the whole process all over again with Amanda.

Chapter Six

Amanda trudged up the steps and unlocked the door of her apartment, her muscles sore from a vigorous aerobics class. Jenny had given them a real workout tonight. She threw her exercise bag in the corner of the closet and stripped off her sweaty gym clothes, showering quickly and pulling on her favorite old cotton gown. It was getting a little tattered, but it was comfortable, and no one would see her in it anyway. Almost against her will, Amanda thought of the sexy black nightie she had shoved down to the bottom of her drawer last Saturday night, and she shook her head sadly. She had so wanted to become Jack's lover, and she was hurt and disappointed it hadn't happened.

Amanda fixed herself a TV dinner and sat down at the table to eat. She tried to read the newspaper, but her thoughts kept returning to the previous weekend, and while she ate Amanda thought once again about what had happened in Burnet. For the hundredth time she asked herself if she had been wrong to walk out on Jack. Should she have gone on acting as if nothing were wrong? Should she have continued to hide her own feelings and become Jack's lover?

Absently Amanda chewed her rubbery fried chicken. She didn't think she was wrong—she simply couldn't allow herself to become any more deeply involved with Jack. If she did, she would do nothing day and night but worry about him. Maybe the fault lay with her—maybe she was overcautious—but she knew herself and she knew that an affair with Jack would tear her apart. She couldn't let herself fall in love with him. She was horribly lonely for Jack. She missed him more than she had thought possible, but she had not been tempted once to call him, such was her conviction that they shouldn't become any more involved than they already were.

Not that Jack had tried to change her mind. Amanda had not heard from him since she had driven off in his truck. She called Eddie from a gas station, and he had picked her up in Jack's front yard. He listened patiently while she sobbed out the whole story to him and took her home to Sylvia, who listened sympathetically and fed Amanda homemade tacos and beer for supper. Eddie had taken Jack his truck keys, and had reported to her every day on the progress, or lack of it, on the investigation. Not once had Jack come to her lab, not even on official business, and Amanda figured that he was trying to avoid her. A part of her was happy he was leaving her alone, but a part of her was disappointed that he hadn't tried to call her once.

Amanda dumped her aluminum plate in the trash and switched on the television. She managed to get halfway involved in a *Miami Vice* episode, accurately predicting the killer thirty minutes before the show was over. She was about to turn off the set when the anchorman for the ten o'clock news came on with the headline leader: "Another suspected poisoning tonight—coming up next on Eyewitness News."

The telephone rang just as Amanda was turning up the television. Without bothering to lower the volume, she picked up the telephone. "Amanda, this is Jack. We've had another poisoning and we need you at the lab."

"Yes, I know. I'll be there," Amanda said, rather sharply, still not able to forgive him for the weekend.

"How did you know?" Jack demanded.

"I just heard it on the news."

Jack swore once, sharply. "Just what we need, the public spotlight on us again."

"I'll be quick," Amanda promised as she hung up on another choice word from Jack. She hurried into her clothes and raced down the expressway toward town. She could understand Jack's frustration—the last thing homicide needed was another poisoning, especially when they couldn't solve the two they had. Briefly Amanda wondered what kind of reception she could expect from Jack but comforted herself with the thought that they were both professionals, and that neither of them was the type to let a personal difference get in the way of the job.

Jack turned into the parking lot just ahead of her. Amanda parked next to him and took one of the evidence bags he was fumbling with. She glanced at Jack's face, trying to catch a hint of his feelings from his expression. But his professional mask was in place, just as hers was, and Amanda had no idea what he was thinking. A stab of regret tore at her when she thought of what they might have shared together, had Jack been different.

"What happened?" Amanda asked as they hurried toward the building.

"A poker game turned lethal."

"I thought this was a poisoning," Amanda said as she unlocked the lab.

"It is." Jack logged himself in while Amanda put on her lab coat.

"Oh. Poker games usually end up being a knifing or a shooting."

Jack handed Amanda a handful of vials with the victims' blood samples. "Not this one. Apparently this was a regular Thursday night game. The men are all stationed at Fort Sam and the stakes are very low, so there's no motive that I can see for one of the participants to be the killer, too. Besides, they all got sick, and they're all sick to the same degree...except for the one who didn't make it."

Amanda prepared the first blood sample and put it in the mass spectrometer. She whistled a moment later. "Jack, come take a look at this."

Jack leaned over her shoulder to read the console. "Is there any old lace to go with it?"

Amanda removed the sample from the machine. "This is interesting. If my memory serves me correctly, arsenic's usually a slow poison. I wonder why they all fell sick so suddenly?"

"Maybe we can tell when we find the vector," Jack suggested.

Amanda rolled her eyes as she unloaded the bags. "Another batch of party food," she sighed. "Jack, can you put on some coffee? We may be here for a while."

"Try the onion dip first," Jack suggested as he rinsed out the coffee pot. "Just in case."

"I intended to," Amanda said shortly. "It's the same brand, even." She prepared a sample and put it in the spectrometer. "Sorry, the onion dip's clean," she announced a moment later.

"It didn't hurt to try," Jack said.

Amanda made her way through two more dips and a sack of chips. "I don't know whether to test the wine or drink it," she commented as she poured out a little sample of the wine. "It may be jug wine, but it's not half bad, and I could use a drink about now."

"Bad week?" Jack asked absently.

"A little hectic," Amanda answered, not adding that she had lain awake every night until the wee hours of the morning thinking about him.

"On second thought, I'll pass on this wine," Amanda declared a moment later. "Jack, come take a look at this."

"Is that a heavy dose?"

"It's enough to kill a horse," Amanda responded.

"Literally?"

"Oh, maybe not literally. But the amount of poison in one glass of this wine would contain what would be a massive single dose for a human. Which of these vials is from the man who died?"

Jack read the names on the vials. "Here," he said, flipping one to her.

Amanda tested the blood in the vial. "There's a higher concentration in this man's blood than in the other one. He either drank more than the others did, or he's ingested some from an additional source." She switched off her machine. "I guess you better go talk to the survivors and find out if Larry Pevetoe went on a bender with the wine."

"So much for any sleep tonight," Jack sighed. Amanda glanced up into his face and was surprised to see big circles under his eyes. "Are you ready to go out to the hospital?"

"Uh, yes," Amanda said. She started to ask Jack if he was sure he wanted her along, but he was out the door before she had a chance to speak.

The victims of the arsenic poisoning were in the same intensive care ward that the last poisoning victims had been taken to. Amanda and Jack carefully questioned each of the four men who were now hospitalized and fighting the effects of a big dose of arsenic. They all got along well, they told them. They were playing for very low stakes, and none of them owed any of the others any money. None of them had any reason to want any of the others dead, they assured Jack and Amanda. They all thought quite a bit of Larry Pevetoe, although the first three admitted that they didn't know Larry all that well, since he had just transferred in from overseas and had only been part of the poker game for the last month or so. And yes, Larry brought the wine tonight.

It was during the fourth interview that Jack and Amanda accidentally stumbled onto something. Joe Grainger, a young corporal from Georgia, was visibly upset as well as ill. "Larry and I were stationed together in Germany for two years," he said as he fought to hold back tears. "He was a real good friend, you know. One of the best." A tear ran down his cheek, and Amanda handed him a tissue.

"I'm sorry you lost such a good friend," Jack consoled. "Mr. Grainger, I want you to think very carefully, since you just might be the only lead we have in Larry's death. Had you resumed your friendship since Larry moved to San Antonio?"

"Sure, we did. Larry even rented an apartment across from mine," Joe answered as he shifted uncomfortably in his bed.

"Mr. Grainger, do you know of anyone who would have wanted Larry Pevetoe dead?"

Joe thought a minute. "No. He was a nice guy. Besides, he'd only been here a month. He hadn't even gotten around to having a steady girlfriend."

Intuition told Amanda to pursue this line of questioning, even if she wasn't sure where it was going to lead. "What do you mean? Did Larry date a lot?"

"Larry would usually date around when he was first transferred, but before long he would have a steady girlfriend that he went with until he was transferred again. He hadn't settled in with anybody here yet. In fact, he had a couple of dates with different girls last weekend."

Jack started to ask Joe something, but Amanda caught his eye and shook her head. "Where did he meet these girls?" she asked Joe.

"One works in an office on base, and he picked the other one up in a bar."

"Did either of them go home with him?" Jack pressed.

"I don't know about the girl on base, but I know the girl from the bar did," Joe said. "I saw her leave the next morning, before sunup."

"Did you get a look at her?" Amanda asked eagerly.

Joe shook his head. "It was too dark to see anything. Larry said later that she was a real knockout, though."

"Did he say any more than that?" Jack demanded.

"No, those were the exact words he used."

Jack and Amanda glanced at one another. Jack continued with the routine questions while Amanda played around with the possibilities. It may have been just a coincidence that Larry and Onion Burns had picked up a woman at a bar within a couple of days of being poisoned, but Amanda didn't think so. She asked if the jug was full when Larry brought it tonight, and Joe said that he thought there was some missing from the bottle.

They thanked Joe and sat down in a deserted visitors' lounge at the end of the hall. "Good questions," Jack complimented. "How did you know to follow that line?"

"I just had a hunch," Amanda admitted. "So what do you think? Is this poisoning related to the other one?"

"I think it's related to both the other ones," Jack said thoughtfully.

"How is it related to the cyanide poisonings?" Amanda asked.

"Stop and think. Both of the intended victims in the last two poisonings have been young men who picked up a woman in a bar. That young man in the first killing—he might have picked up a woman in a bar, too. I haven't a shred of proof on the first one, of course, but I have a gut reaction that says it's related somehow. As far as these last two, either it's a helluva coincidence or we've got a lady out there who likes to make love before she kills."

"Like the black widow," Amanda said softly, shivering a little. "That description of the woman could very well have been Lori."

"If it is her, then we've got another dead end unless someone in that bar saw them leave together and recognizes her," Jack continued tiredly. He stared across the couch with dull, defeated eyes. "I guess I better go on down and write my report."

Amanda started to agree, but she saw an expression of sadness flit across Jack's face before he could stop it. Had that look of unhappiness been because of her? She started to harden her heart, but she couldn't forget the time she and Jack had spent together, or the way he made her blood sing when he kissed her. She had to talk to him—to try to make him understand why she had walked out on him like she did last Saturday. "Would you like to come by my place for a drink?" she invited softly. "You don't have to write the report tonight. We need to talk about last weekend."

Jack ran his hand down the side of his face. "Yes, I guess we do," he admitted. "I'll meet you at your place. The report can wait until morning."

Jack followed Amanda's speeding Mustang down the expressway to her apartment, wondering what she intended to say. He was still angry, but at the same time he was hopeful that maybe, just maybe he could change her mind about him. Besides, he simply couldn't understand why she had been so upset. It had just been a fall from a bull. He had been thrown from bulls lots of times, and he had always been all right. He hoped that he could say whatever it was that would make her rethink making love to him. His relationship with her was special, and he wanted to pursue it. The fight and Amanda's departure had upset Jack more than he liked to admit, and he had spent quite a few sleepless hours since he had awakened Sunday morning from his alcohol-induced sleep with a whale of a hangover.

Amanda unlocked the door and motioned to the couch. "What would you like?"

"Have a beer?" Jack asked. Amanda opened two beers and handed him one. She sat down on the chair across from the couch and drank deeply from her bottle. "Dutch courage?" Jack asked.

"No, I'm not afraid of talking to you," Amanda returned quietly. "It's been a long week, that's all."

"Amanda, tell me again why you walked out on me last weekend. Everything was fine and then you took off."

Amanda took a deep breath. "Everything was fine until you took a foolish chance up on the back of a bull. It frightened me, and it angered me. I admit I shouldn't have taken your truck, but you were treating me like I didn't know my own mind. You acted like I would have changed it in the next five minutes if I had stayed."

"And wouldn't you have?"

"It's been nearly a week, and I haven't changed it yet," Amanda said tiredly. "I still don't intend to become your lover."

"But *why,* Amanda? Why did you change your mind?"

"I'm trying to tell you," Amanda began with exaggerated patience. "I just can't stand it when you take foolish, unnecessary risks with your safety."

"I'm a cop, Amanda, and I don't have a nice, safe laboratory to work out of. I have to take risks. It's part of my job."

"I'm not talking about the risks you have to take on duty," Amanda clarified. "That's part and parcel of a policeman's life. I'm a cop, too, remember, and that sure wasn't popcorn Eddie and I were dodging last month."

"Oh. So it comes back to that. You don't like the things I do for fun," he said slowly.

"You've got it," Amanda answered dryly. "You're right, Jack, I don't like the things you do for fun, because they're dangerous. And they upset me. It tore me apart last Saturday when you got up on that bull, and it's going to upset me every time you do something like that."

Jack drank deeply from his bottle of beer. "I really don't understand," he said quietly. "Why does it upset you so much when I race or ride a bull? It didn't bother you when I stood in front of a crazy sniper with a rifle in his hand. Are you sure you're not just using this business with the bull riding to see if you can get your own way?"

"That's a really awful thing to say, and you know it," Amanda responded hotly. "Why should I want to get my own way? I don't need to do that. Besides, it did bother me when you lured out the sniper. It *does* bother me when you have to take a risk at work, but it's part of your job, and I understand that. But do you have to take chances on the weekends just for the hell of it? You take enough chances because you have to—why do you take them when you *don't* have to?"

"I enjoy racing and riding the bulls," Jack stated simply. "It's fun."

Amanda muttered a curse word. "Never mind, you'll never understand the way I feel," she said as she shook her head. "Go home, Jack."

"No," Jack returned stubbornly as he sat down beside her. "You invited me up to talk, and we're going to do just that. Why does it bother you so much to see me race or ride? There's no danger to you, and I know how to take care of myself."

"Because I *care* about you, you idiot!" Amanda snapped. "Maybe I don't want to see you get splattered all over the racetrack or stomped by a thousand pounds of angry bull. Can't you understand that? I don't want to see you get hurt or killed unnecessarily."

Jack sat quietly for a minute. "I guess I can't, not really." He paused before continuing. "I've never really been frightened by anything I've done. I know in my head that some things are dangerous, but I also know that if I handle myself right, I'll be okay. You see, Mandy, if you approach these things right, they're not dangerous—they're exciting. But I'll try. I'll really try to understand how you feel. Is that good enough, Amanda?"

"I don't know," Amanda said slowly. "Are you going to keep on riding and racing?"

Jack bristled. "You don't have the right to ask me to give them up," he admonished defensively.

"Then I don't think so. I don't want a lover that I'm going to have to worry about constantly. Maybe we'd be better off if we just remain friends."

"And you think you can turn off what's between us just like that?" Jack jeered. "You think you can just up and decide that you don't want me any more?" Before Amanda realized what he was doing, he had slid across the couch and was taking her into his arms. "You think you can just forget about this?" he taunted her as his lips came down on hers.

Amanda's "No, Jack" was muffled by the tender strength of his kiss. Amanda felt herself melting into his embrace, all objections forgotten as he parted her lips and tasted of her sweetness. She didn't want to respond—she fought it as best she could—but her attempt was feeble and it went unnoticed. The attraction and caring between them was too powerful to deny, and Amanda could no more have turned away from Jack than she could have stopped breathing. It was right that they should be together, right and special and like nothing Amanda had ever experienced in her entire life. Her objections forgotten, Amanda gave herself up to Jack's embrace, glorying in the feelings they shared.

Jack moaned as he stroked the smoothness of Amanda's shoulders. She was kissing him as he was kissing her, stroking him, touching his arms and shoulders and back, savoring their embrace as much as he was. Jack's conscience stabbed at him as he deepened their sensual caress, but he pushed his nobler feelings aside as he ran his fingers through the soft thickness of Amanda's hair and pressed his body even closer to hers, letting her feel the strength of his desire. He wasn't playing fair and he knew it, but he needed Amanda so badly he didn't care how unscrupulous his actions were. She was meant to be his, and he intended to claim her.

Jack was astounded by the feelings of tender possessiveness that Amanda aroused in him. He had never felt this way about a woman before in his life—he wanted to take her, to make her his, yet at the same time he wanted to cherish her and protect her from anything that would ever hurt her. And he wanted to stroke her, to feel her body where her clothes sheltered her from his touch. His fingers were gentle as they parted the lapels of her blouse, teasing and stroking the warm skin that covered her collarbones, and when she whimpered and unconsciously arched herself closer, Jack lost whatever restraint he still possessed. His teasing fingers undid her top buttons, and his hand slid across the warmth of one high, firm breast.

"Oh, Jack," Amanda breathed. All her earlier objections forgotten, unconsciously she thrust herself closer to his touch, gasping when his fingers closed over her nipple and pinched it lightly. Jack caressed her, using all the sensual expertise at his disposal to bring her pleasure. He dipped his head and found the tip of her other nipple through the thin lace fabric of her bra, tormenting it until it, too, was hard.

"What are you doing?" Amanda protested when Jack withdrew the tenderness of his lips.

"This isn't enough," Jack whispered as he tasted the soft skin below her breasts. "I need more of you than this." Impatiently, Jack undid the rest of her buttons and pushed her blouse from her shoulders. "You're beautiful," he breathed. "Let me touch you and kiss you."

Amanda nodded, speechless from the wild tremors that shook her. She could do nothing else at this point—she was completely within Jack's sensual web. He unhooked her bra and pulled it from her body, baring her all the way to her waist to his piercing gaze. "Beautiful," he whispered as he took in her soft, warm shoulders and her high, firm breasts. Slowly, almost reverently, he dipped his head and touched one with the tip of his tongue. "You taste so good," he said as he caressed the other with his finger. "You feel good and you taste good and I need you so badly I hurt."

"I hurt, too, Jack," Amanda admitted as she stroked the hard, firm muscles beneath the thin cotton shirt he wore. She wanted him, wanted to touch him with the same freedom he was touching her, to kiss and caress him with the same passion. Amanda's eager fingers stroked his back, his sides, the warm smoothness of his chest, greedily savoring the way his body trembled with passionate response to her touch. Eagerly Amanda unbuttoned Jack's shirt to the waist. "I want to see you," she murmured. "I want to see you the way you can see me."

"I want you to," Jack encouraged as he sat up and shrugged out of his shirt. "Touch me, Amanda. Touch me the way I'm touching you."

Amanda swallowed as she stared at Jack's chest. She could see him and touch him, all right. She could see and touch the mass of yellowing bruises that was left over from last weekend's encounter with the bull. "I didn't realize you had been hurt this badly," she said as she stroked one of the worst bruises with gentle fingers. "They weren't showing that badly when I doctored you that afternoon."

Jack shrugged. "They looked the worst Sunday morning. They were black and blue then."

Amanda shut her eyes against the image. She grew cold inside as she felt herself mentally withdrawing from Jack. "Jack, it's hopeless," she murmured as she turned away, feeling miserable.

"What on earth?" Jack began as he turned her around to face him. "Amanda, what are you saying?"

"It's never going to work," she said as her eyes filled with tears. "I can't even look at you without cringing at the fool things you do."

Jack looked down at his bruised chest and frowned. "I'm sorry if I'm not perfect enough for you," he said stiffly.

"It's not the marks. It's—it's how you got them!" Amanda cried. "I just can't stand the chances you take!"

"What do those have to do with you turning away from me?" Jack demanded. "Why does it mean you can't become my lover?"

"Jack, I'm not your one-night stand kind of woman. I take lovemaking very seriously, and if I make love to you, the chances are that I'm going to fall in love with you. And I'm not going to do that."

Jack stared into her eyes, his bewilderment turning to anger. "You're going to turn it off, just like that, huh?" he taunted. "You're going to let me touch you and caress you like I just did and then send me on my way. There's a name for women like that, Amanda."

"Yes, I know it," Amanda said bravely. "And I guess that tonight it applies to me. But I can't become your lover, Jack. I'm just not willing to commit myself to you like that under the circumstances. I'm afraid to, Jack. I could get hurt too badly if something happened to you."

Jack grasped Amanda by the shoulders. "I could break down that reluctance in about thirty seconds," he insisted as his fingers dug into her arms. "I could have you melting in my arms again, just like you were a few minutes ago."

"Yes, you could," Amanda admitted. "You could have me willing right now. But I wouldn't be willing in the morning."

Angrily Jack thrust her away from him. "You're trying to use sex to manipulate me," he accused disgustedly. "You're just trying to get your way. But it isn't going to work, Amanda."

"I'm not trying to manipulate you, Jack," Amanda answered softly as she reached for her bra. "You can think what you like. I'm only trying to save myself a lot of heartache."

"You can call it what you like," Jack snapped as he grabbed his shirt and thrust his arms into it. "You're trying to use sex to get me to change my mind. But I'm not going to change my mind, Amanda. You are."

"No, Jack," Amanda said quietly. "You're wrong."

"Yes, you are, sooner or later," Jack promised her. "You'll come to me and do it willingly. What we have is too strong for either of us to do otherwise." He buttoned his shirt with trembling fingers. "Maybe not tonight, Amanda." He threw open the living room door. "But you will be mine. Sooner or later."

Amanda stared after Jack as the door slammed behind him. She pulled on her blouse but didn't bother to button it. *Jack's right,* she acknowledged to herself as she shivered apprehensively. She would be his. Sooner or later, she would give in to the powerful, almost magnetic attraction that seemed to draw them together.

Amanda went to the refrigerator and poured herself another beer. She sat down on the couch and drank it almost absently as she thought about Jack. If she hadn't been able to see the bruises, she would have slept with him tonight. She had been granted a small reprieve, but it was only temporary. Jack was right—she would eventually give in to what they shared and become his lover. She could do nothing else. A part of Amanda longed for this to happen and wished it already had, but a larger part of her wondered what it was going to do to her to fall in love with a man like Jack Vance.

***

Jack squinted at the large, elegant home in the exclusive subdivision of Castle Hills. He dreaded the upcoming interview, hating the fact that he was going to go in that house and question a mother and father who had already been hurt beyond belief. But he had a strong hunch that these people might have an answer to some important questions. He put his notebook in his pocket and knocked on the front door. A moment later cool air from the interior of the house surrounded him as Gloria Carroway welcomed him into her home. The woman looked tired and visibly older than she had five weeks ago at the restaurant, and a pall hung over the lovely home she had created for her family. "Come in, Officer Vance," she said as she motioned him into the living room. "I don't know if Roger and I can help you, but we'll certainly try."

Roger Carroway entered from the family room and shook Jack's hand. He, too, looked tired and sad. "Yes, Mr. Vance, we want to do anything we can to help with your investigation," he seconded as the three of them sat down. "It's my understanding that things have pretty well come to a standstill."

"Yes, they have, and it's not because we don't care about catching Bert's and Miss Carroway's killer," Jack replied candidly. "We've turned this case inside out and come up with nothing. But I have a hunch, just a hunch, that this poisoning might be connected with the other two."

"Two? We didn't realize there had been two more," Gloria responded heavily.

"There was another one last night. Have you listened to the news today?"

Roger Carroway shook his head. "No, we haven't."

"What sort of connection do you think there is?" Gloria asked curiously.

"It looks like the other two poisonings were committed by a young woman the victims picked up in a bar. Mr. Carroway, Mrs. Carroway, Bert wasn't too much younger than the second man who was poisoned. Is there any way that your son might have been with a woman like that?"

Jack did not miss the strange expression that flitted across Mr. Carroway's face. Mrs. Carroway shook her head. "No, absolutely not," she assured Jack. "There's no way Bert could have picked up that young woman."

Jack raised his eyebrow. "You sound awfully sure."

"Oh, Mr. Vance, it's not that Bert wasn't fond of the ladies," his mother added quickly. "I'm sure he had his fun. But he had just driven in that afternoon from Waco for dinner. He hadn't had time to go out with anyone here in San Antonio."

Jack tried to keep the Carroways from seeing the disappointment and frustration he felt. "I guess my hunch was wrong," he said quietly. "I thank you both for your time."

The Carroway's telephone rang as they stood up. "You get that, Gloria," Mr. Carroway suggested quickly. "I'll see Mr. Vance to the door."

Roger Carroway followed Jack out, glancing nervously behind him as he shut the front door. "Mr. Vance," he said after a moment's hesitation, "I didn't want to say anything in front of my wife, but there is something you ought to know. The night before Bert died, on the way home from a late meeting I stopped by a bar. I bought a drink for a young woman and we talked for a while that night."

"And?" Jack prompted.

"And nothing. We shared a drink and a little conversation, and I went on home to Gloria."

"So why couldn't you tell me this in front of her?" Jack asked. "Why wait until we're out here?"

"Because Gloria's insecure enough about getting older without her knowing that I bought a girl my daughter's age a drink," Mr. Carroway replied impatiently. "She would be hurt, and I don't want that, especially after all she's been through. Anyway, the point of all this is that the girl gave me her pack of cigarettes. I was out, and we smoked two out of the pack together. She said to keep it—she had more at home—so I did. Anyway, I'm trying to cut down, and I didn't smoke anymore that night or the next day." Mr. Carroway shuddered slightly. "But I did offer the cigarettes around the table after dinner that night. We all smoked a cigarette from the pack."

"Where's the rest of the pack?" Jack demanded. "Did you throw it away?"

"No, the empty pack was wadded up on the table when the police took the evidence. I guess they took it with them."

"Mr. Carroway, thank you," Jack said. "This may be the link."

Jack drove to a pay phone at a convenience store and dialed the lab. "Amanda, this is Jack. Go back through the Carroway evidence and find a wadded-up cigarette case. It may have been the vector."

"I've already tested it," Amanda protested.

"Did you test both ends?"

"No, I cut a piece off the bottom."

"Go back and test the whole wrapper," Jack directed. "I'll call you back in fifteen minutes."

Jack went into the convenience store and drank a Coke that he didn't want. As soon as Amanda's time was up, he impatiently punched in her number. "What did you find out?"

"You're right on target, Jack," Amanda said. "There are faint traces of cyanide at the top of the pack. At least some of the cigarettes in the pack had been poisoned."

Chapter Seven

Amanda flopped over and shut her eyes to the bright July sunlight. "I'm broiling out here," she complained as she felt the warmth of the sun on her stomach.

"Too bad," Jack said good-naturedly as he splashed a little water from the swimming pool on her bare feet. "It was your idea to come to the Fourth of July get-together here at your pool. Now, if you had accepted my invitation to spend the weekend at the coast—"

"—we could be broiling down there instead of out here," Amanda finished for him. "No way, Jack. No weekends together, remember?"

Jack scowled at her. "Stubborn woman," he mumbled as he turned over on his stomach and shut his eyes.

Amanda stifled a smile as she rolled off her towel. She helped herself to a soft drink and slid into the water at the shallow end of the pool, sipping her drink and gazing at Jack's small, muscular body. A familiar wave of longing rolled over her, and for probably the thousandth time, she wondered if she was doing the right thing in refusing to become Jack's lover. It hadn't been easy—holding out against him the last two months—especially when they had drifted back into seeing one another on a regular basis. She had avoided dating him for a while after the argument, always having an excuse for not going out with him, but Jack finally reached the end of his patience and shanghaied her at the lab one night. Over dinner at a lovely restaurant, he said that he wouldn't pressure her about deepening their relationship if she would at least start seeing him again. Amanda seriously doubted his sincerity at the time—and she had been right. But she missed Jack badly and agreed to date him as she had before.

But Jack hadn't had things all his way. He found her surprisingly stubborn about not becoming his lover. Amanda's lips curled into a wicked grin when she thought about how Jack had tried to break down her defenses—wine, candlelight dinners, dancing the night away to slow, romantic music. But every time Amanda sent him away with just a few kisses, even though it usually cost her a sleepless night afterward. It was becoming increasingly difficult to send Jack home, and she could tell that he was probably more frustrated than she.

Amanda finished her soft drink and paddled lazily across the pool. She swam around a young couple wrestling in the water and bobbed in the deep end, waving her arms and legs just enough to stay afloat. She frowned as she squinted through her wet lashes at the little white cloud that temporarily obscured the sun and thought about her feelings for Jack. They had deepened in the last two months in spite of her refusal to sleep with him and her desire to keep their relationship casual. She was falling in love with him. Perhaps she was already in love with him. Amanda sighed as she held on to the side of the pool and hoisted herself out of the water. She didn't want to feel the way she did about Jack, but she couldn't seem to help herself.

Amanda cupped her hands and poured a handful of cold water in the middle of Jack's back, laughing when he came off the towel with a roar. "Come on, get in," she said, laughing as Jack grabbed for her ankle. She fell back into the pool and pulled him after her, chuckling when he came up sputtering.

Not to be outdone, Jack picked Amanda up under her legs and held her out of the water. "What do you think, folks?" he called to the rest of the party. "Should I dunk her?"

"Yeah, throw her in!" a young man encouraged.

"Sure! She has it coming!" someone else added.

"Drop the cop!" another called.

Jack tossed Amanda into the pool and was ready for her when she came up splashing. They played in the water like a couple of kids, and soon others entered into the fun when Jack offered to judge a splashing contest. The sun was low in the sky when they finally called it a day and walked hand in hand up to Amanda's apartment. Amanda let Jack use the bathroom first, and he broiled steaks on the gas grill Amanda kept on her patio while she showered and washed the chlorine out of her hair.

Jack handed Amanda a drink as she came into the kitchen. "Did you have a good holiday?" he asked.

Amanda smiled as she sipped her drink. "The best. Sometimes it's fun just to goof off. How about you? Was it exciting enough for you?"

"It was fine," Jack assured her, although he was sorry she wouldn't come with him to the racetrack. He had been entered in a race in Corpus Christi this afternoon, but when Amanda refused to go away with him for the weekend, he canceled rather than miss the Fourth with her. He hated missing the Corpus race, but he knew he would be able to drive in one here next weekend.

Amanda sipped her drink as she fixed a salad. "Has anymore ever turned up on the poisonings?" she asked. She had been so busy on other cases she had hardly thought about the poisonings in a couple of weeks.

"Nothing," Jack admitted. "Not since I talked to Roger Carroway." He had returned to the Carroway home and taken a fairly detailed description of the woman who had given Mr. Carroway the cigarettes. His description of her was fairly close to Onion Burns's, and homicide officers had visited the bars where she had met her victims. But they learned nothing, and thankfully there had been no more poisonings. The case had even been showcased on a crime-stoppers segment on television without results. The investigation was at a virtual standstill and would remain so until they had a break—or there was another poisoning.

Jack and Amanda shared a delightful dinner and afterward Jack helped her clean up. When they were almost done and she was turning on the dishwasher, he put his arms around Amanda and nibbled the back of her neck. "Want some sugar?" he asked.

"Stop it, Jack! You promised," she whispered, hating the quaver in her voice.

"Aw, come on, Mandy! You've held out on me for two months now," Jack whined as his hands cupped her breasts. "It would be beautiful. You know it would."

"Jack, you're cheating," Amanda warned him.

"Tough," he murmured as he turned her around and took her into his arms. His kiss was tender, passionate, loving, all the things it was supposed to be, and Amanda could feel her resolve weakening as he worked his tender magic on her. Almost of their own volition, Amanda's arms crept around Jack's neck, and she held him close to her for a long, hard, sweet kiss that seemed to go on forever.

Amanda knew if she didn't do something right away, there would be no turning back, so she disengaged herself from his arms.

"That's enough sugar for tonight," she said in a breathless voice as she moved away from him.

Jack's face clouded. "You're as stubborn as a mule," he grumbled. "Why, Mandy? Why are you doing this to both of us?"

"You know why," Amanda returned, her expression hardening as she remembered Jack's refusal to give up the dangerous things he did. "As long as you don't change your mind, I'm not either." Her expression softened when she saw the hurt in Jack's eyes. "Let's not fight about it tonight," she pleaded. "Let's both do some thinking. Will you think about it, Jack?"

"Yes." He pulled Amanda to him and kissed her forehead. "I'll take you out for a drink after work tomorrow, all right?"

"Sure." They shared another kiss, and Jack let himself out.

Amanda sat cross-legged on the couch and played with a throw pillow. *Why am I holding out on him?* she asked herself. She originally refused him so that she wouldn't start to care for him, but she had done that anyway. Could making love with him possibly cause her to feel anymore deeply for him than she did already? Amanda didn't know for sure, but she did know that she was getting tired of sending Jack home at the end of the evening.

***

"Amanda? Are you ready to go?" Jack called from the door of the lab.

"Almost," she answered as she peered into the microscope. Jack logged himself in while Amanda finished with the paint chip she was trying to match. "Are you working on the hit-and-run from last night?" she asked as she turned off the scope light.

"No, Tony's on it," Jack responded. "Does the paint match?"

"Nope. The paint on the little girl's dress came from a car that had been repainted twice. The paint from the Dodge had only the standard factory coats." She picked up the telephone and dialed homicide. "Tony? This is Amanda. No match."

"Good," Tony said.

"Good?"

"Yeah, I didn't want that kid to be a killer," Tony admitted. "Is Jack there yet? He was hot to get out the door."

"Yes, he's here," Amanda verified. She and Tony often made jokes over the phone about Jack deliberately so that Jack could overhear them.

"Did you know that he—I've got to hang up. The other line's blinking," Tony said. "Thanks."

"Your sergeant can be a nice person," Amanda volunteered as she hung up.

"Yeah, if you don't mind Jack Vance jokes," he teased. "Where would you like to go?"

"Anywhere," Amanda responded as the telephone rang. "That is, as soon as I get off the phone."

"Amanda, Tony again. Put Jack on, please."

"It's Tony," Amanda said.

Jack listened for a minute and wrote down an address. "No sign of a struggle? Could they see any wounds on the body?" He tapped his foot. "I'm gone."

"Another poisoning?" Amanda asked.

"He wasn't sure. The call just came through. But it might be. Want to come along in case it is?"

"Can't you ever take me to anything but a murder?" Amanda teased as she took off her lab coat. They fought the expressway traffic to a pleasant neighborhood near Kelly Air Force Base. "I wonder what's going on," she murmured when she saw two squad cars at the curb and neighbors peering out the windows across the street. Another two squad cars were parked down the street, and a van with a television crew was pulling up halfway between the two groups of patrol cars.

They parked next to the nearest squad cars and approached two officers that were positioned behind them. "What's up?" Jack demanded. "Another sniper?"

"We don't know," one of the patrolmen answered. "There was a shooting down the block, and the man who did it ran home and shut himself in his house. He hasn't been seen since, and he can't be reached by phone."

"Do you have an identification on him?" Jack pressed.

"The neighbors all know him," the other officer said. "His name is Ralph Tijerina, and he's only lived here a few months."

"Ralph! I know Ralph," Jack broke in.

"You know him?" Amanda asked.

"Sure, he used to live in the neighborhood I patrolled a couple of years back. He wasn't a bad sort. Let me go and see if I can get this straightened out." Jack started to go around the cars.

"Sir, my sergeant has already called in the negotiators," one of the patrolmen put in hesitantly. "Don't you think it would be better to wait for them?"

"Nah, I can handle this one," Jack said as he stepped around the car and marched up the sidewalk.

"Jack, no," Amanda whispered, but he never heard her protest. She watched in horror as Jack approached the house. He was violating two cardinal rules of police safety: he had let his guard down because he knew the suspect, and he wasn't respecting a barricaded subject. Just last year a veteran officer had been shot and nearly killed because he didn't frisk a suspect he knew from his patrol. Many an officer had regretted taking chances with a barricaded subject. To make matters even worse, Jack didn't have a highly trained SWAT team with him today. If he got in trouble, he had only three officers—herself and these two young patrolmen—to help him.

"What does he think he's doing?" one of the patrolmen asked as Jack banged on the door and called for Ralph.

"Being a hero," Amanda replied bitterly.

"He must be crazy," the other man spoke so softly that Amanda could barely hear him.

The cameraman from the van wandered up and crouched behind one of the cars. "What's going on?"

"We have an officer who's attempting to contact the man inside," one of the patrolmen explained. "The man's potentially dangerous, and we're going to have to ask you to stay away for the time being."

The cameraman peered at Jack. "Say, isn't he that crazy cop who takes all the chances?"

Amanda stared coldly at the cameraman. "I believe the officer told you to stay back."

Reluctantly the cameraman moved out of the line of fire. The three of them drew their weapons and crouched behind a squad car, listening as Jack called out for Ralph. "Ralph, it's Officer Vance. I know you're in there. Come out and let's talk about this."

Amanda held her breath, but nothing happened. "Ralph, this is Officer Vance." Jack banged on the door. "Come on out and talk to me about this."

"Is he trying to get himself killed?" the other patrolman asked incredulously. "That man in there's already killed one man today."

"He doesn't think about that," Amanda said hotly. "He never gives it a thought."

"Ralph, please come out and tell me what happened," Jack called through the closed front door. He reached for the knob and turned the handle.

"Good God, he intends to walk in there," one of the patrolmen breathed.

"I gotta film this," the cameraman said excitedly as he moved forward again and zoomed in on Jack.

"He's crazy," the other one uttered. "Utterly crazy."

"Amen to that," Amanda murmured. She rubbed her sweaty palm on her skirt and transferred her .38 to her left hand so she could wipe her right.

"Are you coming out, Ralph, or may I come in?" Jack called through the open door.

"I'm coming out," a voice yelled from within the house.

Amanda's hand tightened on her weapon as a frightened-looking young man stepped out on the front porch, an old rifle clutched uncertainly in his hand.

"Put the rifle down, why don't you, Ralph, and let's talk about this," Jack coaxed. Amanda shuddered when she realized Jack had still not drawn his gun.

Slowly, Ralph handed the rifle to Jack, and the two of them sat down on the front porch. Just then another car pulled up, and Mike McCormick and Dave Greer, the head of the negotiating team, got out. "What's going on?" Mike demanded.

"We understood there was a barricaded subject," Dave said.

"There was," Amanda responded, returning her .38 to her purse. "Jack talked him out of the house."

"He *what?*" Mike demanded incredulously.

"Apparently he knew the suspect," one of the patrolmen put in. "He just walked up and banged on the door until the guy surrendered."

Mike muttered a string of curse words under his breath. "That careless damned fool's going to get himself or one of us killed someday," he snapped, not bothering to hide his fury.

Ralph and Jack stood up and came down the sidewalk. "Ralph, I'm going to have to put cuffs on you," Jack said. "They'll take you downtown, and I'll call you a lawyer."

"Am I in bad trouble?" Ralph asked.

"Murder's always trouble," Jack replied honestly. "I'll do what I can, though."

The cameraman shot film of the scene as one of the patrolmen read Ralph his rights and hustled him into a squad car. "What was that all about?" Mike demanded.

"A revenge killing," Jack explained. "One of the neighbors took Ralph's sister out last night. Apparently the man slapped her around some, and Ralph was furious."

"That's not what I'm talking about!" Mike thundered. "What in hell do you mean, marching up to that door and yelling at a barricaded subject?"

Jack looked surprised at Mike's attack. "I was doing what I was supposed to be doing. I got him out of there without further violence."

"Yes, and you could have gotten yourself killed in the process. You had no business marching up to that door and demanding to speak to that man. He could have just as easily shot you."

"I knew him," Jack defended. "I knew he wasn't going to shoot me."

"How could you know that?" Mike demanded angrily. "You think that because you've met the man, he isn't capable of killing you? Do you know how many cops have been killed because they thought the same thing? Don't you know the department has rules and regulations for a reason, Vance?"

"Rules and regulations don't always work, Mike," Jack bit out. "So what if I broke a few rules? I got him out, didn't I? Isn't that what you wanted?"

"Not at the expense of your life, or the lives of your fellow officers," Mike snapped. "Vance, you didn't just take a chance with your own safety this evening. You put three other cops on the line with you. If something had happened to you, they would have been forced to go in after you. I'm writing you up, Vance. You're going before the review board."

Jack looked shocked. If the review board ruled against him, suspension would be for at least three days and could go on indefinitely. "I was just doing my job," Jack reiterated, staring Mike straight in the eye. "And I'll tell the review board the same thing. I did the right thing in going up to that house. I got him out of there because he knows me and he trusts me. Neither one of you could have done that."

"We'll let the review board decide," Mike said. "You can go on home. Another team of homicide detectives has already started down there." He and Dave got into their car and left, and Jack and Amanda followed a few minutes later.

Jack gunned the accelerator as he pulled onto the expressway. "Can you believe that?" he uttered in amazement. "I go in there and get Ralph out, and Mike has the gall to threaten me with the review board."

"I hope he hauls you up," Amanda responded tightly. "And I hope they suspend you for a solid month."

"What?" Jack asked unbelievingly.

"I said I hope they send you home for a month," Amanda snapped. "Maybe then you'll think twice before you pull another fool stunt like you pulled this afternoon."

Jack clenched the steering wheel tightly. "Not you, too," he said bitterly. "I honestly can't believe either one of you, Amanda! I got Ralph out without him shooting anybody, didn't I? By the time I was through he didn't even resist arrest. But that's not good enough for you and McCormick. I broke a couple of asinine rules, and you both want to string me up by the thumbs. What's it with you and the rules? I can't believe you're that big a stickler."

"I break as many minor rules as the next cop," Amanda ground out. "But I don't violate important regulations. You took a chance this afternoon, Jack. You took a stupid chance, and you're lucky you aren't laying in Tijerina's front yard with a hole in your gut."

"Oh, don't be ridiculous!" Jack snapped. "Ralph wouldn't shoot me. I know that man and—"

"Yeah, and how many other cops have known the men who shot them?" Amanda demanded. "Besides, he was barricaded. I wouldn't approach my own *mother* if she were barricaded."

"Well, I would," Jack retorted. "I'd approach anybody who I thought I could talk out of a situation like that. And I did it, Amanda! But you're not interested in that, are you? You're upset because I broke some rules and took a chance."

"You took an incredible chance," Amanda declared hotly. "And you involved me and a couple of green kids right out of the academy."

"All right, all right. I'm sorry if you think I put you in danger," Jack said stiffly.

"That's right. Get huffy. I wasn't worried for myself or one of the rookies, for heaven's sake. I was worried about *you.* Don't you even care that I was scared sick for you?"

"Are we back to that again?" Jack moaned with exaggerated tiredness as he pulled off the expressway. "I'm sick of your harping on being scared all the time."

"And I'm sick of you doing stupid things," Amanda snapped as Jack pulled into the parking lot of the police station. *"Yes,* you scared me, and you scared those young cops, too. They really thought you were crazy, Jack. And so do I." She jumped out of the car and slammed the door behind her.

Jack jumped out and started across the parking lot after her. "I'm not crazy! I was just doing my job!" he shouted, following her across the lot. "I didn't do anything I shouldn't have done. But that isn't good enough for you, is it? I acted like a man, a real man, and you don't like that. You'd rather I acted like a lapdog or a wimp."

Amanda whirled around and bumped into Jack, who stumbled backward. "No, I don't want you to act like a lapdog or a wimp. And you didn't act like a 'real man,' you acted like a comic book hero. For God's sake, Jack, act like an adult with a little sense and quit trying to be Superman. The cape doesn't fit you."

"I was doing what I had to do."

"You were acting like a fool!" Amanda cried. "A stupid, careless fool. What do you use for a brain? Jell-O?"

Amanda got into her car and slammed it into gear before Jack could think of a comeback. Her hands trembling, she drove away from the police station, tears running down her cheeks. She wiped her eyes with the back of her hand, still thinking he was a fool—a rash, stupid fool. If only she could convince herself that he wasn't worth her tears, but she knew that was a futile endeavor.

***

Jack swore sharply as Amanda's car left a trail of dust swirling in the hot air above the street. She had no business chewing him out like that, and neither did Mike. He had only acted like a good cop, and he thought he deserved support, not censure. Amanda at least should have stood by him when Mike chewed him out and not torn him apart some more. She was a police officer, too, and she of all people should have understood.

Jack kicked a small rock that was lying in the driveway and swore when it hit the fender of somebody's new Buick. *Amanda shouldn't have had the last word,* he thought, rerunning their argument through his mind. He had some things he wanted to say to her, and there was no time like the present. He pulled his keys out of his pocket and turned around to see Eddie and two other homicide detectives standing on the sidewalk, their arms folded and wide grins on their faces. "We'd clap, but you didn't win that one," Eddie teased.

"Man, and I thought my old lady had a tongue on her," one of the other detectives chimed in.

"She's not getting the last word this time," Jack snapped. "I'm going to her place right now, and we're going to settle this."

Eddie looked down into Jack's livid face and thought of Amanda's temper. "I wouldn't if I were you," he advised mildly. "With the mood you're both in, we would have another homicide tonight, and I'm not sure if you'd be the victim or the murderer. Why don't you come out with me for a beer, and we can discuss it?"

"No, I have to go and talk to her," Jack protested.

"Tell her off, you mean," Eddie observed shrewdly. "Jack, I really wouldn't, if I were you. At least come out with me for a little while so you can both have a chance to cool off. Besides, Sylvia and the kids are visiting her grandmother in Monterrey and I'm lonely."

"What? No wild date? Yeah, I'll come, Eddie," Jack said. "At least for a little while. I'll give her a chance to calm down and see reason. Besides, I could use a drink about now."

Chapter Eight

Jack and Eddie walked to a small, quiet bar that was off the beaten path of the tourists that poured into San Antonio every summer. They sat down in a booth in the back, and a tired-looking waitress took their order. "So do you want to talk about it?" Eddie asked.

"May as well," Jack said. "I'm still so mad I could bite a nail in two. I can't believe that Amanda acted that way. I just don't understand her."

"What happened? As interesting as it was, about all we heard was the bit about your cape not fitting and the Jell-O for a brain."

"You didn't hear the part about being a lapdog, huh?" Jack inquired dryly.

"She said that?"

"No, I did," Jack admitted sheepishly. "We're not above calling names, either one of us."

"Shame, shame," Eddie chided. "So what happened to get you both breathing fire? Did you run out in front of a semi to save a frog?" Eddie's eyes were dancing with amusement.

"No, but the way Amanda and Mike McCormick acted, you would have thought I had."

"Mike? How is Mike involved in this?"

"He and Dave Greer came to the call we answered, and Mike didn't like it that I had talked Ralph out of the house."

"Huh?" Eddie asked. "I'm more confused than ever. Why don't you start at the beginning and tell me what happened?"

Their beer came and Jack drank from his. "I was in the lab when a call came that there had been another homicide. It was a vague report, and we thought it might have been another poisoning, so Amanda offered to go along with me. We got there and found two rookies staring at a barricaded subject, who I knew from my old patrol. Anyway, Mike and Amanda got all bent out of shape because I went up to the front door and talked him out of the house."

"Let me get this straight. You waltzed up to the door of a barricaded subject and knocked on it?"

"Sure. Ralph knew me, and I knew he wasn't going to do anything to me."

Eddie shuddered inwardly at Jack's foolhardy courage. "And I guess Mike and Amanda left you in no doubt about how they felt about that."

"You bet. They both let me know in no uncertain terms what they thought," Jack assured Eddie. "Mike's so mad he's hauling me in front of the review board." He shrugged and drank from his beer. "I don't expect any different from him—not really. He's always been a stickler for regulations, and I did break a couple."

"No kidding," Eddie teased. "But it's not like Mike to involve the review board. He usually makes do with a chewing out."

"He thinks I put other officers in danger," Jack admitted. "But Eddie, I didn't do that. I knew Ralph, and he wasn't going to come out shooting."

"Jack, we never know what a frightened man with a gun is going to do," Eddie reminded him quietly, "particularly one who has just shot another man. Maybe you were sure there was no real danger, but you can't expect another officer on the force to take your word for it, especially when so many policemen have been hurt or killed for doing that very thing."

"I guess you're right," Jack said. "And I'm not mad about Mike, not really. It's Amanda who has me angry. She was nasty, Eddie, really nasty. And that was after she had heard Mike chew me out. You would think she would be a little more understanding."

Eddie pulled a pack of cigarettes from his pocket and lit one while he thought. "Jack, what do you expect from Amanda?"

"What do I expect from her?" Jack was surprised by the question.

"Yes, what kind of a relationship do you expect from her?" Eddie asked. "What are you looking for? I don't mean physically or on a practical level. I mean emotionally."

"I never thought about it, at least not in any depth. I guess I want her caring and support. And I sure didn't get that this afternoon."

"I disagree," Eddie said bluntly. Jack stared across the table at his friend. "I think you got caring, a lot of caring, from Amanda this afternoon, even if you don't recognize it as such."

"How's that? She tore me up for doing what I had to do."

"She tore you up because she *cares* about you, and in her eyes you took a foolish chance," Eddie went on. "You have to understand,

Jack, that a woman who cares about you is frightened for you when you're in danger. I know when I was on the street, Sylvia worried about me from the minute I left the house until the minute I returned. In fact, I used to call her as soon as I got off duty so she wouldn't worry if I went out for a drink."

"But Amanda's a police officer," Jack protested. "She shouldn't be that way."

"Yes, she should, if she cares about you," Eddie said. "It's when she quits worrying about you that you're in trouble. And, too, I'm guessing that she's never complained about any of the usual things that you face on the job. Isn't it your more exotic exploits that she protests?"

Jack nodded his head slowly. "She even told me that."

"So I'd say the woman's doing a pretty good job of caring about you," Eddie concluded. "And as far as supporting you goes, she's never going to be one to croon nice things that she doesn't agree with. If she thinks you're being a stupid fool, she's going to tell you so."

"Wonderful," Jack responded dryly.

"Would you want any less from her?" Eddie quizzed shrewdly.

"No, I guess I wouldn't," Jack admitted.

Eddie drained his beer and lit another cigarette. "I'm going to be honest with you. I've known you both for a long time, and I think you and Amanda are practically perfect for one another. You're both bright, and funny, and have a lot that you can share."

"We also have the hots for each other," Jack added.

Eddie's eyes twinkled. "No kidding. I'm sure that helps. Anyway, you're nothing like that stuffed shirt she used to be married to, and she's not like those dumb china dolls you get bored with in a month. I think the two of you might have something really good together."

"I think so, too, sometimes. But it seems like every time we turn around, we're fighting over either the bull riding or the racing or something like this afternoon," Jack admitted.

"Nothing else?"

"No, just those things."

Eddie stubbed out his cigarette. "Well, if that's all you ever argue about, you have more going for you than most couples I know. Sounds to me like the two of you just need to hang in there and see what happens. The first thing you need to do tonight is to go over and talk to her."

"Not chew her out?" Jack inquired, laughing.

"No. That's probably the last thing she needs right now." He stared at Jack thoughtfully. "Jack, have you ever thought of soft-pedaling it a little bit? Have you ever thought of trying to be a little more careful? Amanda's not the only person who worries about you, you know."

Jack could see the concern in Eddie's eyes. "Don't worry about me, Eddie. Nothing's going to happen to me, honestly." He got out his wallet and laid a bill on the table. "This one's on me. Thanks."

"Sure, anytime," Eddie said. He lit another cigarette and blew a smoke ring as he watched Jack make his way to the door. He should have known his suggestion that Jack take it easy would fall on deaf ears. If Amanda couldn't convince that man to lay off the heroics, he wasn't going to be able to either. Eddie wondered just what it would take to make Jack realize what a fool he could be at times.

***

Amanda sat on the carpet in front of the television and stared at a music video. She had tried to get interested in an episode of *Dynasty*, but she had given up after a few minutes and turned to the country and western music station. The videos were silly, and mindless, and perfect to cry by. Amanda wiped her cheeks and tried unsuccessfully to hold her tears back. *Is Jack trying to commit suicide?* she wondered morosely. Didn't he care that it tore her up when he risked his life like he did this afternoon? He could have been killed so easily.

Amanda wiped her eyes and blew her nose. Vowing that she wasn't going to cry anymore, she got up and went into the kitchen to make herself a sandwich. She didn't really feel hungry, but she could never sleep on an empty stomach, and she knew she was going to have enough trouble sleeping as it was. She had just sat down at the table when she heard a soft knock at the front door.

Amanda put her fingers to her swollen eyes and groaned. She looked terrible. Whoever was out there was going to know she had been crying. Since she wasn't up to giving any explanations, she ignored the knock, hoping whoever it was would think she was in the shower and go away. She heard another knock as she took a bite from her sandwich. "Amanda, it's me," she heard Jack call through the locked door. "I know you're angry, but please let me in. I need to talk to you."

Amanda shut her eyes in despair. "Go home, Jack," she called out the window. "I don't want to talk to you." She wasn't up to facing him tonight, and she didn't want Jack to know she had been crying over him.

"I'm not going home, Amanda, until you let me in," Jack insisted as he banged on the door again.

In response Amanda turned out the porch light and the light in the living room. She sat down in the dining room and tried to eat her sandwich. The bread and peanut butter stuck in her throat. She didn't want to face Jack tonight—she didn't want to face him for a long time.

Amanda forced herself to eat a little of the sandwich and was gagging down the last bite she intended to eat when she saw a small, lithe figure pull himself over the rail of the patio and slide open the plate glass door. "How did you get up here?" Amanda demanded as Jack shut the door behind him.

"I climbed up. Couldn't you tell?" Jack asked grimly. "Why won't you talk to me?"

"That ought to be obvious," Amanda muttered as she turned her back to him. She carried her plate to the kitchen, hoping to avoid Jack's piercing gaze, but he followed her in and blocked her way back out. "Leave me alone, Jack," she demanded, her voice thick with tears. "For God's sake, just get out of here and leave me alone."

Jack whirled Amanda around and stared down into her red face. "You've been crying," he said questioningly as he touched one swollen eyelid with his finger.

Amanda pushed past him and stomped into the living room. "Yes, I've been crying," she answered tightly. And if he didn't leave soon, she was going to be crying some more.

"Is something wrong? Is your mother all right?"

"My mother's fine."

"Then why are you crying?"

"Because you scared me to death this afternoon!" Amanda blazed at him, fresh tears welling in her eyes. "You m—marched up there and y—you yelled at him and you d—didn't even draw your gun," she sobbed, furious with herself for letting Jack see her weakness. "You could have been killed, and I wouldn't have been able to do a thing to stop him." She turned away from Jack and cried into her open hands.

"Oh, Amanda, I'm sorry," Jack said as he turned her around and cradled her in his arms. "I would have drawn my gun if I had needed it. I never meant to frighten you like that. I had no idea it would scare you so much."

"What did you think it was going to do to me?" Amanda demanded as she stared up into Jack's face. "How would you like it if you loved someone and they did something like that?"

Jack pushed Amanda's head down on his shoulder. "You love me?" he asked wonderingly.

"Yes, I do," Amanda sniffed. "I don't want to ... but I do."

"Why don't you want to?"

"Because you do things like today, and I'm scared to death that something's going to happen to you." She moved away from Jack and sat down cross-legged on the floor. "It would kill me if something happened to you, Jack."

Jack sat down beside Amanda and took her hand. "Nothing's going to happen to me."

"You don't know that," Amanda flared angrily. "You've been on the police force long enough to know that it *does* happen—even to the most cautious of officers. And then you go out on the weekend and take every chance in the book to get your kicks."

"I'm sorry I frightened you," Jack returned, speaking quietly. "I thought that approaching Ralph directly would be the best thing to do under the circumstances. As it turns out, it was. But I didn't realize it would upset you this much, Amanda. I honestly didn't."

"Of course it upsets me, Jack," Amanda said as she wiped her eyes. "Let me tell you what it does to me. It knots up my insides so badly that I can't breathe, I can't think, I can't do anything but worry about you. This afternoon I felt utterly helpless. I had my .38 drawn, of course. We all did. But if he had come out shooting or shot you through the door, there wasn't one thing, not one thing, I could have done to help you. And that's a horrible feeling, Jack."

"I never thought about it like that," Jack responded in a hushed tone.

Amanda leaned back against the edge of the sofa and closed her eyes. "I don't understand you," she admitted. "I can't understand why you take chance after chance. Why, Jack? Why do you do some of the fool things you do?"

Jack leaned back, too, stretching his legs out in front of them. "I don't even think about the danger when I'm working. Like this afternoon. I knew I was breaking a couple of regulations when I walked up to Ralph's door, but I never thought I was in real danger. I knew Ralph, and to me, it was the most expedient way to get him out of there without more violence."

"Is that the way you felt the afternoon I met you?" Amanda pressed quietly.

Jack nodded. "I didn't feel in danger that day either. I knew in my head that I was, but not in here." Jack touched his chest lightly. "I just felt a little excited—that's all. And satisfied. Proud and satisfied."

"Proud? Satisfied?"

"Yes, proud and satisfied. It's a good feeling to know that I probably kept Ralph from shooting anybody else, and the day we met I felt good that nobody else was in danger from the sniper." He thought a moment. "It's the kind of thing that would have made my father proud of me."

Amanda looked at Jack with surprise. "Your dad was a cop?"

"No, nothing like that. It's just that he was one to admire courage. He was a brave man himself, and he loved an adrenaline rush as much as I do."

Amanda thought a minute. Do you feel the danger when you race or ride bulls?"

Jack thought a minute. "No, I don't."

"How do they make you feel?"

Jack thought a minute. "Excited. Like when I do something on the job—but more so. Challenged, maybe."

"Does anything else make you feel like that?"

"I don't know," Jack confessed. "I've never really tried to find substitutes."

"Are those the only reasons you like to do dangerous things?" Amanda quizzed on. "Or is there more to it than that?"

Jack thought a minute. "Bigger, maybe? Braver? I've never really thought about it before. I've just gone ahead and done things. Can you try to understand that?"

"I will…if you'll try to understand why it frightens me to see you do them."

"I'll try," Jack agreed.

"Then so will I," Amanda promised him.

"Thanks," Jack said as he squeezed her hand. Amanda's eyes were still closed, but she could feel the warmth of Jack's body the moment before he leaned over to kiss her. His touch was butterfly gentle on her slightly parted lips, teasing and tasting and nibbling before he scooted over and put his arms around her. "I love you, Amanda," he whispered as he cradled her tenderly to his side. "I love you so much, and I'm sorry I made you cry. I never meant to do that."

Amanda's fingers flew up to her eyes. "I must look a mess. I never could cry beautifully."

"You do everything beautifully," Jack assured her as he placed a soft, tender kiss on each eyelid. "I'll get a washcloth for your face."

Amanda watched Jack as he poured ice water from her refrigerator on a washcloth from the bathroom. "Lean your head back so this won't fall off your nose."

Amanda put a throw pillow on the floor and lay down on the carpet. She flinched when Jack laid the cloth across her eyes. "Yow, that's cold!" she complained. "Why didn't you just use water from the tap?"

"This will make the swelling go down faster. It's a trick I learned from my mother."

"Did your mother cry a lot?" Amanda inquired curiously.

"She did."

Amanda lay quietly while the wet washcloth worked its magic. "Do they look any better?" she asked a few moments later when Jack picked up the washcloth and looked at her eyes.

"Yes, they're considerably improved," Jack assured her as he leaned down and kissed her gently. "I'm sorry you cried over me," he said as he stroked the side of her face with the palm of his hand. "I do love you, you know."

Amanda stared at Jack. She searched his face for the truth and found love shining out at her. "You do love me, don't you?"

Jack scooted down so that he lay next to her on the soft carpet. "Yes, I do. I think I've loved you almost from the moment I laid eyes on you."

"I think I've loved you for at least that long," Amanda returned as she turned to Jack and caressed the side of his face. "I was fascinated, at least."

"You just liked my sexy body," Jack teased.

"Me and every other woman watching you that afternoon," Amanda replied, laughing. She turned onto her back and stared at the ceiling. "You do have a marvelous body, Jack, but what I feel for you is so much more than just physical attraction. We share so many things other than that."

"That's true." Jack leaned over Amanda and brushed her lips lightly with his. "But we need to share the physical side of our relationship as well. Have you thought about us, Amanda? Do you still not want to become lovers?"

Amanda lay very still, and Jack could feel her emotionally pulling away from him. "Damn it! Don't do that, Mandy," he pleaded as he bent his head and joined her lips in a soul-burning kiss of love and desire. Amanda groaned, unable to deny Jack, as she met his passion with a matching flame of her own. She opened her lips and let him savor the sweetness he found there, giving and sharing the love they felt for one another. For a long, sweet moment they clung to one another before Jack pulled away and jackknifed into a sitting position.

"Jack, what's wrong?" Amanda demanded as she sat up beside him. "Why did you turn away?"

"I'm not going to use physical attraction to seduce you," Jack said as he ran a trembling hand across his forehead. "I love you, and I want to be your lover more than anything. But I'm not going to do it that way." He turned around, and there were tears shimmering in his eyes. "I love you, Amanda," he repeated quietly. "I love you so much I hurt with it. I told you once, rather arrogantly, I'm afraid, that eventually you would come to me of your own free will. Tonight I'm rephrasing that a little. Amanda, will you come to me? Will you make love to me and let me make love to you?"

Jack waited, tension evident in the set of his shoulders. Amanda felt the last of her reservations melt away like snow in summer sunshine. She loved Jack, she had fallen in love with him in spite of her desire not to, and she needed him as much as he needed her. Without speaking, she smiled and held out her arms.

Jack flew into her embrace, holding her head in the palms of his hands while he covered her face with quick, feverish kisses. "Oh, Amanda, I need you so much," he whispered over and over. "I need you and I love you and I've wanted you for so long."

"Jack, I've wanted you, too," Amanda confessed as she returned his passionate kisses. "I'm sorry I've made us wait so long." She caressed the hard muscles of his shoulders.

"I don't know, maybe it's better that we waited," Jack breathed as his lips brushed her neck. "This way, we know how much we want one another."

They melted into a tender, passionate embrace, holding tightly yet gently to each other. Amanda's breasts were crushed to Jack's chest, and she could feel the strength of his desire for her. Their hearts pounded in a wild, staccato rhythm, and Amanda could feel Jack pushing her down into the carpet, crushing her beneath him, his small body tense with desire for her. "We're wearing too many clothes," he murmured as Amanda caressed his back through his shirt, "and you're not protected."

"We can fix both of those," Amanda said as Jack's fingers tantalized her through her blouse. She made a quick trip to the bathroom. Without speaking they lovingly undressed one another, Amanda pulling Jack's shirt and undershirt from his body as he unbuttoned her blouse and drew it away from her body. His eager fingers trembled a little as he unhooked her bra and took it from her. Amanda laughed when he twirled it around his finger before he tossed it across the back of the couch. "Careful, I spent a fortune on it," Amanda teased.

Jack cupped both of her high, firm breasts in his hands. "I don't know why you bother with a bra," he said as his fingers grazed the tips. "You're perfect without it." He leaned down and touched one nipple with his tongue. "In fact, your whole body's just about perfect."

"No, it isn't," Amanda admitted, suddenly shy even though Jack had seen her in the briefest of bikinis. She was fine on top, but she felt that her hips and bottom were too hefty for the rest of her. "I'm too heavy below my waist."

"I know better than that," Jack insisted as he pushed her down on the carpet. His fingers gently unzipped her skirt, and he removed the garment from her body. He was careful not to damage either her pantyhose or her lacy bikini briefs as he removed them. Amanda waited, a little embarrassed, as Jack stared at her naked body, paying special attention to the parts that were hidden by her swimsuit. "Beautiful, just like I thought," he said as he planted a tender kiss in the middle of her stomach. "Soft and warm and cuddly," he added as his lips drifted lower.

Amanda gasped as she felt Jack's warm, tantalizing breath. Suddenly he sat back on his haunches and unzipped his pants, fumbling a little with them in his haste, and stripped them from his body. He started to move to Amanda, but she held out her hand in protest. "Just a minute. Let me look at you the way you looked at me."

Jack sat back and let Amanda stare at his naked body, a portrait of masculine excellence before her. He was hard and fit, the epitome of strength and beauty. Strong muscles lined his chest and stomach, and the symmetry of his thighs and hips flowed downward into the carved perfection of his thighs and legs. Tonight there were no bruises to spoil his beauty, and Amanda memorized every plane and sinew of him as he had her. "Will I do?" Jack asked hesitantly after a moment.

"Oh, Jack, you're perfect! Don't you know that?" Amanda asked as she opened her arms to him. He came down to her, crushing her to the carpet as he covered her with his hard, warm body. His hands were everywhere, touching and stroking and caressing Amanda into a feverish pitch of desire. His lips tormented her tender breasts as his hands caressed the softness of her waist. When her nipples were two small buds of desire, his lips drifted lower and lower. "Jack, what?" Amanda whispered as he pushed her legs open.

"You haven't made love in a long time, have you?"

"No. How did you know?"

"I just do, and I want to be sure you're ready for me," Jack said as his lips moved beyond the invisible barrier. Amanda gasped at the sensual beauty of his passionate caress—every touch, every stroke was bringing her closer and closer to a place she hadn't been in a long time, if ever. Jack caressed her until she was panting, moaning, nearly mindless with desire for him. Just as Amanda thought she would reach the ultimate without him, he moved over her and joined their bodies together.

They lay still for a moment, savoring their long-sought intimacy. "You feel so good to me," Jack whispered as he began to move within her. Slowly at first, then with greater strength and force, he carried Amanda with him on a passionate voyage that neither of them had been on before. Amanda gasped at the power of their union, her eyes tightly closed as she soared higher and higher, closer and closer to the ultimate delight. She gasped when the tension broke within her, and waves of pleasure flowed through her body. Spurred by Amanda's joy, Jack gave himself completely to the tremors that shook him.

Too moved even to speak at first, Jack and Amanda collapsed in a damp tangle of arms and legs. They lay entwined as their breathing slowly returned to normal. "Amanda, you're something else," Jack said as he raised his head and stared into her passion-clouded eyes.

"So are you," Amanda assured him, caressing his strong, sweaty back. "I didn't get to touch you and kiss you much, though."

Jack placed a tender kiss on her lips. "I wanted this time to be for you. Later you can indulge me." He kissed her once again and eased himself from her, lying down beside her on the carpet. "Hey, do you believe this? We didn't even make it to the bedroom!"

Amanda giggled as a blush colored her face. "I don't think I've *ever* been that eager before."

Jack stared down into her face. "Is that true, Mandy?"

"Yes, it is. I didn't even feel that kind of desire for my ex-husband." She glanced up at Jack. "Was it special for you, Jack?"

In response Jack leaned down and covered her lips in a tender, passionate kiss that left her in no doubt that their lovemaking had been very special for him, too. He lay back on the carpet and pulled Amanda close to him. "Yes, it was special. I've been around a lot, but it's never been that beautiful before."

"Have you ever been in love before?" Amanda asked.

"Not like this," Jack admitted. His stomach rumbled and he blushed furiously.

Amanda sat up and kissed the middle of his noisy stomach. "I bet you didn't get any dinner."

"No, not unless you consider a draft beer dinner. Eddie and I talked for a long time, and I came straight here."

"I can fix that," Amanda assured him. She disappeared into her bedroom and came out in a long, silky robe. "What would you like to eat?"

"Anything you have," Jack said as he rolled to his feet and pulled on his shorts.

Amanda poked around in the refrigerator and the cabinets. "How about steak sandwiches? I have some steak left over."

"Sounds great," Jack returned. Amanda made Jack two sandwiches and herself one, and they sat down at her dining room table. "This hits the spot," Jack remarked with relish as he wolfed down the first sandwich.

Amanda's eyebrow rose. "Looks like you were hungry for more than just me."

"Now, now. Which did I do first?" Jack teased. "And which am I planning to do again just as soon as these sandwiches are gone?"

"Again? My, aren't we in a randy mood tonight," Amanda flipped back.

"Just making up for all that making sure," Jack quipped before he became serious. "Thank you, Amanda. I needed your love tonight." He bit into the second sandwich. "Especially with what I have facing me at work in the next few days."

"The review board?" Amanda murmured.

"Yes, the review board. I'm not looking forward to that."

"I won't testify against you," Amanda said quietly. "I'll tell them you did the right thing."

Jack looked up, surprised. "What will you say?"

"I'll say that you exercised your professional judgment, and that you were right. Which is the truth."

"Never mind how you feel about the professional judgment?"

"Something like that," Amanda admitted as she took a deep breath. "But I want you to do something for me in return. I know you're always going to take chances on the force. It's in your nature and it's your style as a cop. But couldn't you possibly give up some of the dangerous weekend stuff?"

Jack frowned. "Is this an ultimatum?"

"No, it's not," Amanda answered, surprised and irritated and not bothering to hide either emotion. "I gave myself to you freely tonight—there wasn't any price tag involved." She leaned over and grasped Jack's hand. "It's a request, Jack. A request made by a woman who loves you very, very much."

"Then I too have a request," Jack said softly. "Would it be possible for you to learn to accept some of the weekend stuff? Maybe we could meet halfway or something?"

Amanda thought a minute. "I'll think about it."

Jack's face softened into a tender smile. "Then so will I," he responded as he looked at her with love in his eyes. "But let's not talk about things like that tonight." He tugged on her hand gently. "Come sit on my lap and tell me how we're going to spend the rest of the night."

Grinning, Amanda sat down in his lap and started whispering in his ear. "We're going to do that?" Jack teased. "And that? And that, too? My mama warned me about girls like you!" He bolted the last of his second sandwich and carried Amanda to her bedroom, barely giving her time to get the covers turned back before he was stripping the robe from her body and pushing her down on the bed.

***

Amanda lay awake as the gray of early morning began to lighten her bedroom. It was still fairly dark, but she could see Jack's undershorts where she had tossed them on the chair and the empty wineglass from a drink they had shared sometime after midnight. Jack had made love to her a second time, and they had shared a warm shower and a glass of wine before collapsing together and sleeping soundly.

Amanda turned her head on the pillow. Beside her, Jack snored softly, dead to the world. She was glad she'd awakened a little early; it gave her time to contemplate her relationship with Jack Vance. She knew without a shadow of a doubt that she loved him. If she hadn't been sure before, yesterday evening and last night had left her in no doubt about her feelings for Jack. She loved him deeply, and she knew that he returned her love. She was glad they had become lovers—very glad they had finally taken the last step toward total intimacy.

Amanda smiled to herself as she thought of the way Jack loved her. Their lovemaking hadn't been just a physical union: they had joined their souls together as they had joined their bodies. Amanda couldn't ever remember feeling this kind of intimacy, this kind of oneness with her former husband. What she and Jack had was special, and she hoped they could see it to its ultimate. Amanda didn't know—it was too soon to tell—but she was beginning to think that the ultimate with this man might be marriage.

Amanda sighed as she thought about the man who slept beside her, and the passionate, somewhat stormy relationship they had. Everything about their lives seemed to mesh except for Jack's addiction to putting himself in danger. Amanda admitted to herself that she would never understand that. The question was, would she ever be able to accept it? Would they be able to meet halfway as Jack suggested, or would they be battling constantly over the things he did for fun? Did they really have a chance? Amanda knew that she loved Jack dearly, and that she might even like to marry him. She just wasn't sure she could ever learn to accept this constant flirtation with danger.

Chapter Nine

Amanda tiredly climbed the stairs to her apartment and unlocked the front door. "Jack, are you here yet?" she called into the apartment.

"Sure am," Jack answered from the kitchen. "Supper's almost ready."

"Good, I'm starved," Amanda said as she followed her nose to the kitchen. Once there she moved easily into Jack's outstretched arms.

Jack bent his head and kissed Amanda slowly and thoroughly. "You smell like a corpse," he murmured as he ran his hands down her back and patted her bottom.

"How romantic!" Amanda teased. "I guess the mystery's gone out of our relationship."

Jack released her but kept one arm around her waist as he turned back to the stove. "Well, you know how it is," he kidded, his eyes twinkling. "After two months I guess the romance goes out of any relationship." He spooned up some spaghetti sauce. "Here, try this. Does it need more salt?"

Amanda tasted the steaming sauce cautiously. "No, it's perfect. Have we really been together that long?"

Jack nodded and kissed her temple. "Two months today. Happy anniversary," he said as he handed her a small box from his top pocket.

"Jack, you're precious," Amanda exclaimed as she tore the paper from the box. She opened it and found an elegant lady's sport watch. "Jack, it's beautiful. You really shouldn't have."

"Of course I should have," Jack insisted. "Maybe this one will survive you dunking it in the sink."

"I hope so," Amanda responded, thinking of the watch she had recently ruined in the laboratory. She strapped the watch on, and Jack immediately grabbed her wrist and held it under the faucet. "Jack, you idiot, don't do that!" she squealed. "You're soaking it!"

"That's the idea." He held her wet wrist up to his ear. "It's not ticking," he announced solemnly.

"Of course it isn't. It's quartz," Amanda informed him dryly. She held it out in front of her and together they watched the digits change. "It's doing fine," she said. She threw her arms around Jack's neck. "You're so good to me! Thanks."

They hugged one another before Jack turned back to the stove. Since he pretty well had things under control, Amanda escaped to the bedroom to change her clothes and wash her face, thinking how nice it was to come home and find Jack there. She had given him a key about a month ago, and more often than not he beat her here and had supper well under way by the time she drove up. They would spend the evening together, and most of the time Jack brought fresh clothing to wear in the morning and stayed the night. Amanda thoroughly enjoyed the time Jack spent with her and missed him on the nights he didn't see her.

Amanda stepped out of her skirt and pulled off her slip and pantyhose. She left them in the middle of the bed, knowing that Jack would tease her about it later. But she didn't mind—she never minded his gentle teasing. It seemed to be a way for Jack to show affection, and it made her feel loved. Amanda had to admit that since she had become his lover, she hadn't found out anything about Jack that wasn't totally endearing. They had both been pleased and delighted to discover that they liked one another as much as they loved one another. Their relationship had grown deeper and stronger by the day, and they had even discussed the possibility of getting married. But Amanda found herself hedging whenever Jack brought up the issue: he still hadn't given up any of his dangerous hobbies, and she was afraid to marry him if he didn't.

Amanda put on an old pair of shorts and a T-shirt and joined Jack in the kitchen. The spaghetti and sauce were ready, so they made do with lettuce wedges for a vegetable and sat down at the table. "Did I really smell like a corpse when I came in the door?" Amanda asked curiously as she served herself.

"Yeah. Did you spend the afternoon with Dr. Sawbones?" Jack teased.

"I spent part of it with the medical examiner, yes. I took evidence in that shooting last night. Ballistics was able to come up with a match. They made an arrest this afternoon."

"That's good," Jack responded dryly. "I'm glad the department can arrest somebody's murderer."

"Now, Jack, don't be that way," Amanda chided him. "Something will turn up on those poisonings sooner or later."

"I'm not so sure. It's been nearly four months since the last one, and the trail's stone cold. We'll never catch our mystery lady if she doesn't poison somebody else. You know, it's really something. I'm so desperate to solve those murders I halfway hope she'll strike again. I actually hope she'll try to kill somebody else!"

"I think that's only natural," Amanda defended as she wound the long, thin threads of spaghetti around her fork. "Especially with the coverage the department's gotten lately." One of the local stations had run an unfavorable series on the news about the SAPD, and the unsolved poisonings figured prominently in the story. "The public expects miracles, and we can't produce them all the time."

"I wish you'd tell the chief that," Jack complained. "He's putting the pressure on homicide, and our bosses in turn are putting the pressure on us."

"I'm sure he's getting pressure from the city manager," Amanda replied. "The public's stirred up, thanks to the series." She ate a bite of spaghetti. "I swear, this spaghetti's better than that in Italian restaurants."

"Thanks," Jack said. Conversation lagged as they enjoyed the fruits of Jack's culinary labors.

Finally Amanda pushed her plate back. "That was delicious. I love your cooking, Jack."

"I'm glad. Did you like the watch?" he added shyly.

"You know I did," Amanda gushed, love shining in her eyes. "And the gold chain you bought me last month, and the Mustang key ring you found last week, and the bottle of hot sauce that I love but you hate. They're all so special, Jack."

"When are you going to let me buy you that special ring?" Jack prodded quietly. He was sure that he wanted to spend his life with Amanda, and her reluctance to agree to marry him bothered him more than a little. He would buy her a ring tonight if only she would agree to become his wife.

"Uh, not just yet," Amanda answered quickly. She was afraid that Jack intended to press the issue tonight, and she wasn't in the mood to argue with him. Nor was she ready to accept a proposal of marriage. "Let's give it some time before we think about that." She grabbed up her dirty plate and headed for the kitchen.

Jack jerked up his and followed her. "Damn it, Amanda, that's the third time this week you've ducked out when I started talking about getting married," he chastised her as he rinsed his plate at the sink. "Why can't we at least talk about it?"

"We have talked about it—several times in the last month," Amanda said. "I just don't want to do anything official yet." She rinsed her plate and put it in the dishwasher.

Jack brought in the dirty spaghetti bowl and the silverware from the dining room. "Why not?" he pushed as Amanda loaded the rest of the dishes. "Don't you think we have the real thing here?"

"Yes, we do," Amanda admitted as she turned off the light in the kitchen. Jack followed her to the living room and sat down beside her on the couch. "I've never loved a man, not even Brian, the way I do you. And I know that you love me."

"So why won't you let me buy you a ring?"

"You know why. You're still riding, and racing, and last weekend you went skydiving. You said you'd think about compromising on some of the dangerous stuff you do on the weekend, but so far you're going after them as hot and heavy as you ever did. You haven't changed a thing. And I'm trying to be more accepting, Jack, but I'm no closer to accepting them than I was two months ago. I'm sorry, I'm just not. So no, we're not ready for you to give me a ring."

"So why don't we agree to disagree on that the stuff you don't like? Lots of people disagree on things a lot more serious than each other's hobbies!"

"No, we can't agree to disagree on those," Amanda fired back tightly. "And I'd hardly call those things hobbies. We're talking about your safety and well-being."

"Amanda, you're not being fair," Jack argued. "I haven't asked you to give up anything."

"No, but I don't do the things you do. Besides, I haven't asked you to give up your profession, have I? A lot of women won't even marry a police officer."

"No, but you could hardly do that, since you're a cop, too," he said coldly.

"All right. So I'm on the force. But I'm not on the SWAT team, am I? Have I asked you to give that up?"

"No, but why should I give up my hobbies?" Jack replied. "They're no more dangerous than what I do during the week."

Amanda threw up her hands. "You just refuse to understand. The more chances you take, the greater the likelihood that sooner or later something's going to happen to you."

"Amanda, those things just aren't that dangerous," Jack defended, exasperated. "Have you ever thought that if you knew more about them, you might not be so frightened?"

"I doubt that," Amanda replied tartly. "I may learn to accept them at some point, but I'm never going to like that stuff."

"How do you know, if you won't even try to familiarize yourself with them?" Jack challenged her. "You've been to exactly one race and one bull riding contest and decided on the basis of those that I'm some sort of wild-eyed crackpot. Now, is that really a fair trial?"

"No, I guess not," Amanda admitted.

"All right, will you come with me next Sunday? Our club's rented a plane and we're all jumping."

"No way!" Amanda shot quickly. "I'm scared to death in small planes."

"How do you know?" Jack asked.

"I've been up in them several times, and the last time I swore them off for good when we got caught out in a thunderstorm. I've never been so scared in all my life."

"All right. Will you go back to the races with me, then? I'm supposed to race on Saturday."

"Okay," Amanda agreed reluctantly. She wasn't at all eager to go back out to the hot, dusty racetrack, but maybe Jack had a point. Perhaps she hadn't given the racing much of a chance. "To the races it is."

"And what about a ring?" Jack persisted.

"Let's hold off on that for a while, please," Amanda pleaded. "Let me be sure I can make it with you, Jack."

Jack was opening his mouth to argue when the telephone rang and Amanda answered it. "Amanda, this is Tony Pehachek. We've had an attempted homicide and need you and Jack to come in right away."

"Another poisoning?" Amanda demanded.

"Yes, but it wasn't successful," Tony said.

"Thank goodness. We'll be right there." She hung up the phone and started peeling off her shorts. "You got your wish. There's been another poisoning, an unsuccessful one."

"Hot dog," Jack whooped, springing up off the couch. Amanda changed her clothes in record time, and they hurried down to the station. Tony met them at the door of the lab with an evidence bag. "What are you going to have me poking through?" Amanda quizzed as she eyed the peculiar-smelling bag suspiciously.

"His kitchen garbage. Sorry about that. At least he didn't send the evidence down the disposal." He handed Amanda the evidence bag, and Amanda logged the three of them into the lab. "As near as we can tell, he was poisoned when he ate supper."

Amanda made a face as she opened the bag. "Good night, Tony, this smells awful!"

"What in the world is it?" Jack gulped as he tried and failed to stifle a gag.

"I think it's chili," Tony replied. "On second thought, that stuff might have poisoned him without any outside help." He put a second bag on the counter. "There were some spices sitting out on the counter that we went ahead and gathered up, too."

"It's got to be in that chili," Amanda pinpointed as she prepared a sample for the mass spectrograph. "That stuff could disguise the taste of anything." She put the sample into the machine. "Will you look at that! Nicotine. Our murderous lady slipped up this time."

"How's that?" Jack asked.

"Nicotine's a poison, all right, but it won't kill in this quantity," Amanda explained. "So whoever is doing this isn't an expert."

"She's a pretty good amateur, then," Jack put in.

Amanda looked over the bottles of spice. "The chili powder…it has to be in there." Using a cloth so that she wouldn't destroy any fingerprints, she took a sample of the powder. "Right on," she exulted a moment later when the results flashed on the screen. "I'm getting good at this."

"Has anyone talked to the victim?" Jack queried.

"No. I thought you and Amanda would like the honor," Tony responded. "Same hospital, same ward."

"You know what kind of publicity this is going to generate," Jack said disgustedly.

"What do you mean 'going to'? I've already run the gauntlet with the reporters at my door tonight, and I'd be willing to bet you face a few at the hospital."

"Wonderful," Jack replied. "Come on, Amanda, let's see if we can find out what happened to this guy."

As Tony had predicted, there were reporters waiting for them at the double doors to medical intensive care. "Officer Vance, would you like to comment on this new poisoning?" a reporter from the *San Antonio Light* asked.

"Why can't the homicide department solve these killings?" a pushy woman pressed, thrusting a microphone into Jack's face.

"I'm not prepared to comment at this time," Jack said.

"You're Jack Vance, aren't you?" a young reporter from one of the television stations asked.

"Yes, but I'm not doing anything daring tonight," Jack flipped, grinning at her as he pushed open the double doors to the intensive care unit.

"Aw, you should have stripped to your skivvies for her," Amanda teased when they were inside the unit. "She was so disappointed!"

Jack made a face at Amanda as the nurse, who could recognize them by now, pointed to a room about halfway down the hall. Jack peeked in and motioned for Amanda to follow. They introduced themselves and showed the good-looking young man, who was the occupant of the room, their badges.

"I'm Tommy Donovan," the man said.

Tommy Donovan didn't appear to be too ill, so Jack pulled out his notebook. "Mr. Donovan, your chili powder was laced with nicotine. How long has it been since you used the powder?"

"I used it last Wednesday night," Tommy replied. "I make chili at least twice a week. Love the stuff." Amanda wondered privately how a connoisseur of chili could have eaten the wretched-smelling stuff in Tommy's garbage.

"Who's been in your apartment since then besides you?" Jack continued.

"Just a couple of friends…and a girl I took home Saturday night. Surely you don't think one of my friends did it!"

"No, not the friends, but I'd like their names and addresses anyway," Jack said. He wrote down the information Tommy gave him. "Now, may I have the name and address of the girl?"

"I don't know her address," Tommy answered, blushing a little. "I just met her Saturday night at a dance hall." His eyes widened. "Do you think she's the same one who killed those other people?"

"Maybe. What name did she give you?" Jack asked.

"Susan." Tommy thought a minute. "Susan Smith. Real original, now that I think of it."

"That's all right. You had no reason to suspect anything," Amanda said. "Could you describe her to me?"

"She was tall, and her face was pretty but not spectacular, you know? Kind of hard to describe. I think her eyes were hazel, but I never got a good look at them. She was a little hard looking, but that might have been all the makeup. Good body—real good body. That is, what I saw of it. She wanted the lights out before I got her clothes off her. She was kind of inhibited about being seen with her clothes off, but she was really wild once I got her to bed."

"Did you notice any birthmarks or any other identifying characteristics?" Jack quizzed.

"Not really, but like I said, it was lights-out time," Tommy returned.

"Hair color?"

"She had blond hair. But if you ask me, it was a dye job. Her skin and eyes were too dark for a blonde. And cut about this long," he added as he held his hand just to his chin.

"And the next morning?" Amanda asked.

"I fixed her a cup of coffee and she left in her own car, since she'd followed me over here. She was in a new Monte Carlo—a green one."

"Would she have had time alone in your kitchen to poison the chili powder?" Amanda interrogated.

"If she hurried," Tommy replied. "I don't remember leaving her alone in the kitchen, but I could have. Besides, the chili powder's always sitting there. I use a lot of it."

"You like chili, do you?" Amanda asked.

"Like I said, I love the stuff. I can't believe that chili was poisoned. It was the best-tasting batch I'd made in a long time!"

Jack and Amanda suppressed their shudders and thanked Tommy Donovan. They walked through the quiet corridors of the hospital and got into the car. "Except for the hair, 'Susan Smith' sounds a whole lot like our friend 'Lori,'" Jack commented as he started the engine.

"Too bad he didn't get a peek at her bottom," Amanda giggled. "We would have known for sure."

"Yeah, I wish she hadn't chosen Saturday night to get modest," Jack chimed in as they drove out of the parking lot.

***

Amanda walked across the street from the courthouse and ran up the steps to the station. "I think my testimony sewed that one up," she exclaimed gleefully to Samantha, who was bent over the microscope staring at a hair sample. "Do we have a match?"

"No, this hair's entirely different from the one on the victim's coat," Samantha replied. "The suspect has naturally dark hair, and the one on the victim was dyed."

"I guess it's just as important to find out who didn't do it as it is to find out who did," Amanda mused.

"Oh, Jack's been trying to get in touch with you all morning," Samantha added. "He said to call him right away."

"Business or pleasure?" Amanda asked as she dialed Jack's extension.

"Business, I think."

"Jack, this is Amanda. Sorry I was out of pocket. What can I do for you?"

"I can think of a lot of nice things for when we get off duty," Jack teased. "Seriously, we're having a brain-storming session this afternoon on the poisonings. Tony and I wondered if you could spare us a few minutes. We sure would like your input."

"I'd be glad to," Amanda responded quickly. "What time?"

"Tony said two. And thanks."

"You know I'm glad to help," Amanda returned. She drank a diet milkshake for lunch and worked on trying to match a blood sample from a robbery until it was almost time for Tony's meeting. As she climbed the stairs and walked down the drab corridors that led to Jack's office, she admitted to herself that she was glad she didn't have to work up here in this sterile, institutional atmosphere. Although her lab was equally drab, the scientific equipment made it seem more attractive to her. She exchanged greetings with Jack and the other homicide detectives that shared a large, cluttered office and poured herself a cup of coffee from the pot that was on constantly.

The detectives gathered around a large conference table in the middle of the room. Amanda sat down between Jack and Eddie. Tony sat down at the head of the table. Since all the detectives at the table were familiar with the case, Tony skipped the formalities. "All right, gentlemen, I'm open to suggestions. Where do we go from here?"

Ray Torres cleared his throat. "It seems to me that the key to solving this one is going to be in the poisons. Not just anybody has access to this stuff, do they?"

"No, not really," Amanda clarified. "There are pretty strict laws governing what's sold to the general public, although I guess that someone who wanted these substances very badly could find a way to get them."

"We've checked with every chemical supplier in the San Antonio area after each poisoning," Eddie spoke up. "In no case was that particular poison sold to anyone who remotely fit the description of our suspect."

"We're pretty sure that the actual poisons are not being purchased in the San Antonio area," Jack added. "Of course, if our suspect is as smart as she seems, she would know better than to buy them here in town."

"And she would have time between poisonings to secure more from wherever," Eddie chimed in.

"I notice that she didn't poison anyone all summer," Amanda observed. "She poisoned three times in the spring, and then not again until fall. I wonder if that has any significance?"

"It might," Tony answered, entertaining the possibility.

"I keep wondering why so many different poisons," Tom Black threw in. "Most killers stick to one, but there have been how many? Four already?"

"Yes, I've wondered about that, too," Tony said. "It would be hard enough for an average citizen to get hold of one of those compounds, but four?"

"Maybe we ought to approach it from that angle," Jack conjectured. "Maybe our killer isn't just an average citizen. Maybe she's somebody who has access to some of these things in her line of work."

"A nurse!" Eddie and Ray chorused. "They can get all kinds of things."

Several of the other officers murmured in agreement, but Amanda shook her head. "I don't think so."

"Why not?" Harvey Schroeder challenged her.

"Because nurses have access to drugs, not to the kinds of chemicals our killer's been using," Amanda explained. "A nurse would be using things like atropine or insulin or digitalis. She wouldn't be able to get substances like cyanides or the dinitrophenol any more easily than the general public."

"Who would?" several of the men demanded.

"A chemist or someone with some chemical background," Amanda suggested.

"And it would help if said person had access to chemicals, wouldn't it?" Eddie asked.

Tony whistled under his breath. "Amanda, just who would have both the knowledge to commit the murders and access to the poisons?"

"A lot of people would have the knowledge: an industrial chemist at any of the military bases, a clerk at one of the chemical supply houses. And any of the people I've just mentioned would have access to chemicals, but I'm not sure what chemicals they could get. Every lab would have a different stock, depending on what sort of work is done there."

"College laboratories?" Jack quizzed. "Would they have these poisons?"

"Certainly. At least some of those chemicals would be available. Possibly high school labs, too. I'm not sure what's kept in the schools today. And remember, it could be anyone with a little knowledge and access to the chemicals. It wouldn't have to be a trained chemist. In fact, I don't think our killer is an expert at this. She messed the last one up when she didn't give him a strong enough dose."

"That's a lot of people to investigate," Tony said. "It's going to be like looking for a needle in a haystack. Any other ideas?"

"What about attacking this thing from the other angle?" Tom ventured. "So far, our killer has picked up every one of her victims in a bar somewhere. Why don't we see what we can turn up there?"

"You just want to go barhopping," Eddie teased.

"Besides, if you think there are a lot of people with access to poisons, you ought to see how many more there are out trying to make a pickup on Friday night," Jack threw in, laughing.

"Hey, Tom has a point," Tony said. "It's worth checking out the bars again, especially now that we have a better composite picture of the woman. We'll go at it from both angles. Jack, Eddie, I want both of you to find out exactly what labs in town have the particular chemicals in question. Tom, Ray, Harvey, you three are going to get mighty tired of smoky bars. I want you to check out as many as you can."

Ray turned to Tom. "It beats musty old stockrooms, doesn't it?"

"Sure does," Tom replied grinning.

"So where do we start?" Eddie asked Jack.

"I have an idea," Amanda said. "I have several old friends who have jobs as chemists here in town. Why don't we pay some of them a visit and find out exactly what chemicals would be in whose stockroom? You might be able to eliminate a whole lot of your suspects right off if we find out, for example, that a high school lab wouldn't have anything that has been used."

"Amanda, that's a good idea," Jack commended.

"I second that," Eddie said. "Want to be my partner instead of him?"

"Yeah, I'd love to have her up here," Tony declared sincerely. "Any time you get tired of all your ghoulish goodies downstairs, I'd welcome you with open arms."

"Thanks," Amanda said. "You're both nice. Would you like for me to call up some of my buddies and tell them you're coming?"

"I'd appreciate that," Jack replied. "Tony, why couldn't Eddie and I have had the bars? Ray, Tom, and Harvey are going to have a lot more fun than we are."

Tony winked at Amanda. "Because this lady would have my head," he answered sweetly as Amanda stuck her tongue out at him.

***

Jack and Amanda parked in front of the big, pink high school with the American and Texas flags blowing around the flagpole. "Brings back memories, doesn't it?" Amanda asked.

"Not really," Jack admitted. "Pearsall High wasn't this big. Or this crowded," he added, glancing at the packed parking lot.

They entered the building and found the administrative offices. The principal was a little reluctant to let them go back to the science wing until they showed their badges and explained that Marge Cooper, one of the school's science teachers, was an old friend of Amanda's and had agreed to help them with their investigation. The principal offered to take them to Marge, but he was called to the telephone, and one of the students who worked as an office aide escorted them to Marge's room. They stood just outside the door and listened while Marge finished a lecture on equilibrium. "It's hard to believe that I almost went this route," Amanda whispered as she peered in at the rows of bored-looking students.

"I thought you always wanted to do forensic work," Jack said, surprised.

"I did, but Brian wanted me to teach. I finally told him to go jump in the lake."

The bell rang and suddenly the hall was filled with a sea of youthful faces. They waited until Marge's last student had left before entering the large room that served as both a classroom and a laboratory. "Amanda, how are you?" Marge asked as she enveloped Amanda in a huge embrace.

"I'm just fine, but not as fine as you seem to be," she observed as she surveyed her friend's burgeoning pregnant figure. "How much longer are you going to be able to teach?"

"Until the bitter end, I hope," Marge replied. "We need the money. Besides, I called the secretary from the hospital when Susie was born. I can do it again."

"That's super. Marge, I'd like you to meet Detective Jack Vance. Jack, Marge and I took organic chemistry together in college."

"I'm delighted to meet you," Jack returned as he shook Marge's hand. Marge raised her eyebrow at Amanda and Amanda nodded faintly. "Yes, I'm the fellow who's kept her too busy to come out and see you," Jack added.

"Shame on you! Why don't you come out with her?" Marge asked. Marge and her husband had a new place in the suburbs that they were very proud of and welcomed any opportunity to show it off.

"We'll do that," Jack promised.

Marge peeked out the door before she closed it. "I don't want any of the little darlings overhearing us," she explained as the three of them sat down on lab stools. "The last thing I need is for any of them to get any ideas. So tell me how I can help you, and I'll do what I can."

"You've read about those poisonings we've had," Jack began. "We've tried, unsuccessfully, to trace the purchase of the poisons to one of the local supply houses. In a meeting yesterday Amanda made the point that since so many different chemicals have been used, the killer must have both some knowledge of chemical poisons and some access to them. We need to start somewhere, and Amanda thought you might be able to help us. Exactly what chemicals would a high school teacher have in the laboratory? Would they have any of the poisons this woman has used? Do you have a list of chemicals that high school labs stock?"

"We're trying to narrow the list of potential suspects down, and we're hoping that if we check your list, we'd be able to eliminate the high schools as a possible source," Amanda explained.

Marge whistled under her breath. "Amanda, I hate to tell you, but you're out of luck. There is no 'list' of chemicals for the high school laboratory. All of the teachers in the district order their own, according to the particular labs they run during the school year."

"What kinds of things do you order?" Jack asked.

Marge shrugged. "We order whatever we need more of. It's left up to us what to have around as long as we don't have anything highly explosive like elemental sodium or bromine, or any known carcinogens. They came and got those about five years ago when we got the commission's new regulations."

"But what about poisons?" Jack persisted.

"Almost everything back there could be considered a poison," Marge replied. "After the Tylenol killings in Chicago, we were told to get rid of our cyanides, and I did, of course. But that's no guarantee that the teacher in the next school didn't squirrel some back or ignore the directive altogether. When you get right down to it, the individual teacher pretty well has control of whatever is in the stockroom."

"In other words, any of the chemistry teachers in town could have the poisons," Amanda reiterated for clarification.

"Yes, they could. Or if they didn't have them, they could order them," Marge assured her.

"But we contacted every one of the chemical suppliers in the area after each poisoning," Jack spoke up. "Nothing turned up."

"We don't use local suppliers," Marge explained. She handed Jack and Amanda each a thick catalog. "I have institutional access to any of the chemicals in stock at either of these companies. I order them in the name of the school, and the secretary in the front office types up the order."

"And if you ordered a couple of very lethal substances, would anyone know the difference?" Jack pressed.

"It's highly unlikely," Marge admitted. "A chemical name is a chemical name to most people."

"What you're saying, then, is that if you wanted to poison somebody and you didn't have the right poison to do it, you could order it through the school and no one would be the wiser?" Amanda asked.

"Sure. Couldn't you?" Marge countered.

Amanda thought a minute. "I sure could, couldn't I?" Amanda turned to Jack. "I could order just about anything in the name of the SAPD and they would deliver it, no questions asked. I could knock off as many people as I wanted as long as Samantha didn't suspect something."

"It would be even easier for a teacher," Marge said. "We don't have someone like Samantha around to wonder why we're ordering what we are."

Jack turned disappointed eyes to Marge. "We're going to find the same thing at the colleges around town, aren't we?"

"I'm afraid so," Marge answered. "They have the same institutional access that we do. For that matter, you can't even eliminate the middle school teachers. They order from the same catalogs that we do."

Jack and Amanda thanked Marge for her time and got back in the car. Jack banged the front seat with his fist in frustration. "Damn, we can't eliminate anybody, you know that? College profs, lab assistants, purchasing agents, high school teachers—anybody with one of those catalogs who can order in the name of a school."

"And don't forget all the other places I named yesterday," Amanda reminded him. "So what will you do next?"

"Start sifting through the haystack and look for the needle," Jack grumbled as he rubbed the back of his neck and started the engine.

Chapter Ten

"Jack? Is that you?" Amanda called from the bathroom as she heard the key turn in the lock and the front door open.

"No, it's the mailman," Jack hollered back. He pushed open the door of the bathroom and kissed Amanda's wet cheek. "I missed you last night."

Amanda blotted the water from her face and turned to Jack. "I missed you, too," she said affectionately as she strained to kiss him without getting his jumpsuit wet. Jack placed his hands on her shoulders and leaned forward, meeting her lips with his in a kiss that was passionate and tender. "You should have come on over," she lamented when he finally moved away from her. "I was home by midnight."

"I wasn't," Jack replied as he made a face. "That reception didn't break up until three in the morning." They had both provided security for large weddings last night and had agreed to spend the night separately.

Concern flashed across Amanda's face for an instant. "Are you awake enough to drive today?" she asked, hoping she didn't sound like a mother hen.

"Oh, yes, I only got up a half hour ago." He looked around Amanda's apartment. "Some of us don't get up at the crack of dawn to clean."

"Yes, and I can imagine what your place looks like right now," Amanda teased. She had been to Jack's house several times, and although it was really a pretty little house, and nicely furnished, she had never once caught it anywhere near neat.

"Yes, there was a movie producer looking for a post-Third World War set who was trying to rent it this morning," Jack teased. "Have you got any coffee on? I could use a cup."

"Sure, there's some in the coffeemaker waiting for you." She pulled on jeans and a knit top and hoped that Jack hadn't noticed that her lightheartedness and gaiety were forced. She was dreading going to the racetrack and watching Jack drive, but she had given her word. She wasn't going to back out—even though she dearly wanted to. And maybe Jack was right. Maybe she would even learn to enjoy watching him race, after all.

Jack had finished a cup of coffee by the time Amanda was ready. She watched him as he rinsed the cup in the sink, his movements relaxed, his talking and his laughter natural. He wasn't in the least tense or anxious about racing, but then he hadn't been the last time either. "Shouldn't we be getting on out there?" Amanda inquired. "It's almost noon now, and you're supposed to race at two."

"My time got changed to two thirty, but it wouldn't hurt to go on," Jack said. "We could watch a couple of the early races together."

Jack followed Amanda down the stairs and opened the door of the pickup for her. She was trying so hard not to let on that she was nervous. Jack's heart swelled. He loved that she was willing to come with him when she didn't even want to. He just hoped she would understand that racing wasn't dangerous to him. He had always felt like he had a greater chance of getting hurt on the city streets than he did on the racetrack.

The hot September sun was blazing down on the track and the bleachers by the time Jack and Amanda arrived. Amanda could hear the dry grass crinkle under her feet as they walked toward the stands. The wildflowers of spring were long gone, and the grass was wilted and dry from the heat of summer. A hot, dry wind stung Amanda's face, and heat shimmered from the race cars parked in the pit. Jack joined Tom Martinez and his beloved Charger, and they talked cars for a few minutes while Amanda looked around at the other people in the pit. She could feel perspiration on her forehead and her palms. She wasn't sure whether it was from the heat, her nerves, or both. For a minute she wished she had worn her shorts but changed her mind when she saw a couple of drivers leering at her.

Jack came over to her and took her hand. "I don't have to be down here until a few minutes before I race. Want to go up in the stands where we can see better? I can explain a little of what's going on."

"Sure, I'd like that," Amanda replied. They climbed the steps to the bleachers, and Jack bought them each a Coke. They found a couple of seats that promised to be shady for most of the afternoon and from which they still had a good view. "The noise is hard to get used to," Amanda commented as the cars entered in the first race lined up.

"But eventually you do," Jack said in her ear. "I like it now."

The flag went down. Amanda found that since Jack wasn't in this race, she was able to relax. Her eyes were glued to the track as the cars sped around and around, and Jack leaned close to her and provided a narrative of what was going on. Amanda had to admit that Jack's explanation of what was happening made the race interesting and even a little fun.

A fantastic old Chevy Nova painted bright yellow just barely beat out a white GTO. "Way to go, Ray!" Jack cheered as the yellow Nova slowed and came to a stop.

"You know him?" Amanda asked.

"Sure, I know most of the people out here. You want to come and meet a few of them?" he asked, thinking that if Amanda could see how truly nice the other racers were, she might feel better about his participation in the sport.

"Of course, I'd love to meet your friends," Amanda responded. It was going to be a few minutes until the next race, so she followed him down to the pit.

Jack made a beeline for a middle-aged man and his teen-age son. "Jack, you old so-and-so, how are you these days?" the older man boomed in a gravelly voice that was strangely familiar to Amanda.

"Just fine, Johnny," Jack replied warmly. He turned to the boy. "Ready to race me today?"

The young man nodded. "Are we in the same race? I can hardly wait to beat the pants off you again!"

"Yes, we're in the same race. Only this time you better watch out for me." Jack teased. "Johnny, John, I'd like you to meet Amanda Blakeman. Amanda, this is Johnny Howard and his son John."

Amanda's face broke into a smile. "I wondered why your voice seemed so familiar," she told the elder Howard. "I listen to your radio show every morning on my way to work."

"And agree with everything I say?" Johnny asked, his eyes twinkling.

"No, most of the time I think you're outrageous. But you do get me to thinking."

"Good, that's what I'm trying to do," Johnny replied, laughing.

Amanda turned to John. "I'm glad to meet you, and good luck this afternoon."

"Thanks, ma'am," John managed. He seemed almost shy next to his outgoing parent.

"I sincerely hope you win second place," Amanda added teasingly.

The Howards laughed and Jack steered her toward a blue Fury, where a young couple was peering under the hood. "Having problems?" Jack inquired as he leaned down and took a look.

"Nothing serious, I hope," the man said as he extended his hand "Jack, how have you been? I guess the poisonings have been keeping you pretty busy."

"That, and this lady," Jack responded. "Perry, Sue, I'd like you to meet Amanda Blakeman. Amanda, this is Perry and Susan Purcell. Perry and I have been at this together for almost ten years."

"Jack's known Perry longer than I have," Susan added. The girl straightened and Amanda could see that she was pregnant.

"Congratulations on your baby," Amanda offered sincerely.

"Thanks," Perry said shyly. "We're both so happy we don't know how to act."

"I'm sure you are," Amanda answered warmly. "When is the baby due?"

"December," Susan pinpointed. "I'm resigning from my job next month. It's going to be a tight squeeze, but we've managed to work out a budget so that I can stay home with the baby."

"That's wonderful," Amanda said. Although she had never felt that it was absolutely necessary that a mother stay home with a child, she was happy for Susan in her decision to do so.

A voice came over the loudspeaker instructing the drivers in the second race to line up. Amanda glanced at Jack, but he and Perry were bent over Perry's engine, totally absorbed in whatever they found there. "Would you like to go up in the stands with me to watch the race?" Amanda asked. "We really can't see too much from down here."

"Sure," Susan agreed. They climbed the stairs to the bleachers and sat down in the last of the shade. "I get so hot out here," Susan complained as she fanned herself.

"Let me get you a drink," Amanda offered. She bought them both a Coke and handed Susan one.

Susan drank deeply. "I guess I really ought to stay home these days," she admitted. "The heat really gets to me, but I hate to miss Perry's race."

Amanda looked at the girl curiously. "It doesn't bother you when he races?"

"Yes, it bothers me. I get so jealous I could hit him."

"Jealous?"

"Yes, the doctor said I couldn't race anymore until the baby was born," Susan explained. "And I guess he has a point. But I sure do miss it."

"You race, too?"

"Sure, I do," Susan said, grinning. "Shirley Muldowny, move over! Susan Purcell's coming your way!"

"You don't get scared?"

"Yes, I get scared," Susan confessed. "Only a fool wouldn't. But I enjoy it in spite of the fear. And besides, accidents don't happen all that often."

The flag went down and Susan was immediately absorbed in the race. Amanda studied the girl's eager face as the cars whizzed around the track. Maybe Susan and Jack were right. Maybe the chances of getting hurt out there weren't really all that great. Amanda could feel herself slowly relaxing. This racing business might turn out to be all right.

A driver that Susan didn't know won the race easily. Susan tapped on Amanda's arm and pointed across to the pit. "They're getting ready to go," she said as Perry and Jack both pulled out of the pit and took their places in the starting lineup. Amanda could feel herself growing tense again, but this time it was as much from excitement as it was from fear. The enthusiasm of the crowd was catching, and Amanda allowed herself to be caught up in the thrill of the moment.

Amanda's eyes were glued to the orange Charger as the instructions came to start their engines. A moment later the flag went down. Amanda gasped as the Charger roared to life, along with the other cars. She watched as Jack jockeyed with the other drivers for the lead, dodging and trying to find an opening he could pull through. Gradually the cars became more scattered around the track, and Jack found the opening he needed. He roared around a green Riviera and blasted down a free stretch of track. "Come on, Jack," Amanda yelled while Susan cheered Perry on. "You know you can do it!"

The Charger passed another two cars, and Amanda looked up the track. There were only three cars in front of Jack's—one of them Perry Purcell's. Amanda calculated how far Jack would have to pull ahead to beat the other three. He could do it, honestly he could! "Come on, Jack, let's go!" Amanda yelled into the roar of the crowd.

The accident happened so quickly that no one saw it coming. A blue Toronado pulled around Jack, who was fast approaching Perry, and plowed into the Fury on the driver's side. Jack tried to swerve away, but the two cars veered straight into his path and he rammed right into them both. The three cars whirled into the fence and skidded back across the track, finally coming to rest in the grass on the far side of the inner track.

Amanda's horrified gasp was lost in the roar that went up from the stands. She held her breath and strained to see what was happening—whether Jack was moving or climbing out of the wreckage. But all she could see was men running toward the accident. The cars that were not involved continued to circle the track. "Why don't they stop?" Amanda demanded.

Susan turned glazed eyes on Amanda. "They never stop unless they have to. Besides, it's over."

A winner crossed the line and was cheered by the crowd. Amanda and Susan made their way as best they could in the milling crowd to the pit, but a racetrack official stopped them when they tried to get past the gate. "Sorry, ladies, nobody but essential personnel out there."

"But my husband was in that wreck. I have to know if he's all right," Susan protested.

"We need to get out to those cars," Amanda declared firmly, whipping out her badge and showing it to the official.

The man's eyes widened, but he let them through with no further argument. They ran across the track, Susan's pregnancy slowing her down only a little. Within seconds Susan was kneeling beside Perry, who was already laid out on a stretcher. "Perry, say something," Susan begged of her unconscious husband.

Amanda gasped in horror when she realized that Jack was trapped in his car. "Can't you get him out of there?" she cried to a volunteer fireman who was standing beside the cars.

"We're working as fast as we can, ma'am," he assured her. The immediate area around the wreckage had been roped off, and Amanda didn't choose to hamper Jack's rescue by making a pest of herself. She watched as two firemen removed the door and helped Jack from the car. He was swaying on his feet, but he shook his head when the ambulance attendants tried to get him to lie down on a stretcher.

Amanda climbed over the rope. "Jack, lie down," she said, her voice trembling with shock. "You've been hurt."

Jack took a look at her expression and for once didn't argue. Numbly almost, he lay down on the stretcher and grasped Amanda's outstretched hand. Amanda was amazed to feel that he was trembling. "How badly is Perry hurt?" he whispered.

"I don't know, but he looks like he's in bad shape," Amanda admitted.

Jack's face went white and he muttered a curse word. "Could he die?" Jack pressed.

"Yes, he could," Amanda said steadily. "I'm sorry."

Jack swallowed. "It could have been me, couldn't it? He could have hit me and not Perry."

Amanda squeezed Jack's hand in response. On Jack's request she found a paramedic who knew something about Perry's immediate condition. He said that Perry had broken both legs and possibly had some internal injuries. Perry and the other driver, who was also pretty badly injured, were loaded into one ambulance and driven away; Jack, who appeared to have only minor injuries, was put into another.

Amanda followed the ambulance to the hospital and waited in the emergency room while Jack was checked over by the resident on duty. She drank a cup of coffee and tried not to think about what had almost happened, but she could not stop the instant replays in her mind of the cars crashing in front of Jack and him crashing into them. He was right—it could have been him near death and not Perry Purcell. Amanda spared a few moments to worry about Perry and Susan. Even if Perry recovered, he was going to be a long time paying off his medical bills. If he didn't, Susan had a baby to raise by herself.

Finally the door to the examining room opened, and Jack followed the doctor out. He was pale and had a few Band-Aids on his face and arms, but otherwise he seemed all right. He opened his arms and Amanda flew into them. "Jack, are you all right?"

"Yes, they say that I'm fine," Jack said. "But Amanda, I was scared."

"Shh, I know," Amanda comforted as she held Jack's trembling body close to hers. "It's all right now. You're safe. It's going to be all right."

"Is it?" Jack asked grimly. "What about Perry?"

"Let's go up and see," Amanda suggested. They went up to the surgical waiting room, where Susan was conversing with a middle-aged doctor. "How is Perry?" Amanda asked as Susan finished speaking and turned to face them.

"He's got two broken legs, one of which is crushed pretty badly, but the X-rays revealed no internal injuries. He's going to be all right, but it's going to be a long time before he's well."

Jack and Amanda offered to stay with Susan, but she said that her mother was coming and for them to go on home. Jack was still feeling a little shaky, so Amanda drove the pickup to his house and parked it in the garage. "I guess Debbie was totaled," Jack said wistfully as he looked at the spot the Charger usually occupied.

"I would say so," Amanda responded. She followed Jack into the house and moved into his outstretched arms. "I was so scared, Jack. Are you really all right?"

"I think so," Jack replied as he held her almost too tightly. Amanda wrapped her arms around his waist and held him close to her, frantically touching him through the dirty jumpsuit. She wanted to feel for herself that he really didn't have any broken bones or other injuries. "I'm all right, Amanda, honestly," Jack repeated over and over, as much to convince himself as to convince her.

Amanda unsnapped the top snap of his jumpsuit and pulled down the zipper. "I want to see for sure," she said as she pushed the sweaty jumpsuit off his shoulders. "I just want to make sure, Jack."

Jack shrugged the suit off his shoulders and pushed it down his body with Amanda's help. She gasped at the ugly seat belt bruises across his chest and stomach. "Dear Lord, those must hurt," she winced as Jack sat down on the floor to pull off his boots.

"Yes, I'm sore," Jack admitted. "I don't think I hurt like this even when that bull threw me."

"I'll run you a hot tub of water to soak in," Amanda volunteered. She left Jack to struggle with his boots and ran the tub almost full. Jack came in and threw the jumpsuit and his underwear in the hamper. "Get in and soak for a few minutes. I'll fix you some supper."

Jack grasped Amanda's arm as she started to leave. "I don't want supper right now. I want you to stay with me. Get in the tub, Amanda. I want to take a bath with you, and then I want to make love to you."

Amanda gasped at the sensual need in Jack's expression. "Jack, we—we can't," she stammered. "You've been hurt."

"I haven't been hurt that badly," Jack argued. "Please, Amanda. I need you—right now."

There was no way Amanda could refuse Jack's impassioned plea. She pulled off her blouse as he slid into the water, and in just a moment she was standing naked before him. "You get more beautiful every time I see you that way," he breathed as his eyes delighted in Amanda's shapely curves.

"That's only because you love me," Amanda murmured softly as she slid into the water and sat between Jack's outstretched legs. "You need a bigger tub."

"Someday we'll have a tub that we can share comfortably," Jack told her as he slid down into the water. Amanda lathered a washcloth and soaped herself while Jack watched her with eager, excited eyes. She took her time, scrubbing away the dust, the heat, and the fear she had been exposed to this afternoon. When she had finished, she signaled for Jack to sit up, and she lovingly soaped his chest and his back, taking care not to hurt any of the quickly darkening bruises on his body. She reached under the water and scrubbed his legs and his stomach, boldly caressing him until she knew of his desire for her.

"I guess you weren't hurt all that badly," Amanda teased as he responded to her loving ministrations. "I was so afraid," she admitted as she leaned forward and kissed Jack tenderly. He grasped her shoulders and pressed her close to him, her breasts crushing into his chest as she opened her lips to his. The water caressed their bodies as they stroked and touched one another beneath the soapy surface. Every touch was designed to tease, to arouse, to enflame. Before long they were both overflowing with desire for one another. Amanda needed Jack—needed his love and needed to make love to him to prove to herself that he really was all right. Jack needed her, too. He needed the comfort of her body and her spirit tonight. He needed to be one with her, to know her gentle touch and her loving embrace.

In unison they stood, wrapping one another in large bath sheets. They patted and stroked one another through the thick terry cloth, their touch mutually loving, and comforting, and at the same time unbearably arousing. They stared into one another's eyes, and in a moment of unspoken communication and desire, they let their towels drop to the floor and moved into each other's arms, their bodies wrapped together from head to toe as they embraced in the steamy bathroom. Amanda could feel the strength in his thighs and hips, the firm tautness of his stomach, the hardness of his hair-covered chest. His back was firm and strong against her fingers, his bottom hard and tight. Love and longing burst forth in Amanda for Jack as she gasped his name. "Take me, Jack," she whimpered. "Now. Please."

Jack could feel Amanda's wild passion as well as his own. His breathing rapid, he half pushed her to the bed and fell down on top of her, nudging her legs open and entering her with a swift, sure movement. Amanda's welcoming warmth assured him that she was more than ready for him. "I need you, Amanda," Jack murmured over and over as he moved over her. "I need you so badly that sometimes I could cry with it."

"I need you, too, Jack," Amanda whispered as they moved together. "I love you and I need you and I want you to be all right. Ooh," she gasped as Jack rolled onto his back, turning her around so that she was atop him.

"Make love to me, Amanda," Jack pleaded. Amanda moved over him, continuing the rhythm of passion that Jack had set, taking them both on a journey of unbelievable delight. Amanda could feel herself spiraling quickly, too quickly, toward the ultimate satisfaction. She wanted it to last longer—they both did—but desire was too strong between them and they quickly reached their moment of mutual delight. Amanda gasped and moaned as Jack's body tensed beneath her, tenderness and passion and love combining to transport them to the nearest shooting star. The moment seemed to go on forever but was still over too soon.

Amanda laid her head on Jack's shoulder. "That one has to take the world speed record," she complained.

"We couldn't have held that back any more than we could stop Niagara Falls," Jack said gently. "Besides, what makes you think we're finished for the evening? It's early yet."

"That's right," Amanda agreed happily as she moved away from Jack and snuggled down beside him. He flinched when she threw her arm across his chest. "Sore?"

"A little," Jack admitted. "My arm muscles, too. That's why I wanted you to make love to me."

"Why are your arm muscles sore?"

"I was trying to veer off when I hit them," Jack began. "The wheel was jerked in the other direction while I was still holding it, and I guess it strained my arms."

"I'm sure that hurt," Amanda said, thinking that maybe it was just as well that the Charger was totaled. She rubbed Jack's sore muscles for a minute. "Would you like me to get us some supper?"

"I'd love something to eat," Jack admitted. "Let's fix it together." He pulled on underwear and a pair of shorts and handed Amanda another pair of shorts and a T-shirt. "Here, these ought to fit."

Amanda pulled on the cutoffs and shirt, which fit her perfectly. "Did these belong to an old girlfriend of yours?" she asked only half-jokingly as she followed Jack to the kitchen.

"No, they're mine," he confessed, blushing a little. "Big macho man, I'm not."

Amanda looked down and grinned at her own stupidity. "They would fit you, wouldn't they?" She put her arms around Jack from behind and hugged him to her. "Maybe you're not big, but believe me, you're plenty macho. You're the most appealing man I've ever known."

Jack turned around and stared into Amanda's eyes. "It doesn't bother you that I'm short?"

"No, it doesn't," Amanda replied. "Why? Does it bother you to be short?"

Jack was quiet a minute. "Not really, I guess. Not anymore, anyway."

Amanda cocked her head to one side. "What kind of an answer is that?"

"It bothered me a lot when I was a kid. I was horrified when I had my leg X-rayed when I was about fifteen and the doctor said my growth plates had already fused. But I'm okay with it now."

"So what made you decide you're okay with it?" Amanda pressed gently.

"Something my dad said to me that afternoon. He reminded me that there are no pipsqueaks on the back of a bull. He was right." Jack grinned. "And he of all people should have known. He was even smaller than I am."

And probably loved danger as much as Jack did, Amanda thought. Was this it? Was this at least part of Jack's obsession with taking chances? How could it not be, the way he idolized his dad? "You're hardly a pipsqueak, on a bull or off of one," she reassured him.

"Thanks," Jack said, kissing her parted lips lightly. "What would you like to eat?"

"Anything you have—I'm starved."

"Broiled fish, okay?" Jack suggested.

It sounded good to Amanda, so while Jack broiled the fish to perfection, she shredded cabbage for coleslaw and made her very own homemade tartar sauce. The passionate lovemaking had relaxed her, but once in a while the afternoon's events flashed before her eyes and she would become tense for a few moments. She glanced curiously at Jack, who seemed as carefree as he ever was. *Did the accident this afternoon make a lasting impression on Jack, or has he managed to put it from his mind?* Amanda wondered in earnest.

"Here we go," Jack said a few minutes later as he put the delicious-smelling fish on the table. Amanda added her contributions, and Jack poured them each a glass of white wine. "I didn't think beer would go with this," he qualified. He handed Amanda her wine and drank a little of his.

"What? No toast?" Amanda teased.

"Not just yet," Jack said.

Their talk was light and casual over dinner. Amanda had the feeling that Jack wanted to say something to her, but she wasn't sure. She figured that Jack would bring up whatever was on his mind when he was ready to. They finished their meal, Amanda taking seconds on the fish. Jack offered her some of his mother's homemade chocolate cake for dessert. Amanda took a bite of the cake and sighed. "This is delicious. Do you suppose your mother would part with the recipe?"

"She would do better than that," Jack answered quickly. "I'll write her and ask her to make you one of your very own."

"She wouldn't have to do that!" Amanda said. She took another bite of the cake. "On second thought, do you think she would?"

Jack grinned. "I'll write her. She's been dying to meet you," he added softly.

"And I'd like to meet your mother," Amanda returned. "Why don't you introduce me the next time she drives up?"

"I was waiting," Jack said. "I wanted to introduce you as my future wife." He paused a minute. "She's coming next week, Amanda. Could I introduce you to her as my fiancée?"

Amanda swallowed the cake in her mouth. "I don't know." She hesitated. "Do you want—"

"Damn it, don't change the subject on me!" Jack snapped. "I asked you to marry me. I've asked you several times, in fact, if you'll marry me. Why won't you say yes or no?"

"Because I can't!" Amanda cried. "I can't bring myself to agree to marry a man who takes the kinds of crazy chances that you do."

"Are we back to that again? Jack and his daredevil stunts?"

Amanda shut her eyes and leaned her forehead in her hands. "Have you forgotten this afternoon already?" she asked tiredly. "It's only been about five hours since you nearly got splattered across that asphalt track. I haven't forgotten, Jack, even if you have."

Jack's anger faded. "Yes, maybe I did forget for a moment," he admitted. "I'm sorry, Amanda. I shouldn't have gotten angry. But it hurts when you won't say you'll marry me, even though I love you and I know you love me."

Amanda raised her head. "It hurts me just as much when you go out there and put your life on the line." She thought a minute. She was going to take a gamble, and she might very well lose. But she loved Jack and she wanted to marry him, so she had to give it a try. "So what do you say we stop hurting one another?"

"How's that?"

"You lay off the dangerous hobbies and I'll marry you," Amanda said.

Anger flared in Jack's eyes. "That's blackmail. How would you like it if I made our marriage conditional on something? Like you giving up your job?"

"I'd tell you to go jump in the lake," Amanda admitted frankly, "because that would be unreasonable on your part. But my condition's a reasonable one. Furthermore, I don't think it's too much to ask if you love me like you say you do."

"And what will you do if I tell you to go jump in the lake?" Jack demanded.

"I'll walk out of here and not come back," Amanda answered gravely. "I will not—I repeat, *will not*—spend my life like I did this afternoon. I was frightened out of my wits and I don't like the feeling. I'm not going to spend the rest of my life worrying about you. You have plenty of opportunity for thrills and challenge at work," Amanda reminded him. "Jack, I love you, and I want to marry you. But it has to be on those terms. I love you too much to stick around and watch you get hurt or killed." She paused a minute, hoping Jack would respond in some way. "Look, we don't have to settle this tonight. I'll help you clean up, and you can run me on home."

Jack watched Amanda as she loaded the dishwasher with the dirty dishes. Her conditions angered him, but she probably felt that she was in the right. He knew that she had been badly frightened this afternoon. He was perceptive enough to know that seeing her involved in that kind of accident would have frightened him just as much. Besides, he did love her and he wanted to marry her. What could be more important than that?

Amanda turned on the dishwasher and flipped off the light over the sink. "I'm ready to go," she said softly.

Jack pulled her down on his lap and kissed her passionately. "Now, is that any way to act? Running out on the man you're going to marry?"

"Marry?" Amanda asked. "I thought you wanted to think it over."

"I have. For a whole ten minutes. And I could think about it for ten hours or ten days or ten years, and I would still come to the same conclusion. I love you and I want to marry you. And if you don't want me racing or riding or skydiving, then so be it."

"You mean you're willing to give them up?"

"I love you and I want to make you happy. If that's what it takes, I'll do it."

Amanda sniffed back tears of joy. "You've made me the happiest woman in the world," she said as she leaned forward for Jack's tender kiss.

Jack met her lips eagerly, ardently, opening himself to her as she gave herself to him. He could feel the tears of joy that dampened her face, and he knew that his eyes were wet with tears of his own. They had somehow managed to find one another in this crazy world. Jack was sure that there had never been another man as happy as he was right then. She was his. Amanda had finally agreed to be his wife.

"Oh, Jack, I love you," Amanda murmured when Jack finally released her lips. He trailed tender kisses all over her face—her eyelids, her forehead, her chin. He left no spot untouched. Amanda held Jack close to her as she kissed and touched and caressed him. She couldn't believe that she had gambled and won—she had been so sure that he would refuse her. But he hadn't. He had agreed to set her mind at rest and give up the things that frightened her so. She only hoped that he wouldn't regret the sacrifice she was asking him to make.

"I love you, too, Amanda," Jack breathed as his hands lovingly explored her supple back, "We're going to be so happy."

"Going to be?" Amanda asked. "I already am. I'm happier than I ever thought possible."

"I'm glad." Jack's lips met hers for another searing kiss of love and passion, and Amanda could feel desire start to swell in her again. She needed him yet again tonight, and she knew that he hadn't completely slaked his desire for her.

He hadn't. Jack fairly trembled with love and desire for Amanda. She was everything he had ever wanted in a woman, and he loved her like he had never loved anyone before. She could arouse him and at the same time soothe and comfort him until he was purring like a kitten. He loved to kiss her and hold her and touch her. His hands found the softness of her shoulders through the T-shirt that she wore, and he caressed her gently before his hands drifted lower, massaging the firm roundness of her high breasts. He could feel her tremble as her nipples hardened into two points of desire. Amanda gasped as he swiftly pulled the shirt from her body, baring her to the waist. "I want to see you. I want to see you and touch you and taste you. Slowly this time. And I want you to do the same to me."

Amanda nodded. Jack was already bare to the waist, so slowly, tenderly, as though they had all the time in the world, they explored the upper half of one another's bodies. Although the knowledge was new to neither of them, Amanda took great pleasure in touching Jack's small male nipples, watching one harden until it was firm in her hand. She bent her head and caressed the other one with the tip of her tongue. "You're sensitive there," she said as it, too, responded.

"So are you," Jack said as his lips found and tasted Amanda's hard, firm bud. They kissed and caressed one another until they were ready for more intimacy than the chair allowed. Jack led Amanda back to his bed and turned back the covers. "We're going to take it slow this time. We're going to make it last forever," he promised.

"How are we going to do that?" Amanda whispered.

"Like this. You're going to lay back and let me touch you and kiss you. Then you're going to do the same for me." He pushed her down onto the bed and lay down beside her. "I love you, Amanda, and I'm going to show you that love tonight."

Jack leaned over Amanda and kissed her tenderly. He left every part of her face tingling with the passion of his touch before his lips drifted lower, touching and caressing her shoulders, the valley between her breasts, the tips of her nipples that were already hardened with desire. Amanda moaned and squirmed as he drifted lower, leaving a trail of moist kisses on her midriff and around her waist. No man had ever kissed her or touched her with this love, this tenderness, and Amanda opened herself to Jack like a flower blossoming after a rain. His lips caressed her navel and lower, finding and tormenting the essence of her femininity until she was writhing in pleasure. She could feel herself starting to tighten, to tense. She tried to hold back, wanting to share the moment with him. "Don't fight it, Mandy," Jack whispered. "Go on with it. It's all right."

Amanda's body arched and she felt as if her whole body were exploding with pleasure. Stars went off in the back of her head as delight surged through her. Gasping, she lay back and let her body take her where it would. Jack caressed her until the storm was over and stroked her gently until she could catch her breath. "Beautiful," he breathed as he kissed Amanda's face reverently.

"What's beautiful?" Amanda asked.

"Your face at that moment," Jack answered.

Amanda blushed. She pushed Jack over onto his back, touching and stroking him as he had her. "I love you, Jack," she murmured as she kissed his face, his skin rough where his beard was and so smooth where it wasn't. Her lips trailed lower, finding and caressing his shoulders, his hard male nipples, his firm waist and flat stomach. Amanda gulped as her lips drifted lower—she wasn't sure, but she hoped she could please Jack as he had her. Hesitantly at first, she loved Jack as he had loved her, finding and caressing him intimately, her shyness turning to boldness as she heard his gasps of delight.

At the same time, her own desire began to grow within her, so that by the time she sensed that Jack was nearly at the brink, she was ready for him again. She moved up his body and quickly joined them together, their mutual desire quickly satisfied by an explosive, shuddering climax.

Amanda snuggled against Jack, careful to avoid his bruised chest "That was beautiful, Amanda," Jack whispered as he cradled her to him. "No woman has ever made it that beautiful for me."

Amanda smiled shyly. "I'm glad," she whispered back as she lay cradled in Jack's arms. Her even breathing a few minutes later told him that she was asleep.

***

Jack lay still until he was sure that Amanda was asleep. When she snored softly, he kissed her and slipped out of bed, pulling on a robe and heading for the kitchen. He poured himself a stiff drink and carried it to the living room, where he propped his feet and stared at the poster on the opposite wall. His bruises were hurting, and he hoped the drink would take the edge off the pain.

Jack sipped his drink and smiled into the empty room. Amanda had finally agreed to marry him. She hadn't been the easiest woman in the world to convince, but in the end she had agreed to become his wife. And he intended to make her as happy as he knew how. But as he sipped his drink, Jack thought about the promise he had made to Amanda and he frowned. He loved Amanda and had made his promise in good faith. But at the same time, he had to admit that his hobbies were almost a compulsion with him. Would he be able to live up to the promise he had made tonight to the woman he loved?

Chapter Eleven

"Mother, do I look all right?" Amanda asked as she peered into her bathroom mirror. Anxiously she fingered the small tiara of flowers in her hair.

"Amanda, you look wonderful," Jennifer Blakeman assured her nervous daughter. "You couldn't be any prettier, honestly."

"I want everything to be just right for Jack," Amanda said as she smoothed her blusher. "This is the only time he's done this."

"I think you want it to be just right for yourself, too, don't you?" Jennifer asked perceptively.

"Yes, I do," Amanda admitted. "Mom, I want so much for it to work for Jack and me. I love him and I want this marriage to be a good one."

"Oh, Amanda, it will be. Jack's not anything like Brian, and he seems to be so nice. And he certainly doesn't seem to have any of those nasty little habits that some men have these days!"

He doesn't anymore, Amanda thought. In the last month since she had accepted Jack's proposal, he had lived up to his promise to her. He had stayed away from the racetrack and had not gone skydiving or bull riding. He had been pretty busy on the investigation of the poisonings, but he had managed to find alternative entertainment on the weekends that he was free. Amanda smiled to herself. Apparently Jack had every intention of living up to his promise. What better omen could the start of her marriage have?

Amanda put the finishing touches to her makeup and stepped back to look at herself in the mirror. A pretty woman with shining eyes and a glow on her cheeks smiled back at her. The woman wore a simple but stunning off-white dress and had a natural adornment of white flowers in her hair. Amanda smiled back at her reflection. Yes, Jack would be pleased with her today.

Amanda got into the back seat of her mother's Buick, and her favorite uncle chauffeured them to the San Fernando Cathedral in the heart of downtown San Antonio. Since Amanda's first marriage had been set aside by the Catholic Church, and she and Jack both attended services at the cathedral on occasion, the priest had been more than happy to marry them. The wedding plans had started out small, but once word got around the police department that they were getting married, they realized they couldn't leave any of their many friends out. The guest list had grown, and Amanda only hoped that the room they had reserved at the Menger Hotel could accommodate the crowd. She held her hands in her lap and told herself not to be nervous. She and Jack had solved the one problem that kept them apart, and there was no reason that Amanda could think of that this marriage could possibly fail. Still, marriage was a big step for any couple. She whispered a silent prayer that she and Jack would have a happy one.

They arrived at the beautiful old stone cathedral a few minutes early. Although it was late October, the breeze that ruffled Amanda's hair was still warm, and it would probably be even warmer in Cozumel, where they planned to fly in the morning. Since the cathedral had no bride's room where Amanda could wait, she slipped into an old stairwell in the back of the church, peeking out every so often to watch as the cathedral filled with family and friends. Samantha, who had been delighted to serve as matron of honor, joined her a few minutes later and kept her calm as the minutes ticked by. Two altar boys lit the candles at the altar, and at precisely seven the bells tolled and Celia Vance, Jack's beautiful little mother, came down the aisle on the arm of Amanda's cousin. Jennifer Blakeman and her escort followed. Amanda's uncle opened the door and extended his arm to her. "It's that time, Amanda," he said gravely as she stepped out of the stairwell and took his arm.

Jack and Eddie followed the priest out, and the organ began the traditional march. Amanda started to tremble, but she looked down the aisle at Jack and her fears melted in the love that shone from his face. Jack positively glowed with feeling for her, and Amanda smiled at him as she and her uncle started down the aisle. She stopped and kissed her mother and walked the last few steps to the altar by herself. With fingers that trembled only a little, she took Jack's arm and together they turned to the priest who would join them together as husband and wife.

The service was simple but moving. Their voices were strong as they pledged to love and honor one another. The lovely old scripture out of First Corinthians describing true love brought tears to Amanda's eyes. They smiled at one another as they exchanged simple gold bands—identical but for the diamond that graced Amanda's. Jack squeezed her hand when the priest pronounced them husband and wife, and he was tender and loving as he kissed her at the altar. Amanda stopped on the way back down the aisle and kissed Mrs. Vance as she had her own mother, bringing delighted tears to her new mother-in-law's happy face.

She and Jack left the church and Jack stopped on the front steps. "We did it!" he exclaimed as he picked her up and whirled her around. "I love you, Amanda Vance."

"And I love you, Jack Vance," Amanda breathed as she bent her head and kissed him with the passion she had restrained in front of the congregation.

Jack returned her kiss passionately, stopping only when Eddie and Samantha started to clap. "Break it up, you two," Eddie chided them. "You'll have plenty of time for that kind of thing after the reception."

"What reception?" Jack teased. "We're going straight to the honeymoon."

"Come on, you two, we need to get back inside for the pictures," Samantha said. She and Eddie herded Jack and Amanda around to the front of the church, where they waited with the priest for the guests to leave. The photographer they hired made quick work of the group shots, and before long Jack and Amanda were in her mother's car and on the way to the reception.

"I hope the room is big enough," Amanda fretted as she and Jack entered the elegant old hotel where they were to have their reception. Amanda had wanted to spend their wedding night here, too, but Jack insisted that they spend it elsewhere, lest one of their practical-joking friends bribe his way into their room and leave a few souvenirs behind.

"I'm sure it will be fine," Jack said as he patted her hand. "Everything else has gone beautifully. You and your mom have done a marvelous job."

"Thanks," Amanda replied quietly.

They found the banquet room, and Amanda was relieved it appeared to be just big enough to accommodate the crowd. Their mothers insisted on a receiving line so they could each meet all the out-of-town relatives, so for the next half hour Jack and Amanda dutifully shook hands. Amanda was amazed at the number of maiden aunts Jack had, and Jack understood Amanda's outspoken tendencies a little better when he met some of her uncles and cousins. Finally they were able to make their way to the buffet table and serve themselves the delicious hors d'oeuvres the hotel prepared. Now that the ceremony was over and they were actually married, Amanda was excited and very, very happy to be Jack's wife.

Eddie and Sylvia were already seated at the head table when Jack and Amanda sat down. "Well, did you meet all the skeletons in her closet?" Eddie teased.

"I don't know if you'd call them skeletons, but a couple of them make Amanda look bashful," Jack teased as he cut a piece of cold roast beef.

"Jack's relatives are very nice," Amanda sniffed.

"I didn't invite the stinkers," Jack retorted.

"This sort of reminds me of our wedding," Sylvia said as she looked around at the crowded room. "We married at the cathedral, too, and had our reception over at the Hilton. All my relatives came in from Mexico. We had nearly four hundred people there."

"I'll bet it was lovely," Amanda replied. "I wish I had known you then."

"Eddie wasn't even on the force in those days," Sylvia continued. "He had just gotten out of the Army."

"Did you have your wedding night at the Hilton, also?" Amanda asked.

"No, not really," Sylvia said cheerfully. "Oh, we spent the night there, but Eddie got nervous and drank too much and went to sleep on me."

Eddie blushed furiously, and Jack burst out laughing. "Don't say what you're thinking, Jack," Eddie warned him teasingly. "I made up for it the next night." Sylvia giggled and blushed, and Amanda hoped that she and Jack had the kind of marriage that Eddie and Sylvia had forged for themselves.

Jennifer Blakeman sat down in the chair across from Jack and Amanda. "Everything's going just fine, isn't it?" she asked. "Come over here, Celia, and sit with me," she instructed as she motioned to Jack's mother. "I just love your family, Jack," she said as Celia sat down beside her. Celia blushed with pleasure at the compliment.

"Thank you, Jennifer," Jack returned. Amanda's mother insisted from the first that Jack call her by her first name. "I like Amanda's family, too."

"Even Uncle Amos?" Jennifer teased. "He's the one who told Jack he'd take a horsewhip to him if Amanda wasn't happy," she told Celia.

Celia laughed. "You heard the man, son. Better be good to her."

"I'm not worried," Jennifer answered blithely. "I met him just over a month ago, and I've seen a lot of him since, what with getting this wedding ready, and as far as I can see he doesn't do one thing that a mother-in-law could complain about."

Celia glanced first at Jennifer, then at Amanda. Amanda shook her head faintly and Celia nodded, understanding completely. Amanda had told her mother quite a bit about Jack, but she completely neglected to mention Jack's interesting choice of hobbies, sincerely believing that Jennifer didn't need to know about those. Why tell her mother, and get her worried, when Jack had agreed to give them up?

Celia smiled faintly, sensing immediately what Amanda had done. "I'm delighted, too, Jennifer," she assured Amanda's mother. "I'm so glad that Jack's finally settling down with such a lovely young woman. It's such a relief to me—you never know just who your son is going to bring home."

"Mothers worry about the same thing," Jennifer said. She glanced over at Jack and Amanda, who were absorbed in private, wordless communication. "If you think we're happy about this, take a look at them."

"I know," Celia agreed, but she made up her mind to talk privately with Amanda before the girl left on her honeymoon.

Jack and Amanda finished their meal and mingled with their guests, making sure everyone had gotten enough to eat and drink. The combo they had hired started playing after everyone had finished eating, and Jack and Amanda led off the first dance. Before too long the small dance floor was packed. Jack and Amanda danced with their guests for nearly an hour before they cut the cake and threw the bouquet. When the dancing started again Jack put his arm around Amanda and bent his lips to her ear. "Are you about ready to slip away?"

"Slip away, nothing. I'm leaving in a shower of rice and confetti."

Jack rolled his eyes. "Better get changed, then. It's getting late and we have an early plane to catch."

"I guess we'll have to go straight to sleep tonight," Amanda teased.

"It's not *that* early," Jack said, laughing.

Amanda found her suitcase in the private ladies' powder room a few doors down from the banquet room. She slipped out of her dress and washed off her makeup, intending to put more on for her flight from the hotel. She was wearing a mint-green going-away dress and was just sitting down to redo her face when Celia Vance pushed open the door. "Amanda? Could you use a little company?"

"Sure, come on in." She figured that Celia would want to talk to her sometime this evening. "Was everything all right tonight?"

"You and your mother put together a beautiful wedding," Celia assured her. "I loved every minute of it."

"I'm glad," Amanda said. "Mom thinks the world of both you and Jack, and I know she'll be happy that you're pleased."

"I gathered from your mother's comments that she doesn't know about Jack's favorite pastimes," Celia began. "Either that or she's certainly a liberal-minded mother-in-law."

"I didn't tell her," Amanda confessed. "Celia, I didn't see any reason to worry her needlessly."

"I know you want your mother to like Jack, but don't you think honesty would have been better in the long run? She's bound to find out sooner or later."

"I don't think she will," Amanda answered. "And it won't be so bad if she does because they're all in the past. Jack's agreed to give them up. I made him promise before I agreed to marry him."

"He did?" Mrs. Vance didn't sound especially impressed. "I hope he means it. I've always worried about him, you know. Perhaps this marriage will make the difference."

"You think he doesn't mean it?" Amanda asked. "He promised me."

"If he does I'll be surprised. I've worried about that boy since the day he climbed up on the breakfront and jumped off. He was barely old enough to walk at the time. Amanda, Jack's always been the daredevil he is today, and I'm not sure that he'll ever change, no matter how much he loves you. It's just in him to take chances. He's just like his father in that respect. Royce never came across a dangerous pastime that he didn't have to at least try."

"Why?" Amanda asked. "Was he an adrenaline junkie like Jack?"

"Who knows?" Celia said tiredly. "Sometimes I think he did it just to prove himself. He was even smaller than Jack and took a lot of ribbing because of it, and the dangerous stuff was to prove he was just as big a man as the six footers."

"I've wondered about that ever since Jack told me something that his father said to him about being small. Something about no man being a pipsqueak on the back of a bull."

"Royce meant it, too," Celia said. "And the way Jack idolized the man, it's no wonder he picked up where Royce left off. I don't doubt that the adrenaline rush is a big part of it, too."

"So you don't think Jack can keep his promise," Amanda pressed dully.

"No, I didn't say that at all." Celia continued, "Jack's a man of his word—he'll do his best to please you. I'm just saying not to be too surprised if he has a hard time keeping his promise to you."

"I'll help him," Amanda said quietly, "because it's very important to me. I love your son like I've never loved a man in my life. I want him to be around for a long time."

"I hope you do help him," Celia responded sincerely. "And I hope for both your sakes he does keep his promise to you—because I want to see your marriage succeed, and because it would kill me if anything ever happened to him." The two women hugged one another, and then a preoccupied Amanda returned to the task of making up her face.

***

Amanda murmured in her sleep and turned over. "Don't want to play," she mumbled as she swiped at a persistent tickle on the tip of her nose. "No, don't do that."

"Come on, sleeping beauty, wake up," Jack whispered as he nibbled her nose. "It's after eight."

Amanda swiped at her nose again. "Yes, I'll marry you—just go back to sleep," she mumbled.

Jack laughed out loud and kissed her cheek. "I hope you were dreaming about me," he said softly into Amanda's ear, "because if you weren't, I'm going to be mad."

"What? Oh, Jack, I was asleep!" Amanda said as she turned over and snuggled against him spoon-style. "It's not time to get up yet."

"Who said anything about getting up?" Jack asked as he wrapped his arm around her waist. "I would just as soon stay here with you all day, but we have to get up if we're going out to the ruins today." His hand drifted up her midriff to cup one warm breast.

"Is that all you ever think about?" Amanda admonished gently as Jack fingered her nipple.

"What? Ruins?" His other hand stroked her bottom.

"No, silly, sex. We did it twice last night and once yesterday afternoon."

"I'm trying for a world's record," Jack announced playfully as his hands worked magic on her body. "We may die young, but we're going to die happy."

Amanda snuggled closer to Jack. "Sounds like a great way to go," she told him as he flexed the muscles of his chest, rubbing her back with the blond hair she found so sensuous. She and Jack had been in Cozumel for a week now, and every night she had gone to sleep with her head cradled in the soft hair of his chest. "How many times have we made love since we got here?"

"Good grief, I don't know." Jack turned Amanda over gently to face him. "I lost count after the third day." Tenderly he held Amanda's face as he kissed her. "Want to try for one more?"

"What about the ruins?" Amanda murmured.

"If we miss the tour, we'll rent a jeep," Jack said, his lips meeting hers again. Amanda opened herself to him. As Jack sampled her sweetness she could feel desire slowly replacing her lethargy. Although they had made love many times in the week since their wedding, her desire for Jack seemed to grow, not diminish. The mystery in their relationship was slowly being replaced with knowledge, sweet, intimate knowledge. This added understanding of one another's needs seemed to increase their pleasure and their passion. Amanda caressed the small of his back the way he loved for her to, and she gloried in the power her knowledge gave her over him.

But if she had power over Jack, he had at least the same power over her. He had learned just where to touch and caress her. He knew that she loved to have her back rubbed, and that tickling the back of her knees would make her collapse in giggles. He knew that her stomach was incredibly sensitive, and that the smell of herbs turned her on more than expensive perfume. And he knew that no man in the world could evoke the response in her that he could.

Jack knew he'd never abuse the power he had over Amanda, just as he was sure she'd never abuse the power she had over him. They had each vowed silently that they would use what they knew to bring the other only pleasure and happiness. They had waited too long to find one another not to treasure the tremendous passion they shared. Amanda used her newfound knowledge to rouse Jack to heights he had never reached with another woman. She stroked the small of his back, his thighs, the hard, strong muscles of his buttocks, deliberately teasing and tantalizing him.

Jack ran his hands down Amanda's sides as he bent his head to her breasts. He loved to feel her nipples grow hard and warm when he kissed and caressed her. She was all warmth and womanliness, and even when she took the lead and became the aggressor—which she did often in their love play—she made him feel like more of a man than any woman he had ever been with. They were magic together, and in moments like this, when he was touching her and caressing her, he found her instant response to his lovemaking unbearably exciting. Jack fondled her breasts as his lips traveled lower, finding and tormenting the little spot just below her navel that was so sensitive. He could feel her grow tense, but he held back on his own impulses and continued to caress her there until she was moaning. "Make love to me, Jack," she whispered into the stillness of the morning. "I need you so much."

"I need you just as badly," Jack murmured as he gently parted her legs. He moved over her, but instead of taking her right away, he let his fingers torment her as his lips gently suckled her breasts for one more long, sweet moment. She writhed and arched beneath him. When Jack sensed that she could take no more, he joined her with a movement that was pure, sweet pleasure. Amanda gasped at the wonderful intimacy of their embrace and gave herself over to the delights of Jack's lovemaking. He made love to her slowly but passionately, each and every movement a beautiful, natural step to the tumultuous explosion they were sure to reach. Amanda responded with all the passion she was capable of, matching his movements so as to give both her and Jack the ultimate pleasure. She could feel the moment coming—they both could—and when it came they cried out together, their pleasure all the more beautiful because they had shared it.

Jack leaned his head on Amanda's shoulder. "You are more magnificent every time," he said as he pressed his lips against her soft skin. "I love you, Amanda."

"I love you, Jack," Amanda murmured. "But the words seem so inadequate, somehow."

Jack kissed her gently and rolled off her. "They're just fine, especially when you show me you love me like you did just now."

They snuggled close together and dozed for a little while, content just to be with one another. When they awoke again Jack began to badger Amanda a little about going out to see the ruins. "Come on, Mandy, we won't be back down here for a long time, if ever. I'd really like to go and see them."

"I want to lie on the beach and vegetate," Amanda complained good-humoredly.

"We did that yesterday."

"Just for part of the day. We went snorkeling all morning, remember?"

Jack patted Amanda's bottom. "And you loved every minute of it, didn't you?"

"Yes, I did, even when that fish started to nibble my hair," Amanda said, laughing. They spent most of the week scuba diving and snorkeling and had come face-to-face with some of the inhabitants of the shallow coastal waters. "Do you want to go again?"

"Sure, we'll go tomorrow," Jack agreed. "I want to see the ruins today, though."

"All right, we'll go to the ruins," Amanda relented with a sigh. "I get the shower first. Why don't you call down for some coffee?" She rolled out of bed and got her clothes out of the suitcase, totally unselfconscious of her nudity. She and Jack had achieved a state of such intimacy that neither even thought to put on a robe when they were together.

Jack started to ask if she wanted company in the shower, but Amanda had already shut the door to the bathroom, so he dialed room service for coffee and sweet rolls. He turned over and shut his eyes for a moment, and then he got up and pulled on a robe. He opened the sliding door to the balcony of their elegant resort hotel and stood facing the sea. Breathing deeply and staring out at the warm blue waves, Jack was about to go back in when he spotted a man in the distance hang gliding over the water, the breeze lifting the glider higher and higher in the wind. Jack shoved his hands in his pockets and watched, trying to deny the feelings of envy he had for the man. *No, I'm not getting restless,* he told himself. He wasn't regretting his bargain with Amanda. It was just the fact that he was on holiday and away from his job. He would be fine once he got back to work.

Amanda had just pulled on her jeans and shirt when room service arrived with their breakfast. She poured them each a cup of coffee, and Jack disappeared into the bathroom with his while she lounged in one of the chairs and nibbled her sweet roll. She was having the time of her life on this trip, and she was falling in love with Jack more deeply by the day. They were lovers, friends, confidants, all the things a man and a woman were supposed to be to one another. She reveled in the sharing, and she had never been happier in her life.

Jack was finished in the bathroom in record time. He devoured a couple of sweet rolls and burned his mouth on a cup of coffee. "Damn, that's hot!" he exclaimed.

"Hey, slow down!" Amanda said. "We have all day, remember?"

"But the tour starts in just a few minutes," Jack protested,

"Let's forget about the tour and just go out on our own," Amanda suggested. "I'd rather skip the tour guide patter anyway."

Agreeing with Amanda, Jack sat down and ate the rest of his breakfast a little more leisurely. They left their hotel and walked down the long street that ran parallel to the harbor. Amanda was surprised at how few actual sandy beaches Cozumel had. In most of the town the vegetation appeared to drop right off into the crystal-clear water. She and Jack had spent a lot of time in boats since they had arrived, and in most places the water was clear for sixty feet or so.

They walked for several blocks down the busy main street and rented a jeep at another of the hotels. Jack's Spanish was passable, and he was able to get directions to the ruins from the man at the rental agency. "He said it was a pretty wild ride out there," Jack told

Amanda as they climbed into the ancient jeep. "It's through an overgrown bush, apparently."

Amanda glanced at a late-model Cadillac as it passed by. "Mexico is certainly a land of contrasts," she remarked as she thought of the sophisticated nightclub they had enjoyed last night.

Amanda was hot and dusty by the time they had bumped their way out to the ruins. "Is this all there is?" she asked as she looked around at what wasn't much more than the outline of what had once been a Mayan pilgrimage spot.

Jack climbed out of the jeep and wandered around the ruins a little. "It's kind of weird to think that people came here a thousand years ago to worship their gods."

He stared over at Amanda. "I'm sorry there isn't more. I hope you're not too disappointed."

"No, not at all," Amanda assured him. They wandered around the ruins and made their way through the jungle to the highway that would lead them back to town. Once there, Jack persuaded Amanda that they should rent motor scooters, and they spent the next hour exploring the main street of town. When they returned to the hotel they changed into their swimsuits and paid one of the boat owners to take them out into the bay for another afternoon of scuba diving. The water was incredibly clear, and Jack and Amanda spent most of the rest of the day diving around an airplane sunk just off the beach for the filming of a movie.

They returned to their hotel room late in the afternoon, and Amanda collapsed across the bed. "I'm worn out!" she complained.

"I guess those last three dives did you in," Jack teased as he lay down beside her. He kissed Amanda on the forehead. "I'm sorry if I wore you out. We'll lie around on the beach all day tomorrow."

"And the day after that we have to go home," Amanda said, wrinkling her nose. "Back to the old grind." She shut her eyes and snuggled up against Jack. "Do you suppose we could manage to stay here forever?"

"Not unless you want to work as a dishwasher in the kitchen," Jack warned her playfully.

"I wonder what they pay hotel security?" Amanda asked idly.

"Probably not enough," Jack replied. "Does it really bother you to have to go back?"

"No, I just like to complain," Amanda admitted. She turned over on her side. "Wake me up in an hour or so. We can try the restaurant at the Hotel de Leon, if you like."

"Sounds fine to me." Jack lay still beside Amanda and tried to nap with her, but after fifteen minutes or so, he abandoned the attempt and got up. Out on the balcony he sank into a lounge chair and propped his feet on the rail.

There were the hang gliders again. Jack watched them soar above the water, dipping and curving as the riders skillfully rode the wind. Jack could vaguely remember his father in a hang glider, laughing as he came within inches of hitting a tree. Jack envied his father that day, and he admitted to himself that he envied that carefree flier. He knew that hang gliding was dangerous and that Amanda wouldn't like it, but he still wished he were out there, soaring above the town.

Jack tried to convince himself otherwise, but down deep he knew he was getting restless. It had been seven weeks since the accident on the track, seven weeks since he had given his promise to Amanda, and he was getting antsy already. It hadn't bothered him too much before the wedding, because there had been a lot for him to do to get ready for the marriage, and because the extra hours spent on investigating the poisonings had left him very little leisure time. But now the wedding was over, he was away from his job, and he was beginning to feel slightly bored. He missed a feeling of excitement and challenge. He had been so restless today that he had literally worn poor Amanda out. She was sound asleep, and he was sitting here wishing he were out on a hang glider.

But it'll be all right once we get home, he assured himself. Even though he wouldn't be participating in his hobbies anymore, he would have the excitement of his work to fill the need for challenges in his life. Amanda and the police department would keep him busy—or at least he hoped they would.

Chapter Twelve

"Jack, do you want to have a Christmas tree this year?" Amanda asked as she sipped her morning coffee.

"Huh?" Jack responded, looking up from the paper. "What was that, Amanda?"

"I asked if you wanted to have a Christmas tree here this year," she repeated. "I know it's just the two of us, but I thought it would be nice, since it's our first Christmas together."

"I guess so. By the way, did you ever find anything to give my mother?"

"I got her a jade pendant that would go with her best suit," Amanda said. "Do you think she'll like it? It's beautiful, and it didn't put me back an arm and a leg."

Jack looked skeptical. "She's never worn too much jewelry."

"Should I take it back?" Amanda pressed. "I thought she probably didn't have much because she couldn't afford it."

Jack shrugged. "You're probably right. I'm sure that's fine." He jumped up and kissed Amanda's warm lips. "Gotta go," he added in a rush.

"Jack, don't run off yet!" Amanda said as she jumped up and followed him into the living room. "Do you want to go with me after work to pick it out?"

"Pick what out?" Jack asked as he put on his shoulder holster.

"The *tree,*" Amanda answered, her patience sorely tested.

"Oh, sure, hon. See you at the lab!"

Amanda made a face as the front door slammed behind him. She loved Jack, but there were days she just didn't understand him. They had been married for two months now, and although Amanda had never been so happy in all her life, sometimes she felt that Jack was more a mystery to her now than he had been when they were going together. For the most part he was still the easygoing man she had fallen in love with, but now that Amanda was actually living with him, she was aware that he could be a moody person at times. Sometimes he was distant and distracted—like this morning—and occasionally he could be downright snappish. Amanda usually nipped those moments in the bud with a snap or two of her own, but she was surprised that Jack was even capable of being so irritable. She had certainly never been aware of it before they were married.

Amanda finished her coffee and put the breakfast dishes in the dishwasher. If Jack had been willing to wait just fifteen minutes, they could have driven in together, as they sometimes did. But he had seemed restless and eager to leave this morning, and Amanda hadn't seen the point in asking him to wait. Besides, he might have to stay late, and she had too much to do to get ready for Christmas to want to wait for him.

Amanda went into the bedroom to gather up her purse and jacket. She smiled as she looked at their wedding picture framed on the dresser. *Jack's moods aren't really all that bad,* she thought. *He's no more restless than my own father was.* Although Jack sometimes annoyed her, she loved him more each day.

Jack pulled onto the expressway, gunned his truck, and sped past an old Chevrolet. He gritted his teeth, wishing he were on the racetrack and not in the middle of morning traffic—he wanted to floorboard the truck so badly he could taste it. He hadn't realized how much he enjoyed driving fast until he no longer had a legal outlet to do so. In fact, he missed all his hobbies. He missed the thrill of roaring around another car, of free-falling through the air, of staying on top of a bucking bull. He would have given his eyeteeth this morning for just one bull ride.

Jack whipped around an old lady in a Buick and grinned when she made an obscene gesture at him. He could just see Amanda doing something like that when she was old. He couldn't picture his wife ever growing mellow with the years. Although they hadn't had any real arguments since the wedding, she had snapped at him a couple of times when he had gotten irritable with her, and Jack didn't think she would ever change much. He frowned as he thought of Amanda. He loved her more than he ever thought possible. He wanted to make her happy, yet he was beginning to chafe under the bargain they had made. He dearly missed his exciting hobbies and was becoming dismayed to learn that even his deep love for Amanda couldn't take their place in his life.

Amanda spent the morning matching blood samples in a grisly shotgun murder. Since Jack was out on an investigation and couldn't have lunch with her, Amanda ate a taco from a nearby stand and spent her lunch hour in the shops on Houston Street, looking for the perfect Christmas present for Jack. She didn't want to buy him clothes, since he was so particular about style and fit, but she wanted to get him something personal. She wandered through several men's stores and a couple of department stores and was about to give up when she saw something out of the corner of her eye. She whirled around and spotted a small gold pinkie ring, molded into the shape of an old pickup truck. Without bothering to check the price, Amanda hurried into the jewelry store and collared a saleswoman who was about to leave for lunch. "Could you please show me the pinkie ring in the window that looks like a truck?" she asked breathlessly.

The woman glanced over at her boss, who glared at her warningly. She turned back to Amanda, her expression leaving no doubt as to how she felt about having her lunch hour delayed, but she retrieved the ring from the window and showed it to Amanda. The ring was perfectly crafted. It cost more than Amanda expected, but she wrote a check for it without flinching and managed to make it back to the lab only a few minutes late.

Amanda beat Jack home and had supper nearly ready when he drove up. He kissed her thoroughly, scratching her face with his whiskers. "Ouch!" Amanda complained, but she did not try to move away from him.

Jack reached up and fingered the red mark. "Sorry. I'll shave before we go out for the tree."

They ate a quick supper and Jack ran his shaver over his face before they drove to one of the Optimist lots that were scattered across the city. Jack held up nearly every tree in the place for Amanda to inspect. After a little friendly squabbling they settled on a small pine. Their next stop was the five-and-ten, where Amanda picked out several boxes of ornaments, a tree stand, and a string of lights. They had just paid for their purchases when they heard a familiar voice boom across the store. "Jack Vance. Jack! Where have you been, you son-of-a-gun? Everybody at the track misses you."

"Johnny!" Jack exclaimed. He spotted Johnny Howard across the store and made a beeline for him, Amanda trailing behind with the sack of ornaments. "How are you doing these days?" The men shook hands and Amanda freed a hand to shake Johnny's.

"John's winning every race, now that you and Perry Purcell are out of the way," Johnny said. "Where have you been?"

"Uh, I've been awfully busy on the investigation," Jack replied. "The pressure's really on from above. And I've also been busy with my wedding and honeymoon."

"Yes, I'm sorry we couldn't make the wedding, but we had a race in Dallas we'd been entered in for the last six months. I figured you'd understand."

"We did, and thank you for the gift," Amanda put in graciously. "Have you heard from Perry Purcell?"

"He's doing just fine. They had a little girl, I guess you knew. Anyway, according to Perry's doctors, he should be able to race again sometime after the first of the year."

"That's good news," Amanda enthused, missing the look of envy that passed across Jack's face.

"Look, I won't keep you," Johnny said. "I know you have things to do. Merry Christmas. I'll be looking forward to seeing you at the track again."

"Me, too," Jack returned quietly as he started out of the store.

Amanda followed Jack to the truck and dumped the sack of ornaments between them. "I'm glad to hear that Perry's going to be all right." As Jack started the engine she added, "He's a lucky man."

"Yes, he is," Jack said a little sullenly.

Amanda made several attempts at conversation on the way home, but Jack exasperated her by answering in monosyllables. They carried the tree into the house and fitted it into the tree stand. "Do you want it in front of the window?" Amanda asked.

"I don't care," Jack answered irritably. "Put it where you want it."

"I know where I'd like to put it," Amanda snapped back as she dragged the tree across the floor and positioned it in front of the window.

Jack shot her a dirty look as he took the string of lights out of the box. "I don't want to argue tonight."

"And I don't need your surly temper," Amanda retorted, hurt.

"Sorry," Jack mumbled. He tried to untangle the lights but only made them more hopelessly snarled than ever. "Damn these things," he said finally, throwing them on the couch in exasperation.

"Give them to me." Amanda sat down on the couch and started patiently untangling the lights. "What's eating you, Jack? You were antsy this morning, and you're downright cranky tonight. What's the matter? Am I burning the biscuits?" she teased.

"Come off it, Amanda," Jack replied irritably. "I'm not in a mood for your jokes."

"All right...I'm through joking. What's eating you?" Amanda demanded.

"I'm as restless as a frog in hot water," Jack admitted.

"Why?"

"Why do you think?" Jack returned. "I'm bored, that's why."

Amanda flinched. "I'm sorry you find our marriage boring," she managed to say stiffly. "Maybe I should do a striptease to music tonight to liven things up some." She untangled the last of the lights and started to string them on the tree.

"It's not you and you know it," Jack said gently. "I'm perfectly happy with you. I love you, and I love being married to you."

"So what is it, Jack?" Amanda coaxed.

"I miss the racing..." Jack confessed, "and the riding and the skydiving. Don't look at me like that, Amanda. I can't help it if I like those things."

"Jack, you can't mean that you want to go back to them," Amanda said, her voice low with anger and hurt. "You promised me." She clipped a couple of lights on the tree. "You gave me your word."

"I know I gave you my word," Jack snapped. "That doesn't mean I don't miss them." He took the string of lights from her and strung them around the back of the tree.

"I guess seeing Johnny Howard got you all stirred up. You've never mentioned this before tonight."

Jack opened a box of ornaments and started hanging them on the tree. "No, I've never mentioned it before tonight, but that didn't mean I didn't think it or feel it. I broke every speed law in the state this morning getting to work, because I kept pretending that I was racing. I miss it, Amanda. I want to start racing again."

"And bull riding...and jumping out of airplanes, too, I guess," Amanda added bitterly. She picked up the other box of ornaments and hung a few on the tree.

"Yes, I want to do those things," Jack continued. "Or at least one of them. I'd feel a whole lot better."

"No way," Amanda responded through clenched teeth. "You promised me you wouldn't, and you're going to keep your promise."

"Amanda, you're not being reasonable," Jack pleaded. "I didn't say I wanted to go back to all of them, or even to one, on a regular basis. But Amanda, I need to do something. I'm going crazy."

"Take up the guitar. Or join a health club. Learn to play racquetball. Buy a computer that plays video games. Jack, there are any number of things that the rest of us mortals manage to entertain ourselves with. You don't have to be flirting with danger to have a good time."

"Those aren't enough," Jack said coldly. "I miss the things I enjoy. And how do you think I felt when Johnny said they missed me out there? Well, I miss them, too."

"So go out and watch them race," Amanda suggested. "You don't have to race yourself."

"I'd rather take a shower in a raincoat," Jack answered bitterly. "You're not being fair, Amanda."

"Oh, no," Amanda countered. "I'm not the one who's not being fair. You made me a promise, and now that we're married you're trying to renege."

"You made me promise," Jack snapped. "You made me give them up before you would agree to marry me."

"You bet I made you promise. And I'm going to make sure you keep your word. Either you stay away from the dangerous hobbies, Jack—all of them—or I pack up my clothes and my furniture and walk out that door."

"That's really rotten of you, Amanda," Jack said as he shook his finger at her. "You know I'm miserable and you don't even care."

"No, I don't care, because it's your own fault you're miserable," Amanda screamed back at him. "You're too lazy to get up off your duff and go find something that you'll enjoy doing. You'd rather fidget and snap at me because you don't have anything fun to do."

"Maybe if I didn't feel like a bird in a cage, I wouldn't fidget and snap at you. But that's how I feel, Amanda. Trapped. Stuck. Tied down. Restless. I'm sorry if that doesn't suit you, Amanda, because that's the way that I am."

"Tough," Amanda replied coldly, looking Jack in the eye. "I meant what I said. Either you live up to your promise or out that door I go. Make up your mind, Jack."

"What would you do if I called your bluff?" Jack asked angrily.

"I think we both know what I'd do." She put the last ornament on the tree and took Jack's present from her purse. "Merry Christmas," she added as she put the brightly wrapped box under the tree.

"Same to you," Jack returned angrily.

Amanda slammed the door to their bedroom behind her and marched to the shower. There was no way she was going to let him renege on his promise. Amanda trembled with anger as she showered and pulled a nightgown over her head. He had sworn that he wouldn't put his life on the line needlessly, and she was going to hold him to that. If he was bored, that was just too bad. There were a thousand things he could get out and do for fun that wouldn't kill him sooner or later. Amanda turned back the covers and crawled into bed. Somehow she knew that she would be sleeping alone tonight. She knew that Jack was as angry as she was, and that he would probably sleep in the guest bedroom where they had put her bedroom furniture. Amanda sighed deeply as she looked at the alarm clock. It wasn't all that late, but as angry as she was, she knew it would be hours before she could go to sleep. She took a long, involved paperback novel out of the drawer of the nightstand. She had meant to read it sooner or later, and tonight would be a good time to get started.

***

Jack stared down at the drink in his hand. He would have liked another one, but it was late and he had to get up in the morning. He had spent the evening watching reruns and hoping that Amanda would come out of their room and talk to him, but he should have known she was too hardheaded to do that. He had made her angry, really angry, tonight, and he knew she wasn't going to come out of that room until she got over her anger. Jack put his glass in the sink and took a shower in the second bathroom. He started to go into their room to get a pair of jockeys but climbed into the bed naked instead. He wasn't going to be the one to make the first move.

Jack pulled the covers up to his chin and stared into the darkness. He had to admit that he could see Amanda's point. She was honestly worried about him, and he knew that she had a right to expect him to live up to his word. But couldn't she see that he was restless and unhappy? Didn't she care that he was miserable? Couldn't she see that he missed his sports? Jack knew that he was trying to change rules that he had already agreed to, and he knew that it was wrong to do that to Amanda. But couldn't she try to understand the way he felt?

***

"Would you like some more coffee?" Amanda inquired politely of Jack as she poured herself another cup.

"Yes, thanks." Amanda poured some in his cup. He nodded as he sipped it and turned back to the sports page.

Amanda looked at Jack and sighed. He was just as cool toward her this morning as he had been every morning for the last week. For the first few days, that had been fine with Amanda, but in the last day or two her temper had cooled and she hated the strain between them. She desperately wished they could get back to the warm, intimate relationship they had shared before their argument. But she had been no warmer toward him than he had been toward her. And since she wasn't about to change her mind about his participation in his dangerous hobbies, she was very much afraid that the strain wasn't going to ease any time in the near future unless Jack got over his anger with her.

Amanda finished her breakfast and was loading the dishwasher when the phone rang. "Amanda, this is Tony. We need you and Jack as soon as possible. Are you about ready to go?"

"Not another poisoning," Amanda exclaimed.

"Well, we're not sure." Tony gave her an address in the rather exclusive Terrell Hills area. "Can both you and Jack report there immediately? You're reporting officially, by the way. We need a forensic chemist on this case."

"Officially?"

"Yes, the lab will be notified," Tony said.

Amanda wrote down the address. "We'll be there."

"What's up?" Jack asked as he put his dishes into the dishwasher.

"Tony wants us both to meet him at this address," Amanda answered as she handed the scrap of paper to Jack. "There may be another poisoning."

Jack's eyes widened. "Let's go," he said, throwing on his shoulder holster and running out the door.

Amanda gathered up her things and locked the door behind her. "Maybe this will be the break you need," she ventured hopefully as Jack backed out of the driveway.

"I hope it is," Jack replied grimly. "We need some kind of a break. This has gone on too long."

Tony met them at the door of an exclusive townhome. "This is a little strange, but I felt it was worth checking out," he said under his breath. Jack and Amanda stepped into an expensively furnished living room, which contained a fortune in jade carvings in a bookcase along one wall. "Mr. Osterman, this is Detective Jack Vance and our forensic chemist, Amanda Vance. They've been working together on the poisonings. Jack, Amanda, Sid Osterman. Mr. Osterman called us about an hour ago."

Amanda immediately recognized the name of one of San Antonio's most successful corporation attorneys. "Mr. Osterman, it's a pleasure," she said as she extended her hand.

"I bet I took you two away from breakfast," he commented as he shook their hands. He motioned for them to be seated. "I know my story's going to be a little peculiar, and I hope there's nothing to it. But with all that's been happening lately, I thought I better go ahead and contact the police." The well-dressed man blushed and looked miserably embarrassed. "Last night, I met a young woman and brought her back here. When I woke up this morning she was gone. Sneaked out without a trace. And with all the poisonings that have been going on, I got suspicious."

Amanda and Jack glanced at one another. "What did she look like?" Jack interrogated.

"She was a redhead," Mr. Osterman said. "Flaming red hair all the way to her waist."

"How was her hair styled?" Amanda asked. "Is there any possibility that the hair was a wig?"

"Wild...lots of curls. Yes, I guess it could have been a wig."

"We'll check the pillowcases for a hair sample before we leave," Amanda put in.

"What about her face and figure?" Jack quizzed.

"Dynamite figure, what I could see of it. She pretty well managed to stay under the covers," Mr. Osterman replied, blushing again. Amanda wondered whether his discomfort was from prudishness or whether he was embarrassed at being caught going to bed with someone who probably wasn't of his social stature. "Her face was really sort of ordinary. Or at least I think it was, under all the makeup."

"Well, it could be our lady," Jack stated. "Was anything in the kitchen disturbed?"

"No, and I haven't touched anything in there," he said. "Just in case she left fingerprints."

Tony handed Jack and Amanda a pair of gloves. There were no jars or bottles out on the counters that would have been easy to poison, so Amanda cautiously opened the cabinet doors. The cupboard was pretty bare, with only a few cans of food and a jar of instant coffee. "Is this all you have?" Amanda inquired.

"Since my divorce, I've mostly been eating out," Mr. Osterman admitted.

Amanda picked up the jar of coffee and opened it.

"This coffee has white grains mixed in with the brown. Put it in the bag, and we'll test it."

"How about in here?" Jack asked, opening the refrigerator. It was as bare as the cupboard, populated mostly by jars of condiments and cans of beer.

"Take all the jars," Amanda instructed. "If they don't turn up anything, we'll test the top of the beer cans."

"Go ahead and take them if you like," the nervous attorney encouraged. "I won't be able to eat anything out of this kitchen now."

Jack shrugged and packed up the beer. "We'll test all this, and if we find anything in them, we'll need a statement from you."

"I'll be more than glad to cooperate," Mr. Osterman replied quickly. "And I hope I'm wrong—I really do. Trish seemed like such a nice person."

"Trish?" Jack asked. "Did she give you a last name?"

"No. She just called herself Trish."

"Did she say anything else about herself?" Jack pressed.

Sid thought a minute. "She said she worked deep in the barrio."

"Did she say what she did?" Amanda inquired. "Any clues at all?"

"Not in so many words, no. But later she made a joke about dying early from air pollution," he continued. "When I said something about San Antonio having good air, she said that she was exposed to lots of chemical fumes at work."

"Southwest Research!" Amanda exclaimed triumphantly.

"That's hardly in the barrio," Jack said. "That's on the outskirts of town." He turned to the attorney. "Did she say anything else at all?"

"Not really. I asked her to dance, and we spent most of the evening on the dance floor. She was really good."

"Did she know the latest steps?" Amanda asked.

"She sure did. In fact, she said something about the kids teaching her—"

Sid broke off his sentence as the three of them looked at each other in horror. "She's a teacher," Amanda uttered softly.

"She teaches in a barrio school," Jack said. "She's exposed to chemical fumes in the laboratory."

"And the kids teach her the latest dance steps," Sid added.

"She either teaches chemistry or one of the other physical sciences," Amanda declared. "That narrows the field quite a bit."

Sid Osterman looked a little green. "A teacher killing people. That's horrible!"

"Gives me the creeps," Amanda admitted. "I hope it's not her."

Jack and Amanda thanked Sid Osterman and got into the car. "You know, I do hope you find something in one of those jars," Jack stated as he pulled onto Broadway. "If that's our lady, this is the best lead we've had yet."

Jack fidgeted around the laboratory while Amanda prepared a sample of the coffee to go into the mass spectrometer. "My, our lady is imaginative," she said a moment later. "This time she tried to use ergot."

"So it *was* her," Jack exclaimed. "This is the best break yet."

"Does this mean I won't see you for the next week?" Amanda teased.

"Probably," Jack flipped as he sailed out the door.

Amanda shook her head and turned to the rest of the food from the Osterman kitchen, which she would test just to make sure.

Maybe this break in the case was just what Jack needed. It would absorb enough of his time and his energy so that he wouldn't have a chance to get restless or bored, and it would take his mind off the fight they had last week. Maybe now the tension would ease between them.

***

"Is Tony still here?" Jack asked no one in particular as he stepped into the homicide division's drab office.

"He's across the street testifying, but he said he wouldn't be too long and for you to wait for him," Eddie Gutierrez explained as he put on his overcoat. "I'd stay, too, but I've still got to go shopping for Sylvia's Christmas present, and I don't have the vaguest idea what to buy for her. Do you think she'd like an exercise bicycle?"

"She's going to think you're trying to tell her something," Jack answered dryly.

"A fancy negligee? Or would she think the same thing?"

"She might not mind that message," Jack replied, laughing.

"A sexy nightie it is, then," Eddie said. "See you later."

Jack leaned his chair against the wall and shut his eyes. He still hadn't found Amanda anything for Christmas, and it was less than a week away. With the strained atmosphere between them, he didn't feel free to come out and ask her what she wanted. Jack sighed and asked himself if she was ever going to forgive him. He had been angry himself for several days, but he had gotten over his own anger and desperately wanted to get back to the kind of relationship they shared before the argument. But he wasn't much good at backing down, and he sensed that she wasn't either.

Jack was still thinking about how to get back into Amanda's good graces when Tony returned from the courthouse. "Taking forty winks?" he teased when Jack's eyes flew open.

"I wasn't asleep—I was thinking about what to get Amanda for Christmas," Jack explained.

"I know what you mean," Tony agreed. "I had a mink jacket all picked out for Doris, then our whole central heating unit blew up. Now I don't know what I can get her that I can afford and she'll like."

Jack made a face. "That's too bad."

"So what did you find out?" Tony asked as he pulled up a chair.

Jack spread out three profiles on the desk. "I checked with the personnel offices at all the school districts located anywhere near the barrio. This is what I came up with. There are three women teachers at three different high schools who somewhat fit the physical description of the killer. Any one of them would have access to the poisons that have been used, and all three of them are described by their fellow workers as being somewhat quiet and remote."

"What about the men who have been in contact with our killer?" Tony pressed. "Were any of them able to make any kind of identification?"

"Not on the basis of the photographs in the personnel records or in the yearbooks," Jack admitted. "Take a look at the photographs. The three of them look quite a bit alike, when you get right down to it."

Tony looked at the three photographs. "Nothing special, any of them," he said. "I wonder if one of them has a birthmark on her bottom?"

"Remember, only Onion Burns saw that," Jack pointed out. "That's a rather shaky point of identification."

"You're right." Tony looked at the photographs again. "We'd probably have trouble getting a decent identification even in a lineup," he sighed tiredly. "Apparently she disguised herself pretty well before she went out on the town."

Jack took another look at the three plain-looking women in the photographs. "You put a little makeup and a different hairstyle on one of these three, and she'd look entirely different. So what do we do now?"

"It's going to take a lot of man-hours I don't have, but I'm putting all three of these ladies under surveillance," Tony said. "I have a strong feeling that our killer's in this trio, and that it will just be a matter of time until she strikes again."

"It may be several months until she tries something," Jack warned. "Are you really going to keep up surveillance on all three for that long?"

"If I have to," Tony declared. "And I doubt that the brass is going to give me a hard time about it, as much pressure as there is to solve this crime."

"Yeah, I read in the newspaper that this has wrecked the sex lives of most of the single males in San Antonio," Jack put in, laughing. "Everybody's scared to go out and meet people."

"Well, I guess everybody's got their problems," Tony said. "I'll start the surveillance tomorrow. Now I've got to try to find my wife a decent Christmas present for fifty dollars. See you."

Jack picked up the profiles of the three women and read through them again. There wasn't a thing in any of the information that indicated that any one of them was capable of being a killer—nothing in their faces that indicated the kind of cruelty or madness that this kind of killing required. But it was one of them. It *had* to be. Jack shivered a little and put the profiles in the file. Maybe the surveillance would turn up something before she had a chance to strike again. But he wasn't going to worry about it anymore tonight. Tonight he had to worry about finding his wife a Christmas present—and easing the strain that had grown up between them.

Chapter Thirteen

"Amanda? Are you ready to go?" Jack demanded impatiently as he drummed his fingers on the counter at the front of the lab.

"Almost," Amanda replied, turning off the microscope light. "George Hoffsteader needed me to get this match today if I could."

"Did you?" Jack asked as Amanda picked up the telephone.

"No, his suspect couldn't possibly have robbed the house," Amanda said. "George? Amanda. No match. Sorry." She listened for a moment. "Oh, George, how awful! Let me know if you need me to do anymore work for you. Yes, I'd be willing to come in tomorrow if you need me to. Sure, no problem. See you."

"What does George think he needs you tomorrow for?" Jack inquired, a little irritated, as Amanda logged her test results in the book. "Robberies can usually wait until a weekday, can't they?"

"Yes, but under the circumstances I offered to come," Amanda answered rather sharply. "George thinks the old couple might have been robbed by their own child, and that he might try to harm them. The sooner he has a match, the sooner he can arrest the son."

"Ugh, that's sick. No wonder he wants you to come in. Sorry if I seemed impatient," he apologized as he squeezed Amanda's hand. "It's just that tomorrow's the first Saturday I've had free since Christmas, and I was looking forward to spending it with you."

"I know," Amanda uttered softly. "I'm looking forward to it, too. Besides, he probably won't need me. My offer was for just in case."

"Good," Jack said as they got into Amanda's Mustang. "I wish it weren't too cold to put the top down."

"We'd turn into a couple of popsicles," Amanda teased. "I can just see the headlines now—'San Antonio Policemen Frozen in Upright Position.'"

"Mandy, you're cruel," Jack laughed.

Amanda laughed with him, and Jack thought he had never heard a lovelier sound.

***

It had taken them both awhile, but they finally put their argument behind them and were back to the way they had been before. Amanda loved the gold ring, shaped like a rose that he gave her for Christmas. She had worn it every day on her little finger next to her wedding rings. He, in turn, loved the pinkie ring and wore it constantly. Their marriage was on sound footing again and would have been completely happy but for his moodiness and the irritability he didn't seem able to keep under control.

Jack still missed his dangerous hobbies. He missed them more than ever, and he was growing even more restless than he had been last month. Although he desperately tried to hide it from Amanda, he was unhappy a lot of the time. He didn't dare admit to her why he was irritable, so he used the stalled investigation as the excuse for his behavior and hoped that she believed him.

"So are we going out to dinner or to a movie?" Amanda asked.

"Either. Both. Why don't you decide?" Jack suggested.

Amanda opted for a quick dinner in a Mexican restaurant near the neighborhood theater, thinking they would have plenty of time to make an early feature. But they had to wait for a table, and the service was so slow that they hadn't even been served dinner by the time the movie was to begin. "Slowpokes," Jack snarled as the fat waitress waddled away after informing them that their dinner was going to be a few more minutes. "Why can't they get their act together?"

"Jack, it doesn't matter that much," Amanda said softly. "You weren't that excited about seeing a movie in the first place. Why are you so grouchy tonight? Have I done something to annoy you?"

Jack shrugged. "No, it's not you, Mandy. And you're right—it's not that I care all that much about the movie. I don't know what's the matter with me."

"Are you sure?" Amanda pressed gently. "Can't you talk to me about it?"

"I guess the investigation's bothering me again," he hedged.

The waitress finally arrived with their plates, accompanied by an extra basket of tortillas because they had to wait for so long. "You've had those women under surveillance for the last month," Amanda said thoughtfully. "Hasn't anything turned up?"

"All sorts of interesting things have turned up, but not one thing that would shed light on the poisonings. None of them drives a green Monte Carlo. One goes out to a nursing home every week to visit her grandmother, one has her dog groomed every Saturday, one's having an affair with her principal—"

"What?" Amanda asked, laughing.

"You think the police department's the only place that kind of thing goes on?" Jack teased. "Anyway, as I said, we've learned all kinds of things—but nothing that would point to any one of them being a killer. Tony's beginning to think maybe Sid Osterman's date was feeding him a line."

"I don't know," Amanda replied. "Of course, the killer might be a former chemistry teacher who's doing something else now. But what about you, Jack? What do you think?"

"I still think it's one of the three," he affirmed. "And Tony's not going to stop the surveillance on any of them in the near future."

"That's wise," Amanda agreed. They talked a little shoptalk and a little about other things. Since they didn't particularly want to wait for a late showing of the movie, they went by a bookstore in the shopping mall for their evening's entertainment. Amanda spotted the latest marriage manual and insisted that they buy it for fun. Later they curled up together under the covers, intending to read it and laugh. Instead they ended up trying chapters two and three, kissing and caressing and laughing under the covers, until Amanda was exhausted and spent. Overcome by a sleepy haze of sexual satisfaction, she curled up beside Jack and dozed off.

Jack waited until Amanda was sound asleep before he crawled out of bed and pulled on a robe. He made his way to the kitchen, poured himself a drink, and sat down in his easy chair to think. He had lied to Amanda when she asked him why he was so irritable. But how could he tell her the truth? He tried last month, and it resulted in a cold spell that had been forever thawing. He was not going to risk a second round of that. He would lie to Amanda rather than make her that angry with him again. But he didn't know what he was going to do about the increasing restlessness that he felt. He had thought he would get used to not having his exciting hobbies, but he was missing them more, not less, as time went on.

***

"If that's another poisoning I'm going to scream," Jack said groggily as the telephone pierced the early morning quiet.

"I'll second that," Amanda groaned as she picked up the receiver. "George? Yes, you woke me up, but that's all right. Yes, I'm still willing to come in." Amanda made a face. "No one deserves a son like that. See you in a little while."

Amanda hung up the telephone and crawled out of bed. "Sorry, I have to go in," she explained as she started gathering up her clothes.

"I heard," Jack said as he rolled over and put his hands behind his head. "Will you be long?"

"I shouldn't be," Amanda replied. "This shouldn't take more than an hour or two."

"I'll wait for you, and we can go somewhere afterward."

"How about horseback riding at Brackenridge Stables?" Amanda suggested. "We had fun the last time we did that."

"Sure, sounds great," Jack agreed. He dozed while Amanda got ready to go, but once she was gone he was wide-awake—the same old restlessness dogging him. Of all days for Amanda to be called into work.

Jack's restlessness did not improve when Amanda called him at ten and said that there had been a mysterious death overnight involving a prominent citizen's child, and that Tony wanted her to go ahead and do the chemical analyses in that case, since she was already downtown. Jack cleaned the house, not doing as thorough a job as Amanda but finishing much more quickly, and was about to get in the car and go for a drive when Buddy Ecbert called. "Say, Melissa and I are in town, and we thought we'd call and say hello. How have you been?"

Jack assured him that he and Amanda were fine. They talked a little about the wedding and the Ecbert's Christmas, and Buddy spent fifteen minutes extolling the meanness of his new Brahma bull. "You ought to come up and give him a try, Jack," Buddy crowed. "He'd give you the ride of your lifetime."

Buddy finally hung up, after repeating his invitation for Jack to come up anytime and ride his bull. Jack sat down on the couch and tried not to think about the last time he had ridden a bull, but the memory came back to haunt him, like the flavor of a fine wine. He shut his eyes and could feel the rush of adrenaline he always experienced when the bull lurched out of the chute and started twisting in the air. He could feel perspiration dampening his forehead as he tried unsuccessfully to put the longing—the urge to ride—out of his mind. But he couldn't do it. The need, the desire to ride again, was too strong to be denied.

Jack rummaged around in the back of the closet and found his riding clothes. He pulled them on in feverish haste and stepped into his run-down boots. There was a place out south of town that would set up a bull for three dollars a ride. The bull wouldn't be as strong or as mean as Buddy's, but it would be a bull and he could ride it. Just once or twice, just enough to get it out of his system. He would come home and wash and dry his clothes, and Amanda would be no wiser. Jack felt a momentary pang of guilt for what he was about to do, but the desire was just too strong. Besides, what Amanda didn't know wouldn't hurt her.

Jack drove to the small farm that featured bull riding and amateur rodeos. It was too early for the drunken-dare bunch to be there yet, so the only men present were either practicing for competition or sport riders like himself. He paid his money and a huge giant of a farm boy set up a rather old-looking bull in the chute. "Want me to time you?" he asked Jack laconically.

"Sure, if you don't mind," Jack replied as he gripped the rope. His eyes were shining and his cheeks were flushed. This was great! He was riding again!

The old bull gave Jack a better ride than he was expecting, but he managed to stay on the full eight seconds.

He let himself fall off, rolling one way as the bull ran the other. "Purty good, sir," the farm boy said. "Want to wait your turn and ride again?"

"You bet!" There were three bulls in use this afternoon and four riders, so Jack got a different bull the second time he got up to ride.

The second bull was something of a disappointment. Jack rode the eight seconds easily, then quickly got back in line for a third ride. He counted ahead, and the next time he knew he would get the big black bull that looked like he was almost as good as Buddy's bull had been. Jack waited impatiently for his turn to come up, and he eagerly crawled up on the back of the big, angry animal. "Let him go, son!" he told the boy.

The boy opened the gate and the bull ran out, pitching and bucking wildly. "Ooh—ee!" Jack yelled as his hat blew from his head. This was living! He pitched and lurched with the animal as the bull kicked high in the air.

The wind whistled around Jack's ears as he felt himself falling. He pitched forward, tumbling into the dirt. The bull continued forward, kicking Jack neatly in the ribs as he ran past him. Jack cried out as the sharp hoof caught him, and then moaned as he rolled in the dirt. The farm boy ran the bull into the chute as Jack struggled to sit up. He finally was able to push himself into a sitting position, but his chest ached more with every breath he took. Jack unbuttoned his shirt and looked down at a mass of quickly darkening bruises. "Oh, hell," he muttered. "That damned bull broke my ribs."

***

Amanda looked up from the computer console and rubbed her neck. She wished for Tony's sake that the results had been more conclusive. She picked up the telephone and punched in Tony's extension. "Tony, this is Amanda. The blood analysis reveals a combination of alcohol and barbiturates that would be sufficient to kill her, all right. But other than those two bruises the medical examiner told you about, there's no evidence of foul play."

"Wonderful," Tony said dryly. "Is it a murder or isn't it? Her father's demanding a complete investigation." The daughter of a prominent family had been found dead in the early hours of the morning, and the press had jumped on this story, giving it a tremendous amount of publicity.

"I'm glad I don't have your job this afternoon," Amanda admitted. "See you Monday."

Amanda cleaned up the lab and was about to leave when the telephone rang. "May I speak to Mrs. Vance, please?" a youthful-sounding voice asked.

"This is Mrs. Vance," Amanda responded.

"Mrs. Vance, I'm Hugh Green. You don't know me, but I brought your husband in to the hospital this afternoon. He's in with the doctor now. He asked me to tell you to come out right away."

"Is this some kind of prank?" Amanda demanded. "My husband's at home today."

"No, ma'am, this isn't a prank," the voice said quickly. "Mr. Vance really was hurt this afternoon. If you can't get away, I guess I could take him home."

"How was he injured?" Amanda asked anxiously.

"He was injured out at our ranch," the boy explained briefly.

"Oh no!" Amanda cried before she uttered a word that made the farm boy blush. "I'll be right there," she said before she slammed the telephone in the boy's ear.

Amanda broke every speed law in Texas getting to the hospital. "Oh, please be all right," she whispered over and over as she parked her car and raced to the emergency room. "Where's Jack Vance?" she demanded of the clerk at the desk.

The clerk yawned. "You need to fill out these papers," she said as she shoved a stack of official forms at Amanda.

Amanda shoved the forms back at the clerk. "Later," she broke in curtly.

"I'm sorry, the forms must be filled out now," the clerk insisted.

"I said *later,*" Amanda snapped, beside herself with worry. "Where's my husband?"

The clerk took one look at Amanda's face and decided not to argue. "4C," she replied stiffly.

Amanda ran down the hall and pushed open the door to the cramped emergency room. "Jack, are you all right?" Jack was perched on the edge of the examining table. His chest was badly bruised, but otherwise he seemed all right.

Jack looked at her sheepishly. "The doctor says I have three broken ribs. They won't tape them—they say I just have to tough it out."

Relief flooded through Amanda. "How did it happen? Were you out there investigating a murder?"

Jack's face turned red. "No, I was out there riding a bull."

At first Amanda was more shocked than anything else. "You were riding a bull," she began slowly. "But you don't do that anymore. You gave me your word you'd given it up."

"Amanda, I'm sorry," Jack said quietly.

"You broke your promise to me," she accused, more to herself than to him.

"Amanda, I—"

"If you're well enough, perhaps we should go home," she said coldly.

Jack eased himself to the edge of the table and Amanda instinctively reached out to help him down. "I have to fill out the insurance forms," she muttered flatly. "Can you sit on one of the chairs in the waiting room?"

Jack nodded and followed her down the hall to the waiting room. He started to object when she stepped to the window and said that he would fill them out himself, but he changed his mind when he saw her frosty expression. Besides, every breath he took was torture.

The ride home was made in silence. Amanda glanced at Jack several times, but she could see nothing but physical discomfort in his expression. He had broken his promise to her. She considered that promise sacred, and he had broken it. Tears welled in Amanda's eyes, and she bit her lip to keep them from falling. She was just hardheaded enough that she didn't want Jack to see how badly he hurt her.

Jack couldn't tell from Amanda's expression just what she was thinking. He knew he really let her down this afternoon, but the desire to ride again had been too strong to be denied. He tried to keep his promise, but he slipped this time. He was smart enough to know that he would slip again in the future. He was going to have to explain that to her this evening and hope that she would understand.

Jack followed Amanda into the house and lay on the couch. Amanda disappeared into the kitchen for a minute and returned with a stiff drink that she handed to him. "Thanks," he said as he sipped her offering. "I probably don't deserve this."

"You don't," Amanda declared, her face cold. She sat down in the chair across from the couch. "And I don't deserve what you did to me this afternoon."

"Mandy, I'm sorry. I tried to keep my promise to you—honestly I did. I'm sorry I couldn't."

"Couldn't? You just flat didn't," Amanda said. "You went out there, willfully, after you'd promised me you wouldn't. Is this the first time, or have you been sneaking around behind me since we got married?"

"No, this is the first time," Jack confessed. He looked at Amanda. Her expression seemed to demand his honesty. "But it probably won't be the last."

"Thanks a lot," Amanda replied bitterly. "At least I know how much your promises mean. Did you mean any of the other ones you made? The ones to love, honor, and cherish? Or do you intend to break those, too?"

"Oh, for crying out loud, this isn't like that at all," Jack protested. "It's not like I cheated on you or something like that."

"To me it is," Amanda said quietly. "That was a sacred vow to me, Jack, just as important to me as the ones you made at the altar." She sniffed back tears. "And you broke it. I thought you loved me more than that."

"I *do* love you, Amanda," Jack insisted.

"Surely you don't expect me to believe that, if you don't care enough about my feelings to stay out of danger," Amanda returned coldly.

"Amanda, please listen to me," Jack pleaded. "Look, I tried to stay away from everything, honestly I did. But I was miserable. And then Buddy called and I got to thinking how much I loved it. Amanda, it was like I couldn't *help* going out there this afternoon. It was like I had to go—do you know what I mean?"

"No, I can't say that I do. I can't say that I've ever felt the urge to destroy myself that deeply."

"Amanda, it's not like that!"

"Then what would you call it? You're like an alcoholic or a compulsive gambler, Jack. Danger attracts you like a magnet. At work or at play, it makes no difference, as long as you can put yourself in danger and get your kicks. I'm sorry to say it, Jack, but I think you have a psychological problem."

"I do not have a psychological problem!" Jack snapped. "Just because I like—"

"But it isn't just a matter of 'liking' with you," Amanda pointed out. "You couldn't stop yourself from going out there this afternoon—you said as much yourself." Her voice softened. "I think you should talk to somebody about this, Jack. I want you to talk to a professional."

"I'm not crazy!" Jack yelled. He groaned and clutched at his ribs. "This hurts so much."

"I didn't say you were crazy," Amanda said. "I said you have a psychological problem of some kind." Amanda stopped and bit her lip. "You would have to, to be so enamored of dangerous things. You're drawn to them like a moth to a flame, and you need professional help to cope with it. I want you to seek help, Jack. You have to. For the sake of our marriage. I love you, but I can't stay married to you, not knowing when I'm going to have to rush to the hospital again, wondering if someday I might rush there and be too late."

"No way," Jack declared flatly. "There's no way I'm going to talk to a shrink. If I have a problem, then so do a lot of other people. There are a lot of people who race and ride bulls and jump out of planes."

"Rationalizing won't work this time," Amanda answered levelly. "Will you talk to somebody or won't you?"

"No," Jack said curtly.

"Very well," Amanda replied sadly. She got up and disappeared into their bedroom.

Jack lay still for a few minutes, but the silence from their bedroom was deafening. He eased himself up and opened the bedroom door. "What in hell are you doing?" he demanded when he saw the open suitcase on Amanda's side of the bed.

"What does it look like I'm doing?" Amanda said bitterly. "I'm moving out."

"Don't be ridiculous," Jack snapped as he pushed the half-packed suitcase off the bed. The motion sent his chest into agony, and he collapsed into a chair.

"You do that again and I'll punch you in your broken ribs," Amanda threatened as she gathered up her clothes and put the suitcase back on the bed.

"You're not leaving me," Jack insisted through clenched teeth.

"Why should I stay? You broke your promise to me. You promised me that you'd stay away from bull riding, and you went anyway. I can't stay under those circumstances. Don't you see?" She shut her suitcase and took her makeup kit into the bathroom, where she gathered up all her cosmetics.

Jack was still sitting in the bedroom chair when she came out. "You're not going to solve anything by leaving," he said bitterly.

"No, I'm probably not," Amanda admitted. "But I can hardly stay under the circumstances."

"What circumstances? I did something I said I wouldn't and got hurt. Is that worth leaving me over?"

"You broke your promise to me," Amanda cried, tears shimmering in her eyes.

"I'm sorry!" Jack bellowed.

"So am I, Jack," Amanda said as tears started to roll down her face. "If you want to take chances with your life, then be my guest, but don't expect me to live in fear that you're going to be killed. I can't stay here when I can't trust you. I'm sorry, but I'm not going to stick around here and watch you kill yourself. I just can't stand it."

"Amanda, please," Jack pleaded, following her to the front door. "Please don't go."

Amanda turned, tears streaming down her face. "I have to, Jack. Maybe someday you'll understand that. Please, for your own sake, think about getting some counseling."

"I do not have a problem!" Jack snapped bitterly.

"If you say so, Jack," Amanda said. "I'll move my furniture when I find a place to live."

Jack watched in horrified disbelief as Amanda shut the door and walked out of his home and his life. She had done it—she had left him for breaking his promise to her. Jack slowly made his way into the kitchen, where he poured himself another drink. Perhaps it would help take away the pain in his chest, but nothing was going to take away the pain in his heart. He thought she loved him. Had he been wrong?

Jack eased himself down on the couch and sipped his drink. *Yes,* he decided when about half the drink was gone, *she loves me.* But she didn't love him in the right way, or she would have been able to forgive him for today. Instead she had walked out of the door and taken the joy out of his life—all because of a damned bull ride. And he had to admit that he was more than a little angry with her for that.

Jack finished his numbing drink and thought about what Amanda had said before she had left. She had accused him of having a psychological problem, of not being able to control his risk taking. Jack thought about his behavior—about the racing and the skydiving, the bull riding and the chances he took on the force. *No,* he assured himself, *there's nothing compulsive in my behavior.* He didn't have any kind of problem. He just liked those things, that's all.

Chapter Fourteen

"It never ceases, does it?" Jack complained tiredly as he and Eddie left a small house in the barrio, clutching several evidence bags each. They had just finished collecting evidence on what looked like a bad ending to a lovers' spat.

"Murders...or lovers' quarrels?" Eddie asked as they got into the car.

"Both, I guess," Jack replied as he backed out of the driveway. A small dog ran out in front of him and he had to slam on the brakes suddenly. "Sorry," he said as Eddie grabbed the dash.

"That's all right," Eddie returned, glancing at Jack. "Say, I've been meaning to ask you all day how you skinned up your hand like that. I hate to think what the other fellow looks like!"

Jack looked down at his raw knuckles. "I did that falling off a bull Sunday," he admitted.

Eddie didn't try to hide his exasperation. "Jack, when are you ever going to learn? You just got over a bout with broken ribs, and you're back up there again. You could get hurt really badly the next time."

Jack shrugged. "What would it matter?" he asked bitterly.

"It would matter a lot to your wife and mother," Eddie responded dryly.

"Mom's used to me by now, and I don't have a wife anymore—at least not one who cares. Haven't you noticed?" Jack didn't even try to hide his hurt and bitterness.

"I think she cares."

"Then why isn't she with me?" Jack demanded. "Where is she when I get home at night?"

Eddie pursed his lips. "I don't know, Jack. Have you talked to her about it?"

"Of course I have. I talked to her the day she left, and I talked to her again a week later. That woman's as hard-headed as one of those bulls I ride. No, on second thought, she makes the bulls look like pushovers. She refuses to come back."

"She flat refuses?" Eddie pressed. "That doesn't sound like Amanda."

"Well, not exactly," Jack admitted. "She says she won't come back to me unless I seek counseling. She's got this screwy notion that I'm addicted to danger or something asinine like that. She's acting like I'm some kind of basket case."

Eddie was quiet for a moment. "Have you considered that it might be worth going? Oh, not that anything's wrong with you—just to humor her?"

"I'm not going to run up an expensive shrink bill just to humor my wife," Jack replied hotly. "There's *nothing* wrong with me."

"Hey, you don't have to convince me," Eddie said. "It was just a thought." Jack pulled into the department parking lot, and Eddie hopped out of the car. "You go ahead and take the evidence bags to the lab," he directed. "I'll get started on the report."

"Eddie, wait!" Jack called, but Eddie was already on his way across the parking lot. Jack made a rude sign in Eddie's direction and climbed out of the car. This was the third time in three weeks that Eddie had invented some way to throw Jack and Amanda together. Eddie meant well, but sometimes he could be a pain in the rear.

Jack gathered up the evidence bags and trudged toward the lab. He dreaded seeing Amanda these days. It hurt to know he couldn't touch her or make love to her again. He would have given anything to have her back.

Well, almost anything. He had already considered Eddie's suggestion that he visit a psychologist just to please her, but his pride wouldn't let him yield to her demand. There was absolutely nothing wrong with him other than a little bit of restlessness. He refused to spend a bundle of money to have somebody tell him so.

***

Amanda sat with her feet propped up and sipped a cup of bitter coffee. Her body ached and she felt feverish, but she refused to give in to the inevitable and go home sick. She had spent most of the morning giving evidence in George Hoffsteader's case, and she would be in contempt of court if she didn't return at two. Samantha had gone out for hamburgers, but feeling a little queasy, Amanda decided to stay in the lab. All she wanted to do was go to bed and sleep for a week.

Amanda saw the door open out of the corner of her eye, and a familiar blond head look into the room. Her heart started pounding, and she cursed the trembling in her fingers. "Amanda, I have some blood samples for you to check out—" Jack began as she swung her feet to the floor and stood, swaying only slightly. "Amanda, are you all right?"

"No, I'm not all right," Amanda said dryly. "I'm as sick as a dog."

"Then why don't you go home?" Jack asked irritably. "You shouldn't be here if you're sick."

"I would go home if I weren't due back in court at two," Amanda snapped. But at the expression of concern in Jack's eyes, her irritation faded, leaving only deep tiredness in its place. "Believe me, the minute I step off the witness stand I'm going home." She took the evidence bags from Jack and logged them in. "Routine blood typing?" she asked, her stomach becoming even more upset as she eyed the contents of the bags.

"Yes, that's what we need."

Amanda finished logging in the bags and sat back down in her chair. "God, get me through the rest of this day," she moaned. She put her head in her hands, unable to cope with the potent sight of her estranged husband. She had missed him horribly day and night for the last month.

She looked up a moment later and saw Jack still staring at her. "Are you still here?" she asked miserably. "I thought you'd gone."

"I can't leave you like this," Jack protested. "Let me take you home tonight. I can take care of you."

Amanda shook her head. "That's all right. Once I get home I'll be fine."

"Wherever you're staying isn't your home," Jack responded bitterly. "Your home's with me."

"Not anymore, ace. What are you going to be this weekend—an Indy winner or a rodeo star?"

"Neither. I have to work," Jack replied stiffly.

"And last weekend?"

"I rode bulls," Jack said defiantly.

"I'm sure your healing ribs loved that. All happy again, Jack? No more irritable spells, no more restlessness?"

"I'm as lonely as hell," Jack admitted. "Come home, Amanda. Please."

"Not until you at least talk to somebody about this compulsion of yours," Amanda insisted.

"No way," Jack answered coldly. "There's nothing wrong with me. If you think I'm—"

"Well, did you nail him?" Samantha asked as she sailed into the lab carrying a sack of hamburgers. She skidded to a halt when she saw Jack and Amanda together, her eyes wide with curiosity. "Sorry, I didn't bring three."

"That's all right, I'm leaving," Jack said stiffly.

"You don't have to go," Amanda protested as she struggled to her feet. "Give him my hamburger, Sam. I'm going to the ladies' lounge to lie down before I have to go back to the courthouse." She staggered to the door. "Come get me at a quarter till."

"Here, you may as well eat it." Samantha thrust one of the hamburgers at Jack. "She hasn't been hungry for the last three days."

"She's been sick that long and she's still coming to work?" Jack demanded incredulously. "That's ridiculous."

"Not when you have three major subpoenas in three days," Samantha returned coldly. She eyed Jack stonily as she munched on her hamburger.

"I guess she didn't have too much choice," Jack conceded. He ate a quarter of the small hamburger in a single bite. "Is her mother taking care of her?"

"Her mother's on a Caribbean cruise right now," Samantha said.

"You mean she's sick like that and there isn't anybody taking care of her?"

"Well, you're her husband—where are you?" Samantha exploded. "Out riding a bull?"

Jack's face and ears turned a bright shade of red. "If you'll tell me where she's staying, I'll go over and take care of her until she gets better," he said stiffly.

Samantha eyed him suspiciously, but she tore off a piece of paper and wrote down an address. "She lives in this complex. I'm not sure of the number."

Jack shoved the paper in his pocket. "I'll make sure she's all right." Samantha's expression did not soften. "Look, Samantha, I know you think I'm the world's biggest heel, but I do love her."

"So why don't you take her home?"

"I'm trying, Sam. Believe me, I'm trying."

***

Amanda lay on the couch and stared at the ceiling. She needed to get up long enough to get out of her work clothes and take a shower, but every bone and muscle in her body ached. It had been all she could manage to drive her car home and climb the stairs to the dismal little apartment. She had intended to spend the weekend moving her things out of Jack's house and into an unfurnished unit, but now that was going to be impossible. Amanda hated admitting it to herself, but a part of her was relieved that she couldn't do it just yet. As long as her possessions were still at the house, she could pretend that they just might patch things up between them. Moving her furniture into a new place seemed so final.

Amanda jumped and swore as she heard a loud knock on the front door. She stumbled to the door and threw it open, not even bothering to check out the peephole first. "Jack," she said rather rudely. "What are you doing here?"

"I came to take care of you this evening," he replied as he moved her to one side and carried in a small flight bag. "I'm staying until you can manage on your own."

"I was managing just fine, or so I thought," Amanda answered dryly. She swayed with a sudden attack of dizziness and Jack pushed her onto the couch.

"Sure you are," he jeered gently as he pulled off her shoes. "Good night, you're probably burning up with fever. Have you called the doctor?"

"I went yesterday. It's just the flu," Amanda protested.

"Still, your fever's too high," Jack insisted, touching her forehead. He stood her up and marched her into the minuscule bedroom. "A cool shower will start to bring that down."

Despite Amanda's protests, he stripped her and stood her under the shower for several minutes. He dried her, dressed her in one of her oldest and most faded nightgowns, and laid her down on the couch while he opened her a can of chicken noodle soup. With his coaxing she ate most of it and then fell into a deep sleep. Jack sat with her half the night, staring into her feverish face, before he went to sleep.

Amanda's temperature was still high the next morning, but she insisted that Jack go on to work. He agreed only when she gave him a key to let himself in when he came back later, in case she was asleep. Amanda alternated between the bed and the couch all day, dozing a lot of the time and reading a little. Jack came back about four, armed with a TV dinner for him and soup and crackers for Amanda. He sat on the couch beside her as he told her a little about his day. Later he fixed her supper and dosed her with aspirin.

Sometime in the night Amanda's fever broke. She woke feeling extremely thirsty and found her bed and nightgown soaked through with perspiration. She eased out of bed and tried to find another gown in her drawer, but she bumped her knee on the nightstand and swore sharply in the darkness. "Amanda, are you all right?" Jack inquired anxiously as he jumped off the couch and turned the hall light on.

"Yes, I'm fine. I was just trying to find a dry gown."

Jack switched on the bedroom light and gasped when he saw Amanda's nightgown and hair. "Good grief, you're dripping wet!" He fumbled around in the drawer and found another gown. "Lift your arms," he instructed.

Obediently Amanda did as he said. Jack pulled the gown over her head and replaced it with the other one.

"We have to get rid of those sheets, too." Amanda watched mutely as he stripped and remade her bed. "Now, get back in and go back to sleep," he said as he held the covers for her. "You're probably still as weak as a kitten."

Amanda nodded, hating the dizziness that was beginning to overtake her. "Can I have some water?"

Jack brought her a big glass and watched as she sipped most of it. "Now you won't be so dehydrated in the morning," he said. "If you're not awake, I'll try to be quiet so you can sleep."

Amanda nodded and shut her eyes. The next time she opened them, it was nearly noon. She felt well enough to put on a pair of jeans and make herself a bowl of oatmeal. Then she spent the afternoon laughing at the soap operas. She was about to call Samantha and see how things were at the lab when the telephone rang. "Amanda, this is Jack. I just thought I'd call and see if your stomach could tolerate a pizza tonight."

"Sounds fine. But you don't have to—"

"I'll be there within the hour," Jack signed off.

Amanda hung up, her call to Samantha forgotten. Before, she had been too ill to really appreciate how well Jack had taken care of her, but now that she was better, she had to face him—and her feelings for him. A part of her wanted very much to go back to him, but she knew that would be impossible. She couldn't take the constant worrying about him; she couldn't spend the rest of her life wondering if he was safe or not.

Jack arrived exactly an hour later. "You look better," he said, running his hand down the side of her face.

"I feel better," she admitted. "Those pizzas smell delicious."

"I thought you might be hungry." They set the table and Jack poured them each a glass of iced tea.

They were both hungry and managed to make quick work of the pizza. "That was good," Amanda sighed as she refilled her iced tea glass. "I haven't been that hungry in the last mo—since I got sick."

"I thought you looked thinner last night," Jack observed.

Amanda blushed. "I needed to lose a few pounds."

"You've always looked just fine to me," Jack said softly.

Amanda got up abruptly and put her plate in the sink. "I'll wash these later."

"No, I can wash them," Jack insisted. "You go sit down."

Amanda sat down on the couch and listened to Jack's humming and splashing as he cleaned up the dishes. When he was finished, he sat down beside her on the couch. "I've missed you, Mandy," he murmured.

"I've missed you, too, Jack," Amanda admitted as her eyes filled with tears. She cursed her weakness and wiped them from her eyes.

"Come home, Amanda," Jack pleaded, reaching for her.

Amanda stood up quickly and stepped away from him. "I can't do that, Jack. We've been through this over and over again."

"What if I promised you that I would give up all my hobbies and kept my promise this time?" Jack asked.

Amanda bit her lip and turned around to face him. "Jack, we've been this route already. You tried, and you were miserable. You were like a junkie without a fix. You could promise me a million times that you weren't going to do any of those things anymore, and you would break your promise every time. Don't you think I know you wanted to keep your promise to me?"

Jack winced at her insight. "I guess you have a point," he answered heavily. "Do you think you could try to accept the hobbies if I'm careful?"

"I don't care how careful you are—they're dangerous," Amanda returned. "And I don't care how much you protest, that's what draws you to them in the first place. The danger. The thrill of taking a chance. Of beating the odds one more time. But someday your time's going to be up, Jack, and something bad's going to happen to you. I just can't spend the rest of my life wondering if today's going to be that day."

"I see." Jack fiddled with his wedding ring.

"Have you thought anymore about talking to someone about this?" Amanda pressed softly.

"I'm not crazy," Jack protested.

"I never said you were. I just think it might be helpful to at least look into it."

Jack looked at her for a moment. "Is that what it's going to take to get you to come back to me?"

"Yes, I guess it is," Amanda admitted. "Well, are you angry?"

"Yes," Jack responded levelly. "I don't like living my life dancing to meet your conditions and requirements, Amanda."

"And I don't like living mine worried sick about you. I'm not trying to run your life, Jack. I just want you to be around to live it. Is that so wrong?"

Jack shrugged. "I guess not." He stood up and kissed her cheek lightly. "I'll see you sometime in the next few days," he said. "Call me if you need anything."

"Sure." Amanda locked the door behind him and watched him drive away. At least they hadn't yelled and screamed at each other this evening, but she felt that they were just as far apart as they'd ever been. She couldn't understand his compulsion to participate in dangerous, thrilling sports, and he couldn't understand her fear every time he did so. Amanda sighed and wiped fresh tears from her eyes. Maybe she ought to go ahead and move her furniture out of his house, divorce him, and get on with her life. It didn't look like they had any kind of a future together.

***

Jack coughed and sniffed as he locked the door of his house and got into the car. He hoped this was just a cold and not Amanda's flu. The last thing he needed right now was to be as sick as she had been. It had been three days since he had left her at that dismal little apartment, and he missed her more now than he had when she had first left him. His time with her, even though he had only been nursing her through the flu, had been precious to him and had only intensified his longing for her.

Jack's forehead knit into a frown as he pulled onto the expressway and fumed as usual at the bumper-to-bumper traffic. He had put in a lot of time thinking since he had seen Amanda last about her insistence that he talk to a professional counselor of some sort. She had not been upset this time when they had talked, so he had to dismiss the notion that she had been hurling accusations in anger. Apparently she really thought he had some kind of problem. And it wasn't like Amanda to imagine neuroses around her all the time.

Jack scratched the space between his eyes and took a cloverleaf. Was it possible that he did indeed have some kind of compulsion? He had known for a long time that he didn't have the same response to danger that other people had. He simply did not feel the queasiness, the hesitation, the terror that they did. In fact, the only time he could remember being really frightened by something was the day Perry Purcell had been seriously injured on the racetrack, and that day his fear had come only after the accident.

But did that mean he had a problem? *Well,* he thought, *whether I have a problem or not, seeing a counselor might be the only way I can persuade Amanda to come home to me.* It didn't look like she was going to change her mind and come back to him on any other terms. Even his promise wasn't good enough for her anymore. He would have to think about it, but maybe after they got this investigation of the poisonings out of the way, he might find a psychologist and make an appointment.

Jack took the downtown exit and pulled into the parking lot. He ran up the stairs and loped into his office only a few minutes late.

"Sorry," he mumbled when he saw the rest of the poisoning team already assembled.

"No rush," Tony said. "Pour yourself a cup of coffee and sit down."

Jack got his coffee. "Is Amanda in on this one?" he asked as he pulled out a chair.

"She would have been, but she had a bad backlog of work waiting for her this morning," Eddie replied. "Samantha went home sick the day after Amanda did."

"Besides, we really won't need her expertise today," Tony began. "What we've got to decide is what to do about the surveillance on the chemistry teachers. So far we've turned up nothing but one affair, and it's costing us manpower we could sure use somewhere else. Do we abandon the surveillance, or do we continue it?"

"Have any of them gone out besides the one who's carrying on with her boss?" Tom Black asked.

"Yes, all three of them have gone out a few times. Jennifer Bradley, the one who's having the affair, likes to go to country and western clubs. The other two have been to several different nightclubs and bars. But none of them appear to be really into the singles scene, and none of them so far have actually gone home with anyone."

"Were any of them dressed strangely, or did they appear to be trying to disguise themselves?" Ray Torres inquired.

"One of them, Marianne Sharp, likes to affect the punk look, and of course the one who goes to the country bars tries to look like Annie Oakley, but no elaborate disguises, no," Tony qualified.

"Were they approached?" Jack asked.

Tony looked through the reports. "Apparently they talked to a few men while they were there. But half the single women in San Antonio do that."

"So you're saying that no one really came on to them while they were out," Jack said thoughtfully.

"Our men weren't close enough to overhear what was being said, but in their opinion none of the conversations ever got to the your-place-or-mine stage," Tony replied. "Jack, correct me if I'm wrong, but I have the feeling you have something up your sleeve."

"What if the next time one of our lethal ladies goes out on the town, she has a man put the make on her? What if we give her a chance to poison someone?"

"One of us, huh?" Eddie mused. "And I don't have to guess twice who that man will be."

"Jack, I'm not sure I like it," Tony put in.

"Why not?" Jack demanded. "It sounds perfect to me. I pick her up, take her back to my place, and the next morning we check the place for poison. If she's left me a little souvenir, we arrest her."

"Amanda's going to love this one," Eddie chimed in dryly. "Adultery with a murderer."

Jack flushed a deep shade of red. "I wouldn't actually go to bed with her. There's such a thing as drinking too much and going to sleep, you know. I've done it for real a few times in my life, and I think I could fake it. And if I can't, Eddie can show me how."

"I'm sure you can manage to fake it on your own," Eddie shot back.

"And there are other last-minute excuses," Jack said. "Lots of them that I could use."

"Jack, it's not your morals I'm worried about," Tony said honestly. "It's your safety. She could poison anything in your kitchen. She's been pretty inventive so far. I'm worried we won't find it before you get hold of it accidentally."

"That's easy," Jack explained. "We test everything in the kitchen. Everything. Plates, knives and forks, condiments in the refrigerator, towels, paper napkins. We don't leave one thing in that kitchen untested. And I call you the minute she leaves. I won't touch a thing until you get there."

"I guess that'll take care of your safety," Tony conceded reluctantly, "but I can't help feeling like this is too risky."

Jack grinned wickedly. "I've got to liven this department up somehow," he teased before he covered his mouth and coughed.

"Going to seduce her, or take her home to nurse you?" Eddie inquired sarcastically.

Jack coughed again. "I hope to convince her I have the sexiest cold in San Antonio."

"Well, try to get over it before the weekend," Tony said. "One or the other of them is bound to go out again, and if you really want to, you can try to pick her up and see what happens."

"Yes, I want to," Jack answered, his eyes gleaming at the prospect.

"Jack, there's a call for you on line two," one of the men called from one of the inner offices.

Jack disappeared into the office and shut the door behind him. "Are you really going to let him stick his neck out like that?" Eddie asked Tony under his breath.

"I don't like it, but we've gotten nowhere so far," Tony replied. "Besides, it's his neck, and for all the chances he takes, he's never gotten hurt yet."

"Amanda's going to skin him alive when she finds out about it," Ray declared. "Hell, that's why she left him, or at least that's what I heard. I don't even want to be in the building when she gets the word."

"Fellows, that's their problem, not ours," Tony said. "And if he can pull it off, more power to him."

***

Jack sat in front of the television set and blew his nose as he tried to get interested in the newest episode of *Miami Vice*. His cold was getting worse, and he wished he could go to bed. But Tony promised to call him if one of the teachers went out tonight, and he had three sets of clothes laid out just in case he got the call. He had carefully gone through the house and removed everything that might even hint that he was a police officer. He started to remove all evidence of Amanda, too, but decided that it might be more practical to have an estranged wife in the background. He was going to need an excuse for not going through with a seduction, and an attack of guilt would work just as well as going to sleep. Jack had to have an out of some kind—he had no intention of breaking his marriage vows with any woman, especially a murderer.

The telephone rang just as the late movie came on. "Jack, Laura Simmons just parked in front of Extravaganza. She's not wearing a wig, but she's heavily made up and she has a red rinse on her hair. She's wearing a blue lame jumpsuit."

"I can be there in ten minutes." Jack dropped the telephone and jumped into the flashy set of clothes he had laid out. He shoved the others under the bed and ran out to the sporty Datsun that Ray had insisted he borrow. He made it to Extravaganza in record time and gave his breathing a chance to slow as he sauntered into the reverberating disco. A dozen pairs of feminine eyes turned in his direction from the bar, admiring him openly for a moment before they turned back to their drinks and their conversations. Jack scanned the room and groaned inwardly when he saw the woman he knew to be Laura Simmons engaged in what looked like an intimate conversation with a good-looking young man. He hadn't gotten here in time. Well, he could watch her and see if she stuck with the man for the evening. If she did, they would just have to ring the man's doorbell in the morning and test his kitchen for poison.

Jack ordered a club soda and lounged by the bar. Laura and the man visited for a few more minutes before the man paid for their drinks and excused himself. Jack eased his way across the room and gestured to the empty chair at her table. "Is this seat taken?" he asked as he looked into Laura Simmons's eyes.

"No, and I'd love for you to sit down," Laura returned, her voice a smoky alto. "Come here often?"

"Sometimes," Jack replied as he sat down across from her, continuing to maintain eye contact. If this woman indeed was their killer, Jack was surprised that none of the other men had noticed her eyes. They were amber—yellow, almost—and shone with the light of intelligence and something else. What was that elusive something he could see in her eyes? Was it just excitement, or was it a little bit of madness? "How about you?" he asked. "Are you a regular?"

"Hardly. But I come here sometimes. What's your name?"

"My friends call me Max," Jack said. Eddie and Tony had called him that all week to get him in the habit of answering to it. "How about you?"

"I'm Suzi."

A thrill ran through him when Jack heard her give a false name. That was definitely a strong indication she was the woman he was looking for. "Well, Suzi, how about letting me buy you a drink?" Jack offered as calmly as possible.

"Suzi" nodded and Jack ordered her the whiskey sour she asked for and a scotch for himself. They sipped their drinks and exchanged the friendly, flirtatious banter that was standard conversation at a singles bar. But underneath her pleasant and rather funny conversation Jack could sense some undercurrents from Laura that made him more and more suspicious. There was just something strange about her. Jack tried to maintain his professional objectivity about the woman, but he had a hunch, a very strong hunch, that this one was his killer.

The throbbing rock music faded into a slow, sensuous number. "Care to dance?" Jack asked.

"Love to," Laura said. She slid out of the chair and Jack nearly gasped at the spectacular proportions of her figure. No wonder the men had been so enamored of her body. Jack felt a momentary qualm as he held out his hand to her—investigation or no, it just didn't feel right to hold another woman's hand or to dance with anyone but Amanda. But he was on duty, he reminded himself as he took Laura's hand and led her to the dance floor. It was just play-acting, at least on his part.

Laura slid into his arms and pressed her body close to his. Jack's arms tightened around her and suddenly his heart was pounding. Was he dancing with a killer? Was the beautifully built woman in his arms responsible for the poisonings that had rocked San Antonio for the last ten months? A delicious sense of excitement overtook Jack—not sexual excitement but the rush that always came over him whenever he took a chance. This woman might try to kill him tonight. If she did, he was going to catch her and bring her to justice.

They finished one dance and shared another before returning to their table. Jack deliberately kept the conversation light, not wanting to have to make up a long, involved lie about himself, and Laura appeared quite content to do the same. They talked and flirted and danced and drank, and as the evening wore on, Jack was more and more convinced that this woman was the killer. He couldn't put his finger on anything in particular about her that made him feel the way he did. Her behavior was quite calm and sane and normal. But there was something about her—maybe the unnatural brightness of her eyes—that made Jack believe she was the one.

They danced and they drank until almost closing time. "Want to take a chance on me tonight?" he asked, thinking she would favor the direct approach. "I don't think this cold's still contagious."

"Sure, I'd love to. Is your place all right? I have a roomie."

How convenient, Jack thought. "Want to ride with me?"

"I have my car here. How about letting me follow you? It's new, and I hate to leave it overnight."

She has the lines down pat, Jack thought. He escorted her to a new Topaz, ignoring the undercover policemen waiting in the shadows, and kissed Laura as she got into her car. "Don't get lost on the way," he said.

"Never," she promised him.

Jack took several deep breaths. She had taken the bait. She was coming to his house, and she was going to try to kill him tonight. Now the only thing to do was to decide what ruse to use to get out of actually sleeping with her, and then give her a chance to leave her poison behind. He started the engine of the Datsun and headed toward his house, the only outward sign of his excitement the whiteness of his knuckles as his hands gripped the steering wheel. Laura was the one. She had to be the killer. And tonight he was going to catch her in the act.

Chapter Fifteen

Jack flipped on the light and stood aside so that Laura could enter the house. "Would you like a drink?" he offered.

"Sure, if you don't think you've had enough," Laura replied. "Nice place. You live here alone?"

"More or less," Jack admitted. "My wife moved out awhile back. What would you like to drink?"

"Do you have the ingredients for a Tequila Sunrise?" Laura asked.

"I think so." Jack paused. "Let me check."

"Bathroom?"

Jack pointed down the hall. Laura ducked into and out of the bathroom and followed Jack to the kitchen. She watched him as he rummaged around in the cabinet and checked in the refrigerator. "Suzi, you're in luck," he said as he got out the orange juice. "Two Tequila Sunrises coming up."

Laura looked over the kitchen while he mixed the drinks. "Are you divorced, or just separated?" she inquired as Jack handed her the drink.

"Just separated for now," Jack replied as he sat down on the couch beside her. "Why? Do you have a thing about the divorce being final?"

"Oh, no, nothing like that," Laura assured him. "I just don't want an irate wife storming in on us." She snuggled closer to Jack. "I want your complete attention until morning."

"Believe me, you'll have that," Jack vowed as he put his free arm around her. He drank deeply from his glass and pulled Laura close to him. "You'll be the only woman on my mind until morning." *And all day tomorrow and probably the day after that,* he added silently to himself.

He downed the rest of his drink, and Laura took the glass from his hand and set it on the coffee table. She kissed him, her breath warm and smelling of her drink. *I may be kissing a killer,* Jack thought as he pulled her into his arms and crushed her to him. He felt a rush of adrenaline, the same rush he felt in the bar when he had danced with her. Jack's face grew flushed and his eyes bright, and Laura had no way of knowing that his excitement was from the thought of catching her, not the prospect of making love to her. *I'm going to nail her,* Jack thought as he ran his fingers down the hollow of her spine. *I'm going to nail this lady to the wall.*

They kissed for long moments, and Laura started to unbutton Jack's shirt. Jack looked down at her eager hands as she pulled his shirt from his body. Jesus, he was going to have to come up with something to stop her before she went much further, he thought as her long fingers raked through the thick hair on his chest. He wasn't about to actually have sex with her, and Amanda deserved better out of him than his letting this killer feel him up. "God, if the rest of you's this good, I can hardly *wait,*" Laura uttered, eyeing him as a hungry cat eyes its food. She pushed his shirt off his body and ran her fingers down his side. "Beautiful, just beautiful," she whispered, like a rich woman admiring a jewel she has just bought. "I can't believe your wife left a gorgeous specimen like you."

And there he had his out. A truthful out, actually, Jack thought as he let himself stiffen. "Damn, did you have to mention *her*?" he demanded as he backed away from Laura. "That's the last thing I needed to hear right now."

"What's with you?" Laura demanded. "You just said I'd be the only woman on your mind until morning."

"I thought you would be," Jack said as he made himself look guilty. "Damn it, Suzi, did you have to remind me that I'm still married? Now I don't know if I can even go through with it."

"Whoopie damn do," Laura said disdainfully. "A boy scout." She moved away from Jack as he re-buttoned his shirt. "I gather the whole thing's off?"

Jack hoped he looked sheepish. "I guess so, Suzi. Sorry."

"In that case I'm out of here." She grabbed up her purse and headed for the front door.

"You don't have to go running out of here, you know," Jack said quickly. "Why don't you sit back down and at least finish your drink." Damn, she hadn't really had a chance to leave her poison behind. Somehow he had to give her that chance.

Laura stopped and eyed the unfinished Tequila Sunrise. "Don't mind if I do." She picked up the drink and curled up into the chair across from the sofa. "So tell me—why *did* your wife leave a hunk like you?"

When lying, stick as close to the truth as possible, Jack thought. "She doesn't like my dangerous hobbies and I don't like her telling me what I can and can't do."

Laura's eyes narrowed. "I know that feeling," she said enigmatically. "I hate it when someone else thinks they can order me around. So tell me about these hobbies she hates so much."

Much to Jack's surprise, they talked for almost an hour. Jack gave her a carefully edited version of his life as a stock car driver and bull rider, and Laura talked about an almost idyllic upbringing in East Texas. Jack wasn't sure if it was his imagination or not, but it seemed like the strangeness in her eyes he noticed in the club had disappeared, and he hoped it hadn't just been his imagination all along. He deliberately let her go into the kitchen by herself to freshen their drinks, hoping she would feel free to leave behind her lethal souvenir.

When she finally wished him a good evening and left the house, Jack gave her five minutes to get out of the neighborhood before he called Tony.

"She's gone now. You can come on over."

"Took you long enough," Tony replied dryly. Tony and Eddie had been waiting at Tony's, which was just a few blocks from Jack's. "I gather she had a chance to leave something behind?"

"I gave her every opportunity," Jack declared. "Come on over and I'll tell you about it."

Jack had touched nothing in the house, including the drinks in the bedroom. "How was it?" Eddie asked as he came in the door.

"I had a sudden attack of conscience and we ended up talking for the better part of an hour. She wanted to know why my wife left and I gave her a carefully edited version of the truth. And then she told me all about her wonderful childhood."

"You're kidding," Tony exclaimed.

"Didn't you get even one kiss?" Eddie wheedled.

"Of course," Jack retorted scornfully.

"And...?" Eddie prompted eagerly.

Jack shrugged. "She's all right, but I'd rather kiss Amanda."

"Eddie, if you and Jack could save show and tell for later, we could get this kitchen cleaned out," Tony interrupted.

The three of them packed up everything in Jack's kitchen. Jack had thinned out the contents of his cupboards considerably in anticipation of this, but there were still a lot of things to put in the evidence bags. They would have Amanda test the food first; if that turned up nothing, they would test the silverware, china, and pots and pans. Jack hoped that she had poisoned some article of food because that would save Amanda a lot of work.

"That's the kitchen," Tony finalized as they sealed the last evidence bag. "How about the rest of the house?"

"That ought to take care of it," Jack put in. "When is Amanda going to start running the tests?"

Tony looked at his watch. "It's nearly four now. I'll call her first thing in the morning."

"Can't you go ahead and call her now?" Jack pressed eagerly before he coughed into his hand.

"No, I think we could all do with a couple hours of sleep before we get into this," Tony said. "Come on. You can lie down on my couch."

"What did you think of Laura Simmons?" Eddie asked. "Do you think she's the one?"

Jack nodded slowly. "Yes, I do. I really do."

"How do you know?" Tony demanded.

"I can't tell you," Jack admitted. "There wasn't any one thing I could put my finger on, but I really think you're going to find poison in one of those evidence bags."

"I hope we do," Tony replied wearily. "God knows I hope we do."

***

"You did *what?*" Amanda cried incredulously as she faced Jack and Tony. Her face was a picture of disbelief and fury.

"I set the woman up," Jack responded calmly. "I took her home and gave her a chance to poison me."

"You took her into our—your home and you let her try to poison you? Jack, are you completely out of your mind?"

"And you let him do it, I guess?" Amanda asked, turning to Tony.

"It's not your place to question my decisions in homicide," Tony said stiffly. "Besides, it was his idea."

"I'll question any damned thing that puts one of your detectives in unjustifiable danger!" Amanda snapped angrily as she advanced on Tony. "Especially one who doesn't have enough sense to stay out of it himself."

"Calm down, Amanda," Eddie spoke up, soothingly. "Jack was never really in danger as long as he didn't touch anything in the kitchen."

"We looked out for him, honestly," Tony added placatingly.

"Amanda, could you get on with the tests?" Jack pressed anxiously. He got out a handkerchief and blew his nose. "I'd really like to know if she's the one."

"That's all you care about, isn't it?" Amanda asked bitterly. "What do you want me to test first?"

"The food, then the rest of the stuff," Tony directed.

Amanda eyed the bags warily. "There's a lot in those bags. This is going to take me some time. You can go home if you want, and I'll call you if I find it."

Tony and Eddie opted to go home, but Jack decided to stay. Amanda tackled the contents of the refrigerator first and then spent the rest of the morning and the early part of the afternoon testing everything that Jack left in the cabinets. Jack peered eagerly over her shoulder for much of the first hour until Amanda finally snapped at him to go get himself a magazine to read. He returned a few minutes later with the latest issue of *Playboy* and pretended to read it while he watched Amanda out of the corner of his eye.

"That stuff's as clean as a whistle," Amanda announced as she straightened and rubbed the ache in the small of her back. "How about breaking for lunch?"

"Couldn't you keep looking?" Jack asked.

"I don't imagine that you care, but I didn't get any breakfast this morning," Amanda snapped. "Tony called me at the crack of dawn."

"Sorry," Jack apologized stiffly. They walked over to Market Square, and he bought her a plate of Mexican food for lunch. He didn't rush her while she ate, but he hustled her out the moment the check came. Amanda tackled the plates and cups and saucers with renewed energy, but as she made her way through the utensils Jack became more and more anxious. "Haven't you found anything yet?" he quizzed several times.

"I'd have said something," Amanda assured him over and over.

Jack watched her run the last series of tests. "There has to be something here," he said. "There just has to be. I know it was her. I could tell."

"Maybe she left it under your pillow," Amanda suggested sarcastically. "How does it feel to make love to a killer?"

Jack flushed. "I didn't make love to her, Amanda."

"Sure."

"I had an attack of conscience. Couldn't go through with cheating on my wife."

"Convenient," Amanda said sarcastically.

"And honest at the same time," Jack clarified. "She was pissed at first, but calmed down and stayed to talk for almost an hour. I made sure she had a chance to leave the poison. I deliberately sent her into the kitchen by herself to mix a second drink."

"So what did you talk about for almost an hour?" Amanda asked.

"How my wife left me because she doesn't like my dangerous hobbies," Jack said flatly.

"I know, stick as close to the truth as you can," Amanda said tiredly. She took a sample from the last skillet and tested it. "Sorry, Jack, I couldn't find anything in the kitchen. Are you sure she wasn't just out for a good time?"

"No. She's the killer," Jack declared, absolutely certain in his own mind.

Tony stuck his head around the door. "Anything turn up?"

"Nothing. And I was so sure it was Laura," Jack responded, his disappointment written all over his face. "Does this stuff need to stay down here?"

"Not so fast," Amanda spoke up. "Have you tested everything she could have possibly poisoned? You have other things she could have gotten to, you know."

"Amanda, this is everything out of the kitchen," Jack said.

"I want to go over there," Amanda insisted. "I want to look around some myself."

"Amanda, that isn't necessary, honestly," Tony said.

"I want to go and check it out myself," Amanda persisted. "I know you both are thorough, but because of my training I might see something you missed."

"All right," Jack relented, "if it will make you feel better."

"It might not be a bad idea, Jack," Tony agreed. "I'll go back with you and we'll look the place over again."

Amanda felt strange walking into the house she and Jack had shared for such a short while. In some ways it was like she hadn't been here for a million years; in other ways it was as though she had never left. She felt an aching longing to come back here, and she had to bite her lip to keep from crying. "All right, what did you leave in the kitchen?" she asked briskly.

"That's just it," Jack began as he threw open the cabinet doors, "I thinned it out last Wednesday. You tested everything I left in here."

Amanda looked over the kitchen with sharp eyes, yet she had to agree that there was nothing left that could be poisoned. Jack coughed again and blew his nose. "You sound worse than you did this morning," Amanda observed. "I hope you don't have what I had."

"I think this is just a cold," Jack said. Amanda followed him out of the kitchen and into the bedroom, where Tony was poking around. "I've been taking cold capsules and gargling regularly." He stepped into the bathroom and took the lid off the mouthwash. "Maybe this will help."

"Give that to me!" Amanda screamed as she grabbed the mouthwash out of his hand, spilling a few drops on the counter. "Did she come in here?"

"Yes, but just for a min—oh, hell," Jack gasped, stunned, "she could have put it in here."

"You bet your sweet arsenic she could've," Amanda agreed as she capped the bottle. "A bathroom's a perfect place to leave something. Good grief, how could you three stooges have missed the bathroom?"

"Good question," Tony admitted, looking as shocked as Jack. Jack had brought a couple of evidence bags with him just in case, and when those were full they started putting the plastic pill bottles in a shoe box. They rode in silence back to the lab. With trembling fingers Amanda prepared a sample of the mouthwash and put it into her machine. Jack and Tony waited, holding their breaths, as the mass spectrometer made its analysis.

Amanda gasped as the results flashed across the screen: potassium cyanide, 98.2 percent. If he had gargled with that mouthwash, he would probably have been dead within a few minutes. "Will you look at that?" Jack marveled. "She really did it."

"Is that the mouthwash Amanda took away from you?" Tony asked, white-faced.

Amanda got up abruptly, pushing her chair out from the machine. "Yes, that's the mouthwash I took away from him," she said bitterly. "If I hadn't, he'd be dead by now." Overcome by a rage she didn't know she was capable of, Amanda grabbed Jack and shook him by the shoulders. "Did you hear that, you fearless fool? If I hadn't stopped you, you would be dead right now. Did you hear that? Dead! Dead, damn it! And you're too crazy to even be scared!"

Amanda backed away from Jack, too overcome by fury to stop the tears that spilled from her eyes. "You've got to be the hero, don't you?" she screamed as she reached in the shoebox and threw a pill bottle at Jack's head. "Big, brave Jack, going to ride a bull or jump out of an airplane or use himself as bait for a killer!" She grabbed another plastic bottle and hit him in the face with it, even though he dodged. "You don't care who loves you, or who's worried about you, or about anything but getting your kicks with danger, do you?" She hit him in the chest with a bottle of vitamins in spite of the tears that clouded her vision.

"Amanda, what are you doing?" Jack asked incredulously as she threw a bar of soap at his head.

"You could have died tonight, but you never thought of that, did you?" Amanda demanded as she narrowly missed him with a shampoo bottle. "You don't care—as long as you get your kicks! I bet you weren't even scared, were you? You don't even have sense enough to be scared of a killer!"

"Amanda, stop it!" Jack snapped as he ducked a tube of toothpaste. "I'm all right, honestly."

"No, you aren't—you're...*crazy!*" Amanda cried as she threw the last item, a sack of disposable razors, at him. "Just plain crazy!" She collapsed at her desk, sobs shaking her body. "Y—you're going to get yourself killed someday," she repeated over and over.

Jack stared in horror at Amanda, and he started to shake as he realized just how close he had come to gargling with the poison. She was right—he almost died tonight. He would have died, in fact, if she hadn't taken the gargle away from him. And the most frightening part of the entire episode was that up until this moment the whole thing had been a huge game to him. He hadn't really taken seriously the fact that Laura Simmons was out to take his life. He had felt no fear whatsoever at the prospect of tangling with the woman—when in fact he should have been scared out of his wits.

And that was wrong. Just plain wrong.

Amanda was right about him. There *was* something unhealthy about the way he craved danger and sought thrill after thrill. No rational man would have invited a suspected murderer into his home without a single qualm. No rational man would have faced Laura Simmons without feeling fear. No rational man would strip to his underwear and taunt a killer without being afraid. No rational man would march up to a killer's house and ring the doorbell and not be frightened. No rational man would race time and time again, repeatedly jump out of airplanes, and climb on the back of bull after bull *and never feel one iota of fear.*

No rational man would behave the way he did and not be afraid.

He was not a rational man.

He needed to make some changes.

He needed help.

Jack reached out and put his hand on Amanda's head. "Mandy, I'm sorry," he said as he stroked her hair.

"Are you really? Are you really sorry? Or just sorry that I'm mad at you?

Jack flinched at the hurt and bitterness in her eyes. Now was not the time to try to talk to Amanda. They would talk later, after he'd had time to think, and think hard, about what he needed to do. Right now he desperately needed to be by himself for a while. "I'll make that report now," he told Tony. He backed out of the lab and ran up the stairs as though the devil were on his heels.

Amanda rested her head in her hands. "Why did you let him do it?"

"I thought it might work—and it did. But I never would have done it if I had realized how close he would come," Tony admitted. He started picking up the soap and the bottles strewn around the lab. "You can test the rest of this stuff Monday," he suggested. "The mouthwash's enough to get a warrant. Go home, Amanda. You look beat."

Amanda helped Tony clean up the mess and locked the lab behind them. She made it as far as the car before she started to cry again. This time she shed tears of fear and despair rather than anger. That woman had almost killed Jack, and he hadn't even been frightened. Amanda shuddered as she cried softly into the night. She had managed to save him by the skin of his teeth this time, but who would save him the next time he put himself within inches of death and dared fate? She knew that she wouldn't be around to do it again. She would see a lawyer next week about a divorce.

***

Jack parked in front of Amanda's apartment and sat quietly. He stared at Amanda's front door as he tried to build up the courage to knock on her door and talk with her. She had left a message at the station that she wanted to get her furniture over the weekend, and that she had a Monday appointment with an attorney. Jack's palms felt sweaty and he wiped them on his jeans. He had been too hardheaded for too long, and he only hoped that it wasn't too late for him with Amanda. It looked like she was ready to go through with a divorce. Jack only hoped he could change her mind. He grimaced at the irony. She left him because she didn't think him capable of fear, yet tonight he was more afraid than he had ever been in his life.

Jack took a deep breath and ran up the stairs to Amanda's front door. He knocked and fidgeted until Amanda pushed aside the curtains. "Can I come in and talk for a few minutes?"

Amanda blinked and tried to swallow the lump in her throat. What was Jack doing here? She glanced across the room, but her telephone was not off the hook. She hoped that he wasn't going to object to her moving her furniture out this weekend—she had a chance to move into an unfurnished unit just three doors down, and she needed to make the psychological break with him. She took the chain off the door and opened it. "Come on in," she said, trying to disguise the trembling in her voice.

"How are you?" Jack asked as he sat down on the couch.

"Fine." Amanda seated herself in the chair across from him. "How about you? Over your cold?" she inquired, hating the small talk but not knowing what else to say.

"I finally got over it yesterday. And, yes, I got the kitchen and the bathroom put back together." Amanda had not found poison in any of the other articles out of the bathroom, but a further analysis of the mouthwash revealed that a single mouthful would have had enough cyanide in it to kill Jack.

Jack shifted uncomfortably on the couch. "Did you get my message?" Amanda asked.

"What message?" Jack lied. "I came by to tell you what finally happened with Laura Simmons."

"I've wondered about her," Amanda said quietly. The news clips had shown an eerily calm woman being led from her house in handcuffs, and Jack and the homicide department had been roundly cheered by the media for finally cracking the case.

"It's a weird story—and a sad one, really. The district attorney just got back to us with a preliminary psychiatric evaluation, and it looks like they're not even going to be able to try her. She's apparently completely, utterly insane. When she applied for a job with the school district, she was able to hide the fact that she'd been hospitalized some years back for trying to poison her father. She was released a couple of years ago when the doctors decided that she was no longer dangerous. It looks like they were wrong about her."

"Good Lord," Amanda responded quietly. "What on earth could have caused her to end up like that?"

"The psychiatrist doesn't know for sure, but he suspects that the father she tried to poison abused her when she was a child. She couldn't handle that, and she became what she is today. It's sad, really. She has a very high IQ, according to the tests they gave her, and her principal insists she's one of his best teachers."

"How awful," Amanda said softly. She was sure, with the media attention this case had received, that somewhere along the line a book would be written about Laura Simmons and the San Antonio poisonings. "I'm glad you managed to solve the poisonings. I'm sure it's a load off your mind."

"Yes, it's a relief," Jack replied. "It will mean fewer hours for me in the near future."

"Are you going to be off this weekend?" Amanda asked. "Would it be convenient for me to move my furniture?"

Jack swallowed. "I'm not going to be in town," he answered slowly. "I put in for a transfer to the negotiating team, and they're sending me to Houston for a training seminar." *Take the bait, Amanda, please,* he thought.

"Negotiating? How can you be on negotiating? You're already on SWAT," Amanda returned.

"I asked to be moved off the SWAT team. I hate to admit it, but Mike McCormick was glad to see the last of me. I wasn't one of his favorite officers."

"Why did you ask to get off SWAT?" Amanda pressed quietly. "I thought you loved it."

"I do. My therapist suggested that it might be a good idea," Jack admitted.

Amanda stared at Jack. "Is this what you really came over to tell me?"

"Yes, I guess it is." Jack shifted again in the chair. "I thought you might not want to talk about us at first."

"Jack, of course I would have wanted to talk about us," Amanda chided him.

"But you're seeing an attorney—"

"You said you didn't get my message."

"I lied," Jack confessed sheepishly. His eyes filled with tears as he looked at her. "Is it too late to talk about you and me?"

Amanda shook her head, her eyes full of unshed tears of her own. "No, it isn't too late. I don't think it would have ever been too late."

Jack stood up and put his hands in his pockets. "I did a lot of thinking last Saturday night and Sunday," he began. "I went back to the house and I tried to sleep, but I kept reliving the moment you grabbed that mouth wash out of my hand. I also thought a lot about my evening with Laura Simmons. You were right, Amanda. I wasn't scared when I was with her, giving her a chance to kill me. I never once felt afraid."

"How did you feel, Jack?" Amanda asked, biting her lip.

"High," Jack admitted. "Like I was on some kind of trip. I felt a rush when I danced with her and when I kissed her, not because of sex but because I was holding a dangerous woman in my arms. I had my arms around death, so to speak, and I wasn't frightened. I even kind of liked it. And that's not a normal response to danger, Amanda."

"No," she agreed quietly. "It really isn't."

"I should have been scared to death, but I wasn't. I *liked* the feeling of flirting with death. And that got me to thinking about the other things—the chances I've always taken on the job, the racing, the bull riding, the skydiving. They all give me a high, and they give me the biggest high when they're the most dangerous. But that's just it—I'm not scared. I'm just plain excited by them."

"What does your therapist say?"

"Oh, he agrees completely that I have an unusual response to danger," Jack replied as he sat back down on the couch. "He says I was probably born that way to begin with, and then my dad made it worse by cheering me on so much and telling me it made up for being little. He says I have to learn to control it. He didn't think I needed to quit the force, but he suggested that I get off the SWAT team."

"How do you feel about that?" Amanda pressed softly.

"I don't want to, but I think I better. I've taken a few unnecessary chances there, too, remember?"

"Yes, I remember," Amanda murmured, shuddering at the thought.

"I don't think I've thanked you for saving me," Jack said. He got up off the couch and knelt beside her chair. "Thank you for saving my life, Amanda."

"Oh, Jack, don't thank me," Amanda cried, her eyes filling with tears. "I love you and it would have killed me if anything had happened to you."

"Do you love me?" Jack asked as he pulled her head forward and cradled it on his shoulder. Amanda slid out of the chair and sat down on the carpet beside him. "Do you still love me, or have I killed everything you ever felt for me?"

Amanda shook her head. "No, you haven't killed what I feel for you."

"Then can you forgive me for scaring you to death so many times?" Jack begged. "Can you forgive me for all the months you've worried about me?"

"What about the dangerous hobbies?" Amanda questioned warily.

Jack shut his eyes briefly. "They're out. They have to be. And I don't know what I'm going to do when I start missing the thrills again, but I can't go back to them." He put his arm around Amanda. "It's not going to be easy on me, Mandy. I'm going to be hard to live with for a while like I was before, at least until I get used to not having them. I'm basically restless as well as fearless. Not the most pleasant combination."

"The restlessness didn't bother me all that much," Amanda returned thoughtfully. "Dad was restless, so I'm used to it. But are you really going to give up the hobbies, Jack? Do you even think you can?"

"I have to," Jack affirmed starkly. "The therapist's most insistent on that. What I'm going to do in their place, I don't know."

"We'll go for a swim in the neighborhood pool. Or go up to the lake and water ski. That will get the adrenaline flowing, and it's not all that dangerous. We could buy a boat, if you like. There are a lot of things that are exciting but not all that dangerous."

"You said 'we,' Amanda," Jack said softly. "Does that mean you'll come back to me?"

"I—I want to, Jack," Amanda stammered. "I want to come back to you so badly." She put her arms around him and hugged him, her tears wetting the front of his shirt.

"I don't want to give up my career, so I won't be able to eliminate all the risks in my life," Jack murmured as he kissed Amanda's temple. "But I'll eliminate the unnecessary ones, Amanda. I'll eliminate the ones that are just for thrills. I have to. Will you come back to me, Mandy?"

"Of course I'll come back to you," Amanda replied, holding him tightly. "That's all I ever asked of you." She lifted her face to his, and her eyes were smiling through the tears. "I love you so much, Jack! I never wanted to hurt you, but I couldn't—"

Jack silenced her with a finger to her lips. "I know you couldn't stay with me before. You loved me too much to stick around and watch me self-destruct. We had a long talk about you, Amanda."

"We?"

"My therapist and I. He said that you had done the only thing you could. I'd like to keep going to him for a while, if I can. He's not cheap, but I think that in the long run he'll prove to be worth it."

"I'll pay for it myself," Amanda said. She stroked the hard muscles of Jack's back. "I've missed you."

Jack held her tightly against him. "I've missed you, too, Amanda," he answered as he caressed the back of her neck with light, tantalizing fingers. "I don't know how many times I've reached for you in the night and you weren't there. Are you really coming back to me?"

"Yes, I'm coming back to you," Amanda affirmed quietly. "I love you, and I want to help you whip this thing." She ran her hands down Jack's chest. "I'll help you, Jack. We'll find things to do together."

"I know one thing we can do together," Jack said as he pulled Amanda on his lap. "I've missed kissing you and holding you and making love to you. Make love to me, Amanda. Now. I need the warmth of your love."

"Wouldn't you rather go back to the house?" Amanda asked as she looked around the dismal apartment.

"No," Jack replied, starting to unbutton her shirt. "I need you too badly to wait until we go back there." He pushed her shirt off her shoulders and caressed one nipple through the fabric of her bra. "I need for you to show me that you're really coming back to me. I won't really believe it until I've made you mine again."

"But it's so dreary here," Amanda protested.

"Do you really think we're going to notice?" Jack asked quietly as his lips met hers. Amanda melted into him, forgetting everything except that she was in Jack's arms again. They kissed softly at first, not really believing that they were together once more. But as passion flared between them they increased the intensity of their embrace, Jack crushing her to him and teasing her lips open. Amanda gave herself willingly to his passion, tasting his sweetness as he tasted hers. Her lips caressed him as her fingers undid the buttons of his shirt. Her eager fingers caressed the soft hair on his chest. As Amanda stroked his chest she remembered his evening with Laura and pulled away from him. "Did you kiss her the way you kiss me?" she demanded.

"I kissed her a couple of times, yes," Jack admitted. "All I could think was that I was going to nail her to the wall. And my so-called attack of conscience wasn't far from the truth. I couldn't have made love to her. I love you too much." He caressed the hair at her temple. "I would have rather kissed you."

"Did you really? She had a knockout figure."

Jack shrugged. "She was hardened and cold, Amanda. No woman could be more different from you." Amanda smiled and pulled him closer to her.

His eyes shining, Jack took Amanda's hand and led her to the bedroom. "I haven't made love since you left me, and I need that tonight," he said as he threw back the covers. "I've missed holding you." He unhooked Amanda's bra and threw it on the dresser. "I've missed taking off your clothes and taking a shower with you and waking up with you next to me."

"I've missed you, too," Amanda whispered as she pushed the shirt from his shoulders. "I've missed watching you shave in the morning." Boldly she unzipped his jeans. "I've missed seeing you naked and sleeping with my head on your chest. I've even missed being irritable with you."

Jack stepped out of his jeans and left them in a heap on the floor. "We're never going to be separated again," he promised. "We're going to be together forever."

Amanda shed the rest of her clothes and joined Jack in the bed. She forgot about the dingy bedroom. She forgot everything but her love for Jack and her desire to be with him. Jack turned her over so that her back was cuddled against his stomach. "I missed waking up with you snuggled up with me," he said as his lips caressed her neck. He stroked the softness of her bottom before his hands cupped her taut breasts. "God, I can hardly believe we're together again. I was so afraid I'd killed everything you ever felt for me."

"I don't think you could do that," Amanda assured him as he caressed her nipples into twin peaks of pleasure. "I don't think there's any way you could kill what I feel for you." She was quiet for a moment. "I left only because I had to. I couldn't stand to stay and watch you hurt or kill yourself. Will you ever be able to forgive me for leaving?"

"There's nothing to forgive," Jack said as one hand drifted lower. "I understand why you left, and I don't blame you for going." His hand stroked her gently, teasing the skin of her inner thighs.

"I've missed you so badly, Jack," Amanda whispered as shivers of pleasure rippled from her head to her toes. Jack's fingers were working magic on her, and she moaned in response to his ministrations. "Let me touch you, please."

"In a minute." Jack continued to caress her. His every touch and kiss seemed to convey his love for her. Amanda basked in the tenderness of his feelings and gave herself over to the pleasure he was bringing to her. *He's come back to me,* she thought in wonder.

He finally understood her, and he had done what she had asked him to do. And what better demonstration of his love could he give her?

Jack touched and caressed Amanda until she was writhing in pleasure. He finally turned her over to face him, kissing her long and passionately as he stroked the smooth skin of her back. "I want to kiss you and hold you all night," he whispered, his breath stirring the hair on her forehead.

"I want to touch you," Amanda said as she stroked his shoulders and his chest. Her fingers sought to make up for lost time as she reacquainted herself with each contour of his muscular body. She explored his chest, the flatness of his stomach, the little dimple just above his buttocks, each touch and caress expressing her deep love for him and her joy that they were together again. Jack bent his head and touched one nipple with the tip of his tongue. Soon her nipple was taut and rosy with passion. He made his way down the slope of one breast, nibbling and caressing the softness of the valley between her breasts, then he caressed her other nipple into a similar state of excitement. His lips drifted lower. With love in every touch he caressed the softness of her waist and stomach, nibbling and touching and tasting her.

For long moments they reacquainted themselves with the delight of one another's bodies as they reconfirmed their love for one another. Tonight there was no room for coyness or shyness—they gave to one another freely and openly. Jack pushed Amanda's legs apart and ministered to her in the way she loved so much, bringing her to throbbing heights of pleasure, and Amanda caressed Jack intimately with her lips, glorying in the delight she could bring him. When they both sensed that the time was right, they completed their union, sliding together with a passionate power that left Amanda gasping. They moved together, soaring quickly to the heights and cascading off the edge together.

After a moment Jack moved within her yet again, slowly at first and then with more power, and they climbed the mountain again, more slowly this time and without the urgency that had driven them before. This time the delight was so piercing, the pleasure so intense, that Amanda cried out Jack's name as wave after wave shook her body. Jack stiffened and called her name out hoarsely, and they collapsed together in a sprawl of arms and legs.

They lay together as their breathing slowly returned to normal. "Better?" Amanda asked.

"I've never been this good in all my life," Jack answered dreamily. He kissed Amanda's cheek tenderly as he stroked her back. "I do love you, and I'm so glad you're coming back to me." He turned over and put his hands behind his head. "All our problems haven't gone away, you know," he said quietly. "I'm going to miss the danger something awful at first, and I might not be the easiest person to live with for a while. Do you think you can put up with it?"

"Of course I can," Amanda assured him. "I'll just yell back at you!" She leaned over and kissed Jack on the tip of his nose. "Seriously, we'll make it, Jack. I'll help you find some other outlets for the restlessness. We're going to work it out together." She snuggled back down under the covers.

Jack lay still for a minute before he threw back the covers and got out of bed. "Jack, where are you going?" Amanda asked.

"I'm packing your things and taking you home where you belong. You're not spending one more night here."

"Jack!" Amanda protested, but she got out of bed and started helping him pack. Half an hour later Amanda's car followed Jack's truck out of the parking lot. At last she was going home—for good.

Epilogue

2015

Jack lifted Amanda's mountain bike up on the car rack and strapped it securely beside his. "Is that the last of the packing?" he asked as Amanda tossed her duffel bag in the folded-down back seat of her spanking new crossover.

"Nope, but once we get the cooler in the car and we go through the checklist one more time we're good to go," Amanda said. "Sorry about the late start."

"Not much you could do about it. We couldn't very well go off and leave Heather to get our idiot son home from the emergency room last night, not with a cast halfway up to his ass and her seven months pregnant. I swear, Amanda, one of these days I am going to strangle that boy. What in the hell possessed him to try to walk across a two by four barn rafter twenty feet up?"

Amanda's lips twitched. "What possesses Jack Blakeman Vance to do anything dangerous, oh-father-of-his? At least Heather made him sell that damn crotch rocket before she would get pregnant, and I have a feeling once the baby's here he'll be too busy to get into very much trouble." Her face softened. "You sure were."

"And you think it's funny, now that I'm getting back some of my own," Jack groused as he ran his fingers through his silvery-white hair. "Yes, the little one will definitely cool that boy's jets. And it's not like he can get into much trouble on the job. It still surprises me that Blake became a trial lawyer and didn't go into something where he could flirt with danger a little."

"It shouldn't, Jack." Amanda took Jack by the hand and together they started toward the house. "You made your living talking people into things and so does he."

"No, I made my living talking people *out* of things," Jack clarified. "Like shooting up the cops waiting outside to arrest them."

"Same difference." Amanda glanced with loving eyes over at Jack. "Same adrenaline high."

And for Jack it was an adrenaline high, almost as good as riding a bull. He had surprised everyone at first, himself included, with his talent as a mediator, and over the years earned the reputation of being the most skilled negotiator in South Texas, earning the nickname "Silver Tongue" for his uncanny ability to talk even the most strung-out perps down off the ledge, so to speak, and into custody. It became the ultimate challenge to him—to get inside the head of a desperate criminal or a potential suicide and slowly but surely ease them away from an anticipated disaster. Even though they had both retired from the police force several years earlier, Amanda as the head of the CSU and Jack with the rank of lieutenant, Jack still made himself available on a consultant basis if there was a difficult situation to be resolved, and just a couple of months earlier had talked the daughter of a prominent family out of jumping off a water tower.

"If you say so. So, are we ready for six weeks of another kind of adrenaline high?"

"Ready to hit the bike trails, are we?"

"Among other things." Jack patted her butt as she ducked in the front door. "I can hardly wait to try out that new camping mattress."

"Horny old coot," Amanda teased. "You're as bad as you were thirty years ago."

Jack shrugged. "What can I say? You have a bicycle butt to die for and I've always fantasized about wild sex with a gray-haired grandma."

Amanda made a face and shot Jack the finger. He grinned as he picked up the checklist and together they went over the items on it one more time, making sure they had everything they needed for a six week long thirtieth anniversary camping trip, to be spent wending their way through the west and riding every challenging mountain biking trail Amanda could find on the Internet.

And Amanda was more than happy to go—as far as she was concerned, mountain biking had probably saved her marriage all those years ago. Although Jack meant and kept his promise to her to stay out of danger, he had been restless at first and at times downright miserable with no real way to get the adrenaline fix he craved. Boating, water skiing, hiking, even rock-climbing were too tame for Jack, and Amanda had begun to despair of Jack ever being truly happy again until they noticed a peculiar bicycle parked outside a Ranger station in a Colorado state park. The owner of the bike explained that it was specially designed to be ridden off-road and let Jack take it for a spin, and the look on Jack's face when he returned the bike to the owner told Amanda all she needed to know—Jack had *finally* found something that would challenge him, thrill him, tire him out, and not kill him in the process. She bought Jack his first bike the next weekend, and Jack came home from his first ride happier than she had seen him in a long time.

At first Amanda happily and willingly sent Jack out the door to ride, but after a few months of riding by himself Jack had come home with a second bike for her, and after an outing or two Amanda was as hooked as he was. Over the years they, and later they and their two boys, had ridden trails all over the United States, and were constantly on the lookout for the new trails that were opening up all the time. And yes, thanks to all the biking they did, she and Jack were both still slim and fit, and looked damn good for a couple staring sixty in the face.

Jack carried the cooler to the car and Amanda locked the house. "So, where to first?" he asked, his eyes snapping with anticipation as Amanda got in the passenger seat.

"Big Bend Ranch State Park. And there's a good trail at Davis Mountains State Park and another in Guadalupe Mountains National Park, and then we can start hitting the challenging ones in New Mexico."

"Sounds like a plan." Jack leaned across the seat and planted a swift, hard kiss on Amanda's lips. "I love you, Mandy. Thanks for not giving up on me all those years ago."

Amanda smiled gently at Jack's oh-so-beloved face. "I wouldn't have missed it for the world, Jack. Now, let's go find us a bike trail."

ABOUT THE AUTHOR

The author of twenty romance novels, Emily Mims combined her writing career with a career in public education until leaving the classroom to write full time. The mother of two sons, now she and her husband Charles split their time between central Texas and eastern Tennessee. For relaxation she plays the piano, organ, dulcimer, and ukulele. She says, "I love to write romances because I believe in them. Romance happened to me and it can happen to any woman—if she'll just let it."

Did you enjoy this book? Drop us a line and say so! We love to hear from readers, and so do our authors. To connect, visit www.boroughspublishinggroup.com online, send comments directly to info@boroughspublishinggroup.com, or friend us on Facebook and Twitter. And be sure to check back regularly for contests and new releases in your favorite subgenres of romance!

Are you an aspiring writer? Check out www.boroughspublishinggroup.com/submit and see if we can help you make your dreams come true.

www.ingramcontent.com/pod-product-compliance
Lightning Source LLC
Chambersburg PA
CBHW051456170626
46811CB00002B/513